The Secrets of Tintern Abbey

A Historical Novel

Gordon Masters

The Secrets of Tintern Abbey: A Historical Novel

Scripture quotations taken from the New American Standard Bible®, copyright © 1960, 1962, 1963, 1968, 1971, 1972, 1973, 1975, 1977, 1995 by The Lockman Foundation. Used by permission. (www.Lockman.org)

Cover and interior photos © 2007 Carolyn Masters.

Author photo © 2008 Prestigious Images.

Published by Wheatmark®
610 East Delano Street, Suite 104
Tucson, Arizona 85705 U.S.A.
www.wheatmark.com

Publisher's Cataloging-In-Publication Data
(Prepared by The Donohue Group, Inc.)

Masters, Gordon.
  The secrets of Tintern Abbey : a historical novel / Gordon Masters.

  p. : ill., maps ; cm.

  Includes bibliographical references.
  ISBN: 978-1-60494-074-9

1. Tintern Abbey—Fiction. 2. Cistercians—Wales—Fiction. 3. Monastic and religious life—Wales—Fiction.   4. Wales—History—To 1500—Fiction. 5. Historical fiction. I. Title.

PS3613.A8 S42 2008
813/.6

Library of Congress Control Number: 2008933785

To the monks of Tintern Abbey, whose perseverance over four centuries was my inspiration.

Contents

Part I
The Making of an Abbey

Part II
The Church and the Castle

Part III
The Great Mortality

Part IV
The Last Monks of Tintern Abbey

Further Notes and Resources

Preface

IN MORE MODERN times the most famous visitor to the Wye Valley and Tintern Abbey was William Wordsworth. None have captured the essence of that enchanted world more than he. Many who have visited this abbey two times or more have felt compelled to write about it. This writer is one who visited Tintern Abbey only once, but spent the ensuing eight years poring over documents, pictures, descriptions, medieval histories, Welsh church records, chronicles, maps, wills, diaries, the Domesday Book, Celtic mythologies, Gaelic, Cymric, and Celtic names, Saint Bernard's writings, medieval medicines, and records referring to the lives of medieval monks. Special attention was given to those Cistercian monks who poured out their very souls for four hundred and five years at Tintern Abbey, asking only that their souls be saved along with the souls of those for whom they prayed.

The monks, nobles, ladies, and others who are found in this work are composites of historical people. The story, although written as a novel, is inspired by actual actions, events, dreams, persons, and the beliefs of those who occupied the medieval stage during those troubled times. The setting is medieval Europe, narrowed to medieval England, narrowed further to Wales, and finally narrowed to the Wye Valley from 1131 to 1536.

My purpose was to make those nobles, ladies, abbots, priors, ordinary monks, soldiers, peasants, master masons, and bishops live again, sacrifice again, praise again, and finally die again.

A SPECIAL THANKS goes to the monks at the Assumption Abbey in Ava, Missouri, who answered many questions during my stay there.

My thanks also go to Dr. Maynard Sisler and Dr. Scott Ringenberg for reading the manuscript and advising me on medical terms and practices. Spending many hours reading the manuscript and offering valuable technical information were teachers Ava and Jim King. Our gratitude also goes to John Daniel of John M. Daniel Literary Services, who served as our overall manuscript editor and consultant.

This work would not have been possible without the help and support of my children: Steve Masters, Carolyn Masters-Ringenberg, and Mary Freeland. Carolyn was also instrumental in guiding the manuscript through the editing and publication phases.

Finally, my heartfelt appreciation goes to my late wife, Martha L. Wallace-Masters, who read the manuscript many times, offered suggestions, and put up with my constant pestering. This book is a part of her legacy to me.

Prologue

DOCTOR LEWIS PAUSED in his lecture and looked up from his podium at the rapt faces of the students who crowded the tiers of the large theater-style classroom. The room was nearly full. If his lecture series kept growing like this, Magdalen College would have to find a bigger room for him, or even put him in the auditorium. Samuel Lewis did not want an auditorium; he had always enjoyed making eye-contact with his students, although with a crowd like today's—there must have been over a hundred of them—he would be able to touch base with only a handful.

That fresh-faced redhead in the front row, for example, the young woman who had bumped into him in the hallway that morning. Not for the first time, either. Sam had been careful to mention his wife and children back in America at the beginning of every lecture.

Or that older man up in the back row, the one in the clerical collar, with a wise smile on his face. Sam hadn't seen that fellow before.

Sam realized his attention had been wandering. He shook his head slightly and looked back at his notes. Where was he? Five minutes into the lecture, and already he had lost his place. He had felt utterly at sea, ever since his wife's phone call the night before.

SAMUEL GORDON LEWIS, M.D. was, at forty-five, the youngest Distinguished Professor in the Harvard University School of Medicine, and the Associate Director of the Harvard Institute for Disease Control. This spring he had taken a working sabbatical to deliver an eight-week lecture series to premedical students at Magdalen College, Oxford University. The lectures were on the history of infectious diseases, each week focusing on a different pandemic. The first three were cholera, smallpox, and tuberculosis; still to come were malaria, influenza, polio, and AIDS.

He was, at this moment, trying to find his place in the fourth lecture, the one about bubonic plague. Unfortunately, his mind would not stay put on the pile of paper on his lectern. The words swam on the pages. He picked up the sheets, tapped them into an orderly pile, and set them down again. He took a deep breath.

"I'm sorry," he said. "I seem to have lost my place. Forgive me if I just wing it a bit." He looked out at his audience again, and they looked concerned but still attentive. "Don't worry; I've given this talk before. And, as with all the other scourges we've been talking about, I pose the same questions: Where did the pestilence come from? Could it have been prevented? Could it be treated? What effects did the devastating disease have on society? And how did it change history?

"Of course we don't know the origin of the bacterium *Yersinia pestis*; it may be older than our own species. We do think we know how the disease was transmitted, and how it became a human problem. I say 'think,' because it's always a mistake in any science to assume we have learned all there is to know, but we're confident that we can thank rodents and fleas for the problem.

"Unfortunately, the teamwork involved in this complicated transmission— germs, rats, fleas, and people—has only been understood for a little more than a hundred years. Those victims of the Black Death pandemic of the fourteenth century throughout Europe had no idea what or whom to blame, much less what to do about the problem."

Doctor Lewis rambled on, "Yes, the disease could have been prevented if there had been any way to eradicate all the rats and all the fleas, but since there was no way to do that, and since they didn't know rats and fleas were the culprits (or fellow victims, to be more precise), they didn't even know to try.

"Could the plague of the fourteenth, fifteenth, and sixteenth century have been treated? Unfortunately, medical science wasn't yet up to that task. There were doctors, physicians whose only real skill in this regard was identifying the disease, and whose other main talent, not to be sneezed at, was compassion. But in time, what it took to eradicate the disease, or to put it to rest temporarily, was time. Genetic selection certainly helped, as did a gradual improvement in social sanitary habits.

"Meanwhile, Europe was devastated, as were enormous patches of Asia. In this fair land, England, a quarter of the population—over four million people—succumbed to the bubonic plague. As a result, society changed forever. The economy, which had depended on a vast supply of low-paid peasant farm workers, was in ruins. The social structure had to be revised, and with those changes came political changes, some perhaps for the better. Some perhaps for the worse."

Sam knew he'd lost his train of thought, was just bouncing from one idea to the next, but he kept going. Without having to look at his prepared speech, he could concentrate on the faces of the future doctors, who had stopped taking notes and were watching him with fascination.

"But those of us who enter the field of medicine—all of you, I hope—care most about how people suffered at the individual level, because that's where most of us can do the most good. We care intellectually about the origins and effects of disease, but in the existential moment, it's the individual human suffering that touches us most deeply. Not only those who died—wracked by screeching pain, high fever, foul odor, and shame—but also those who watched their loved ones suffer. Who watched, waited, and worried while their sons and daughters, their fathers, their...."

Doctor Samuel Gordon Lewis took a deep breath and let it out in a shaky rush.

"...their *mothers*...." Samuel looked to the back of the classroom. The elderly priest was no longer smiling, but was staring across the distance with intense concern.

Sam pinched the bridge of his nose with his thumb and forefinger.

"I'm sorry," he said. "Forgive me, please. I've said all I have to say for today. I shall see you all next week, when you'll have the dubious pleasure of hearing about malaria."

THAT EVENING, AS usual on Thursdays, the days he delivered his lecture, Sam Lewis ate dinner in the restaurant of his hotel, The Randolph. He had tried to rest that afternoon, but sleep would not come. Instead, another phone call from his wife doubled his worries.

Still, the rack of lamb had been superb, and so were all the extras, from the vichyssoise to the crème brulée. And the excellent Bordeaux. Sam had ordered only a half-bottle, a decision he now regretted and planned to revise. He looked up, saw a man in black approach his table, and held up a hand to order another half-bottle.

When the man in black reached the table, however, Sam realized he wasn't the waiter or the wine steward, but a priest. The same priest who had sat in the back row of Sam's lecture that morning. He began to rise to his feet, but the older man smiled and said, "Stay put. Don't get up. I just wanted to thank you for that fine talk this morning. Most illuminating, I must say."

"Won't you sit down?" Sam said. "I was about to order a half-bottle of claret, but if you'll join me, we could make it a bottle."

"That's very kind," the priest said, pulling a chair back from the table. As he sat, he said, "Blame the maître d' for telling me where you were. He and I are friends, you see. I thought I might find you here. The University's putting you up at The Randolph? Good for you, sir. Good for you."

The wine steward appeared as if by magic and Sam asked for a bottle and another glass. Then he turned to his companion and said, "I'm curious, Father. What brought you to my lecture? Are you a physician as well as a priest?"

The priest chuckled and shook his head. "Not by any means. I'm not a practicing priest anymore for that matter, although they still call me Father Ignatius. No, I'm the curator of the Special Collections room at the Magdalen College Library. And I have a strong interest in the history of the Black Death. So you see, you and I have a common interest."

"Are you interested in the disease from a theological standpoint?" Sam asked. The steward arrived and opened the bottle of wine. Sam tasted it, smiled, and motioned for the steward to pour.

Father Ignatius sipped and nodded. "Not bad at all. Yes, I suppose there's a theological element to my interest. I'm a historian, too. I'm particularly interested in the history of monasteries in England. There used to be a good many of them, you know, but we lost quite a few thanks to…well, thanks to guess what?"

"Our friend the bubonic plague?"

"Indirectly, yes. That was one of the far-reaching societal changes you alluded to in your lecture. Anyway, I would like to invite you to come visit me in my office tomorrow. I want to show you a volume, the prize of our collection in my opinion. You will be fascinated."

"Oh?"

"Oh, yes indeed," Father Ignatius said, smiling like a child with a secret. "Among other things, it contains a chronicle of the plague, a firsthand account of how it nearly decimated an isolated community."

"Sounds fascinating. There aren't many of those, at least that we know of."

"Doctor Lewis, I've read all of them that I could get my hands on, and this one is my favorite. And nobody knows about it. I want you to make it known to the world."

"Because of what it has to contribute to our knowledge of the disease?" Sam asked.

"Well, I confess it may not add much in that department," the priest said. "But that's where the theology comes in, you see."

Sam Lewis did not see, but enjoyed talking with this man who was temporarily taking his mind off the troublesome news updates from Boston. He refilled their glasses and took a sip.

Father Ignatius left his glass on the table. He relaxed his smile and said, "Doctor Lewis, I couldn't help noticing this morning, you seem to be troubled by something."

No. Sam wasn't going to get into this discussion. Instead, he replied, "Tell me more about this volume in your library."

The priest nodded and paused. "Very well. It's a set of chronicles of the Cistercian Monks who lived at Tintern Abbey from eleven-thirty-one to fifteen-thirty-six. Monastic orders fascinate me, and the Cistercian Order intrigues me most of all. I'm sure you've heard of Tintern Abbey? The Wordsworth poem and all that? It's a lovely place, really, set in the Wye Valley, just inside Wales."

"So I've heard."

"Well, I thought you'd be interested in this volume for two reasons. For one thing, much of the work is the chronicle of the plague by a monk named Brother Araud, a talented writer, or perhaps he could be called an inspired writer. Also, Doctor Samuel Gordon Lewis, there's a coincidence that is too evident to ignore, and that was the reason I simply had to attend your lecture this morning."

"Yes?"

"Yes." The joyful smile was back on the old man's face. "You see, three men are mentioned in the document who deeply cared about the health and well-being of the Tintern Abbey monks and nearby villagers. Their names were Samuel, Gordon, and Lewis. I think you were meant to read this chronicle, Doctor, don't you? Do you read Latin?"

Sam put down his wine glass and blinked. "As a matter of fact, I do."

"I'm glad," Father Ignatius said. "And Brother Araud had excellent handwriting, once you get used to it. Now. Forgive me, Samuel. May I call you Samuel? Forgive me, but what in the world is troubling you?"

Okay, Sam thought. A lifelong Presbyterian, he had never taken his problems to a priest before, but this priest had sought him out. And whether it was because of the wine or because of the kind face across the table, Sam felt like talking to this man. No, it was because he needed to talk, and here was somebody who offered to listen.

He talked. He told this friendly stranger about the sudden news of his mother's abdominal emergency. "It came as a surprise to everyone in the family. When she couldn't get out of bed, couldn't uncurl her body from the pain she was holding inside, my father rushed her to the emergency room of Mass General, where they put her through an M.R.I. and a battery of other tests, then rushed her right into the operating room. They removed a tumor the size of a tennis ball. She survived the operation, but now they have to wait for three more days for the results of the biopsy and all the other tests.

Who knows how long she's been suffering? She's like that. She suffers silently. People shouldn't suffer silently. I'm sorry, I don't mean to burden you with my problems."

Father Ignatius shook his head. "Don't apologize," he said. "People shouldn't suffer silently."

Sam sighed loudly. "The problem is, at this point, there's nothing I can do but worry. My mother's in the care of one of the best gastroenterology departments in America. My family wants me to stay in England for now. So I'm stuck here, unable to help."

Father Ignatius smiled. "I do think you should come see me in the morning. Perhaps Brother Araud's chronicle will be good for you. Don't ask me how."

SAMUEL ARRIVED AT Father Ignatius's office at nine o'clock the following morning. He wore informal clothes, khaki slacks and a sweater, but he carried his expensive attaché case and felt like an official visitor. Which he was, he supposed.

The priest greeted him cordially. "So glad you could come. I was hoping you would. Any news about your mother?"

"I telephoned my wife last night, after you left," Sam said. "Nothing new. My mother is resting well and pretends to be in good spirits. She says she can't stand the hospital food, and that's a good sign. But we won't know her test results until Monday or Tuesday. It's going to be a tense weekend for me."

"I expect it will be indeed," Father Ignatius said. "Well, today at least you have something to take your mind off the subject. Are you ready to dive into some light reading? I'm joking, of course. The volume weighs twenty-two pounds."

"I'm ready and eager," Sam answered.

"Very well. I'll have to ask you to leave your luggage outside the room. That's one of our rules. Also, no ink is allowed into the room. No matches or tobacco, no scissors, well, you can imagine. Also no photographic equipment. I hope you don't mind."

"That's fine." Sam took the pen out of his shirt pocket and stowed it inside his attaché case, which he left beside the priest's desk.

"Very well. Follow me, then."

Father Ignatius unlocked a door at the back of his office and led Sam into a chamber of wonders. The north wall had two large windows, but all the other walls were lined with bookshelves, from the floor to the ceiling, and all the bookcases had glass fronts. Freestanding glass-topped display cases formed a phalanx on one side of the room, and two long dark oak tables stood on the other, surrounded by austere but elegant chairs. The room was lit by overhead lamps.

A large volume rested on one of the long tables. Beside it were a yellow tablet and two pencils.

"There you are, sir," the priest said. "I've given you a pad and pencils, in case you wish to take notes. I need not tell you, of course, that no marks are to be made in the book itself. I've put a slip of paper in the volume to mark the beginning of Brother Araud's account of the plague. You're welcome to read the whole thing, of course, but there may not be time today. Unless, of course, you can speed-read Latin."

Sam laughed. "Hardly. That's a pretty big book, I must say."

"It's quarto size, of course. It has been in the Magdalen collection since Tintern Abbey closed and one of the monks came to Oxford. It has been bound twice since it's been in our possession. The most recent binding was in the mid-nineteenth century. That's full Moroccan leather, tooled and stamped with gold foil. We don't see much of that nowadays.

"Very well, I'll leave you, then. Enjoy yourself. Feel free to come back to my office if you'd like a cup of coffee, or if you need to use the loo."

Left alone, Samuel sat down, carefully opened the book on the table, and stepped back into the fourteenth century.

He was surprised at how quickly his Latin came back to him. It was if he had a dubbed soundtrack, reading aloud to him in Brother Araud's voice....

We are prepared to lose some of us, Prior Frank told me, but we shall never be prepared to lose all of us! Make the spirits of the fair ladies buried under our abbey floor live again, he said! Make the spirit of the noble knight Lord Bigod live again! Make the spirit of our founder, Abbot Henry, live again! Make the spirit of our six-fingered knight live again! Make their chants, Vigils, Lauds, Vespers, and Complines live again!

AT ONE IN the afternoon, Samuel became aware that he was quite hungry. He marked his place in the chronicle with the piece of yellow paper, then closed the book carefully. He walked out into Father Ignatius's office, waved to the priest who was on the telephone, and stepped out into the street. Two blocks away he found a student cafeteria, where he ate bangers and mash, washed down with a bottle of cider. Thus refreshed, he hurried back to the library, where the curator once again greeted him cordially and let him back into the Special Collections room.

It was nearly five o'clock before he reached the end of Brother Araud's journal concerning "The Great Mortality," as he called it. By that time Sam was glad to stop reading. His eyes were giving out and his brain was numb. Once again he closed the book carefully. He gathered his notes and the pencils and returned to Father Ignatius's office.

"Good," the priest said. "I was hoping you'd finish up in time for tea. I was just about to put the kettle on the hot plate, and I've had some scones sent 'round. I do hope you'll join me."

"You're very kind," Sam replied.

"Not all, my friend. It gets lonely sometimes in this office. Now tell me. What did you find out?"

"Those poor brothers really went through the wringer, didn't they?" Sam said. "Choir monks and lay brothers as well. With no cure, no help whatsoever."

"No?"

"No antibiotics is what I mean. No rat poison, no insecticides. All they had was prayer, all those Te Deums and Magnificats, fasting, confessions, chanting, Scripture readings, more prayers, marching around in the rain...."

"Well," Father Ignatius said, "that's something."

"Of course," Samuel said. "But did it do any good? Other than give these poor men false hope, I mean?"

Father Ignatius's silent shrug was long and elaborate. "Who

knows?" he said at last. "I do believe it gave them hope, true or false. And isn't that the way it always is with remedies? You never really know if what you've done helped or not. But you have to do it, don't you? And these monks had to do *something*, didn't they? Ah, good. The water's boiling."

"Yes, of course," Samuel agreed.

The two men enjoyed their tea and scones in companionable silence. When they were finished, Samuel said, "Father, thank you so much for your hospitality. I'm sorry if I sounded irreverent. I really am grateful for the chance to spend time with Brother Araud. I didn't meet all the physicians you mentioned, but perhaps I might come 'round tomorrow?"

"The library will be closed tomorrow, Samuel. You're certainly welcome to come next week. I think you'd enjoy...wait!" The old priest grinned. He turned and went to the filing cabinet behind his desk. He opened a drawer and pulled out a ring binder full of British-size typing paper. "Silly me! I should have shown this to you at the start, but I suppose I was just too eager for you to see the original first."

He handed the binder to Samuel, who opened to the first page and read the title: "The Secrets of Tintern Abbey."

"It's my English translation of the entire volume," Father Ignatius said, his face beaming with pride. "Would you like to borrow it for a few days?"

Sam's jaw dropped. "Of *course!*" he said. "I'll read it tonight!"

"If I might make a suggestion?"

"Yes?"

The priest wore a sly smile. "The Randolph is probably not the proper atmosphere for this tale. Why don't you take it to the source?"

"The source?"

"Tintern itself is not that far from Oxford," Father Ignatius said. "Do you have an automobile?"

"A rental," Samuel answered. "I've hardly used it."

"Well, there's a good inn at Monmouth, a very pleasant city only a short drive from the abbey itself. The Queen's Head. Georgian, I believe. They have a well-lit parlor for reading."

Samuel tucked the binder under his left arm and held his right hand out for the priest to shake. "Father Ignatius, I can't thank you enough. How lucky I am to have met you!"

The old priest winked. "I suppose luck had something to do with it. That would depend on what you call luck. Have a good weekend. I'll be praying for your mother."

"Thank you, Father. Do you think it will do any good?"

"I can't say for sure," the priest answered. "But I am sure it will do no harm."

SUNDAY MORNING, DOCTOR Samuel Gordon Lewis sat on a tree-filled hillside in Southeast Wales, near the limestone outcropping locals call the Devil's Pulpit. He looked down through the mist of May on the green Wye River Valley and the village of Tintern, with its grand old ruin of an abbey nearby. The valley was still and quiet, except for the strange croaking of frogs unlike any frogs Sam had ever heard before.

He thought about his mother, and trusted that she would receive whatever fate she was allotted with grace; she was, after all, in the care of one of the best medical teams in the United States. She was, after all and after that, in the hands of God.

He thought about his dear wife, his Mary. How she had encouraged these trips—to Oxford for the spring, and to Wales for the weekend. She held his life, his heart, his sanity in her hands. Dear Mary.

And he thought about the manuscript he had read the night before, in the reading parlor of the Queen's Head Inn in Monmouth, just up the River Wye. A truly remarkable story of truly remarkable people, covering four hundred years of piety, solitude, and survival. This spot in this valley, once the home of Celts, then of Romans, then of Saxons and the Welsh, was for four hundred years the home of a community of holy men, the white-robed Cistercians, who had come here through the wilderness with their brown-robed lay brothers, to build an abbey, a stone church, a place in which to pray for the souls of all men and women.

As Samuel sat, the morning sun rose above the mountains in the east and burned away the mist in the valley. He looked down and watched the village of Tintern fade away before his eyes. The abbey church stood alone, no longer a skeletal carcass of a ruin, but a full, solid sculpture of a building, with clean stone walls and bright colored windows, and a bell whose mellow tone echoed softly through the valley.

Before his eyes, the church faded out of sight, turning to a cluster of wooden structures that dotted a green meadow.

Down by the river a boat was landing at a dock. Men got out of the boat and made their way toward the wooden buildings. As they walked, single-file, toward the center of the meadow, thirteen of them were dressed in white robes, and ten of them wore brown. Before they reached the wooden structures, the men formed a circle in the center of the meadow, where they chanted their Te Deum as if with one voice. The sound of their song of praise and thanks was as eerie as the croaking of Welsh frogs, as melodious as the bong of the abbey bell bouncing through the valley....

High overhead flew a golden eagle....

PART I
The Making of an Abbey

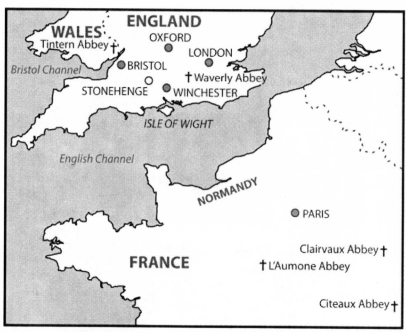

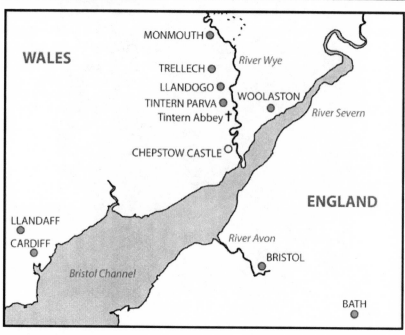

1
Beginning

THERE WAS NOTHING shy about Henry. He did not fit the mold for an Abbot. On the other hand, he did fit the archetype of "first among equals." Was Henry of noble blood? Possibly, but we may never know. Rumors were that he had been a brigand, a highwayman, or maybe even a killer. His face, though clean-shaven, was a bit rough-hewn. The piercing blue eyes disclosed nothing but took in everything. Even Abbot Henry's white robe did not hide his powerful Anglo-Saxon frame. No one who ever met Abbot Henry would ever forget him.

But was he right for the task? His undertaking required him to take twelve monks and ten lay brothers into the rugged wilderness of Wales and build an abbey. The monastery, envisioned by the Lord of Chepstow Castle, Walter Fitz Richard of Clare, already had a name. It was to be called Tintern Abbey.

Tintern Abbey would be only the second Cistercian house in Britain. Lord Walter Clare was of a new generation of British noblemen, who were far more impressed by the ideals of the Cistercians than by those of the Benedictines. Cistercians' white robes contrasted dramatically with the black robes of the older order. These white-robed monks delighted in going to the most remote, inhospitable, wild, isolated, hostile, primordial, back-country lands. One of their spiritual leaders, Saint Bernard, had prohibited traditional forms of revenue enjoyed by the Benedictines, and so the Cistercians rejected all sources of wealth and luxury, including revenues from manors, rents, labor services, mills, churches, and even tithes.

Lord Clare knew that wherever these white robes settled, the wilderness became tamed by villages, towns, and manors where sheep and grain flourished. Had not Gerald of Wales told Lord Clare this a few months earlier? "Just give them a forest or wilderness, and in a few short years you will have a dignified abbey in the midst of plenty." Lord Clare knew the isolated, heavily wooded slopes of the Wye Valley would more than meet the criteria for the Cistercians and Tintern Abbey.

Less than a month ago, Abbot Nicholas of L'Aumone Abbey in France had received the letter from Lord Clare of Chepstow Castle in Wales with the news that the land survey had been completed by two Cistercian Abbots, one from Waverley Abbey and the other from Citeaux. The recommended wood structures had been completed, including a wood frame church, refectory, dormitories for monks and lay brothers, a guest house, and a porter house. More permanent stone buildings were to commence in the spring of 1132.

The departing party of twenty-three men knelt before Abbot Nicholas to receive his farewell blessing. "I send you forth as sheep among wolves. I pronounce upon you not an ordinary but an extraor-dinary blessing because you are all volunteers. I pray that each of you will hold steadfast to the Rule of Saint Benedict. I lay upon each, both the choir monks and the conversi, the responsibility of praying one for another. Lord God, I pray that You will lay upon each brother boldness and humility. Keep their bodies pure as they praise and glorify the Blessed Virgin. May they find hospitality from all as they journey to Wales. May every house they enter as they journey receive a threefold blessing. In the name of the Father, the Son, and the Holy Spirit..."

Crossing themselves, the travelers responded together, "Amen."

As the pioneers gathered to leave, Abbot Nicholas made one final statement. "I shall journey to your abbey next spring for my required annual visit. Until then, God bless you and protect you."

WEATHER WAS FAVORABLE in the spring of 1131. It took four days for the traveling party to reach the English Channel by way of the old Roman road commissioned by Julius Caesar. A boat took the holy men to the Isle of Wight. The next day they were in Portsmouth. Following another ancient Roman road, they traveled on to Winchester. Abbot

Henry had heard many stories associated with this area about a legendary King Arthur.

At Winchester, the arriving party was greeted with fondness and joy by Diocesan Bishop William. Bishop William's family was related by marriage to Lord Walter Fitz Richard of Clare. This bishop had established the first colony of White Monks in 1128 at Waverley Abbey, which stood a day's journey northeast of Winchester Cathedral. Abbot John, the first and only Abbot of the Cistercian's Waverley Abbey, had come to Winchester to greet the pilgrims.

After three days' rest, climaxed by a Mass led by Bishop William asking for their safe journey, the pilgrims traversed through Sarum along another trampled Roman road. Bishop William furnished several horses to help carry supplies during the hundred-mile trip to Chepstow Castle. The weather was still favorable for travel; despite the dark overcast skies, no rain had fallen.

Their journey took them through the New Forest, where the Roman road was lined with ash-hazel trees. Towering oaks pushed their way through the ash. Evidence of man's influence could be seen in the New Forest. The Saxons had discovered that stumps of fallen trees produced shoots that quickly grew upwards, and so they deliberately cut trees to cause large numbers of straight poles to emerge from each stump. Such poles were used for arrow shafts, tool handles, roof rafters, shafts for carts, and poles for fishing.

Leofric, the group's able translator, asked Abbot Henry, "Why were some of the stumps cut so high?"

"Smaller and shorter shoots make tasty meals for deer, pigs, and cattle," answered the Abbot. "The stumps are deliberately cut a full six feet above the ground to prevent animals from eating them."

"Yes, I remember now, this technique is called 'coppicing.' I learned the word while in school in Paris. But this is the first time I have actually seen the practice." Leofric had a small round head, dark hair, and sparkling hazel eyes. Although usually a shy man, he tended to blurt out what he thought and felt, especially when his emotions ruled. He had learned to control his emotions better since joining the Cistercians, yet he was still prone to outbursts.

For the most part the caravan moved along quietly, except for the sound of horses' hooves striking the ground, although they were surrounded by the sounds of chirping birds—English sparrows, hoopoes, and chimney swallows. High on an oak limb an orange-red sparrow hawk eyed some smaller birds below. Through a break in the forest, Abbot Henry spotted a golden eagle gliding in a wide circle. Ancient animal lore claimed that the sighting of this bird could be a sign of either benevolence or impending danger. The Abbot was an intelligent man, but he found the eagle's presence unexpectedly concerning. He comforted his thoughts by reciting a favorite passage from Isaiah:

> *Yet those who wait for the LORD*
> *Will gain new strength;*
> *They will mount up with wings as eagles;*
> *They will run and not be tired,*
> *They will walk and not become weary.*

Despite his private encouragement, however, the Abbot's unease continued. A movement to his left caught his eye and distracted his ominous thoughts. A doe stepped back, as though uncertain of how dangerous these newcomers might be. Abbot Henry's natural instinct was to reach for his bow, but he wore no bow. He was now an Abbot, not a hunter. He had traded his bow, arrow, and sword for a cross.

By the middle of the morning, the skies had turned dull and threatening. Clouds were gathering and moving southeast. Henry told Prior Geoffrey to have the monks search for some kind of shelter. The group left the edge of the New Forest and entered the rolling plains of Sarum, where they began seeing clues telling them that they were well into old Celtic country. A few yards to the left were some rows of waist-high stones, clearly not placed there by nature. Still farther, they ambled through a ring of standing stones. The huge sarsens, or standing stones, were rough, not finished as a monument should be. Four adult men standing on each other's shoulders could not equal their height.

Breaking his silence again, Leofric asked Prior Geoffrey, "Who could have made these and stood them up? Pagans or the devil?"

"Pagans, inspired by the devil," the Prior replied.

Abbot Henry only smiled as he turned away. He realized he had a superstitious Prior.

The monks were now urged to pick up their pace. By afternoon, the party had reached the River Avon. Finding a shallow stone crossing, they continued their northwesterly direction. At a rise on the ridge, they hurried between six monuments that were smaller than the ones they'd seen but still taller than the combined height of two men.

Lightning flashed and thunder echoed from the north and northwest. As they rounded the top of the ridge, the group paused at the sight that stretched a mile ahead of them. Stones of unbelievable size jutted out of the land and formed a great circle. The combination of lightning, the deafening clap of thunder, and the massive looming silhouettes of rock terrified the men, as though the very gates of hell were opening before them.

"We must make haste," shouted Abbot Henry, urging the group toward the stones. "The rage of the storm is upon us. The only shelter is among those huge stones. Quickly!" he cried.

The holy men and the frightful storm were in a race to the megaliths. Galandas, who was usually quite calm by nature, darted ahead and nearly knocked over the hesitant Alfred. Abbot Henry started to scold the young monk, but by then it was impossible to be heard over the sound of the brutal weather.

Terrifying winds whipped around them. Slow drops of rain escalated into sheets of water. A blinding bolt of lightning struck a mile away, just as the group reached the stones. The deafening sound of thunder encouraged everyone to find the best shelter he could.

Abbot Henry counted heads to make sure all had arrived at the shelter. Still frightened, Alfred stayed as close to the Abbot as possible. When the winds died down and the thunder passed, the monks gathered themselves together under the horizontal beams connecting the massive upright sarsens. The rain was now coming straight down, so the lintels offered some protection from the water. Under the horizontal beams, the holy men wrapped themselves in their robes, leaned their backs against the sarsens and prepared for slumber. Despite the uncomfortable conditions, exhaustion hastened the men's sleep. Abbot Henry dozed off last, choosing to let the group forego the night's sacred readings.

A little after daybreak, on a damp, clear, cool morning, the monks joined together for Prime, the ritualized prayer held about sunrise. Abbot Henry thanked the Blessed Virgin for their delivery from the fierce and threatening storm. William of Coventry, an ordained priest, led the group in Mass. After a breakfast of hard bread and some wine, furnished by the Bishop of Winchester, the pilgrimage continued northwest. They were less than two days' journey from Chepstow Castle.

AFTER CROSSING THE River Severn, which was the passageway to Wales, the column of men was only a few miles from Chepstow. Cistercian monks were noted for moving about their activities in silence, and Alfred and Leofric had already been cautioned about their loose idle chatter; but Alfred broke the silence once again. "Abbot Henry," he whispered, "some of us have heard many bad things about the Welsh. Most Welsh have Celtic blood running in them. They are known as the wild people of the Marches. Rumors are that even the Romans were not able to civilize them. If the Celts are supposed to be Christian, then why do they insist on having a circle around the center of their cross? I have even heard that the great Archbishop of Canterbury has been unable to change them. How then, could our small group of unarmed men survive in such an wild and wicked land?"

"The Marches that you mentioned is nothing more than the border between England and Wales that is separated by a twenty-five feet high dike that stretches for miles," Abbot Henry replied. "It is hardly haunted or ominous. The circle on Celtic Cross is there because circles are an ancient sacred symbol of the Celts. When they became Christian, they combined their old circle symbol with their new one, the Cross of Christ, producing the Celtic Cross. The Celts have been Christian for over seven hundred years. Their land is sparsely populated. We are going there to bring Christ to the land, to build it up, and to help make it prosperous. God willing, it will be a trial of our faith. We will be protected by the Virgin Mary, Christ, and Lord Clare. Look at this as an opportunity for inward and outward faith-building. Have no fear.

"Wales was once near the westerly border of the Celtic speaking peoples," the Abbot continued. "They once ranged over the Ukraine, the Iberian Peninsula, and the whole of Northern Europe. First the Germanic peoples, then the Romans, and finally the Saxons pushed the Celts to the end of their world. Once they got to Wales and Ireland, there was no room for further retreat. The Welsh saw themselves as Celtic heroes in the same mold as Vercingetorix, a great Celtic hero, whom they believe will rise up someday and throw the oppressors back into the sea. Vercingetorix was defeated at Alesia fifty-two years before Christ and was taken to Rome as a prisoner. Seven years later Vercingetorix was ordered by Julius Caesar to be strangled. Now the conquering Normans are building castles and abbeys along every stream, in every valley, and on every meadow in Wales."

Abbot Henry realized that other monks were listening too, and so he continued his discussion of Wales, to help them all become acquainted with their new homeland. "Remnants of over six hundred hill forts have been identified throughout Wales. Welsh villages have Celtic names. It has been said the heavy forests of Wales still have markings and echoes of Druid priests. The springs, wells, and rivers have been known to give up panoplies of swords, lances, human heads, armor, shields, cauldrons, gold, silver, flagons, Roman coins, and more. The Celts sacrificed all these valuable items to their many gods, including Lleu and Cernunnos, trying to pacify these deities."

Although the Abbot did not mention this to his flock, he was well aware of the dangers awaiting them in the Wye Valley where Tintern Abbey was to arise. Was danger the meaning of the ominous golden eagle he'd seen circling in the sky? Henry considered the previous sighting. The eagle's presence had been the prelude to the horrific storm amongst the giant stones. What other threats would he and his pilgrims face? Despite his own doubts, Abbot Henry was steadfast in his dedication and devotion to his mission.

Lord Clare had posted riders along the Severn River road east of Chepstow to signal the coming of the monks. Abbot Henry was the first to spot the approaching horsemen. Philip Courtney, a close relative and high-ranking soldier of Lord Clare, led several riders who carried with them clear water, wine, and some freshly baked bread. "We knew you would be coming down this road. My plans were to give you a short rest by this old marker," said Courtney. A small feast was served beside an old Roman road marker that pointed the way to the deserted Roman fort of Caerleon, after which Philip Courtney rode ahead to alert the castle of the upcoming arrival of the seasoned travelers.

Stone castles had not existed anywhere in Wales prior to the Norman invasion of Britain in 1066. The border between Wales and England was called the Marches. The Marcher lords were Norman nobility placed on the border to make this land peaceful and profitable for King William the Conqueror. Marcher lords' dominion swung in a great arch from Chester in the north of Wales to Chepstow in the south. William the Conqueror gave Lord Clare wide powers to subdue south Wales. From his relatives and friends, King William drew a formidable force of fighting men, whom he placed at the mouth of the River Wye, where the river joined the Bristol Channel, a strategic location that the Romans had recognized long before. Chepstow Castle became the focal point of the Norman settlement of south Wales and a springboard for future expeditions into Welsh lands. One important way to subdue the Welsh people was to build a group of Norman abbeys. Tintern Abbey's site would occupy a vital location in the Marcher lords' wars for the suppression of Wales.

The band of twenty-three pilgrims approached the grounds of Chepstow Castle from the northeast. The imposing great tower stood confidently high on the hill, taking full advantage of the natural defenses of a deep ravine on the south and the steep river cliff at the north. Like most of the castles of its time, Chepstow had high walls surrounding a bailey, an open courtyard with exercise areas, parade grounds, and emergency corrals.

Instead of an environment of attack, an impressive welcoming line greeted the monks in the bailey. Lord Walter Fitz Richard of Clare was the first in line. He was flanked by his chaplain, Father Gilbert, and Philip Courtney. Behind the three stood a host of servants eager to make the holy men welcome. Except for Abbot Henry and Prior Geoffrey, these monks had never had such a greeting.

Lord Clare was a leader who knew how to get the most out of people whether they were holy men or soldiers. He stated he wanted to personally greet each man in the caravan.

"Certainly," replied Abbot Henry, surprised by this novel approach for a nobleman. As he introduced the attentive band of pilgrims, the Abbot was also impressed that the lord stepped in front of each man, extended his hand in welcome, emphatically repeated the man's name, and expected a response.

"This is Brother Geoffrey, our Prior. He has been a humble and able warrior of God, after his return from the Crusades." In an unusual gesture, the lord extended his hand. Reflexes brought Brother Geoffrey to attention.

"Tell me, were you among those who reached Jerusalem?" asked Lord Clare.

"I was, Your Lordship," replied Geoffrey.

"Two other monks among us also defended our faith during the Crusades, and they, too, reached the Holy City," Abbot Henry told Lord Clare. Taking a couple more steps, he said, "This is Brother and Father William of Coventry, an ordained priest. He was a crusader who reached Jerusalem."

Lord Clare greeted the monk with a nod and the two men shook hands.

"And here is another Brother William," the Abbot continued, moving along the line. He introduced William the Templar, an honored crusader. "He was at Jerusalem when the heathen walls were breached. To his credit, this Templar was one of those who helped calm the killing frenzy that occurred against both the Moslems and the Christians. Now, although he was a high-ranking Templar, he has set aside his glory and battle array for the white cloak of the Cistercians."

"You are privileged to have seen the Holy City," said Lord Clare, "and to have returned safely when so many others lost their lives."

"This is our Cellarer, Ralf," said the Abbot, continuing down the line. "Brother Ralf is the third son of Duke Ehudes of Burgundy. Handling his father's estates makes him well qualified to administer large holdings."

"Next is Brother Ordric, our Sacrist. He came to the abbey of Cluny as an oblate. Brother Ordric often leads us in our services and sacred readings. We are pleased to have him. He is well schooled in Latin, in the sacred writings and readings."

"It is an honor to welcome someone like yourself who has great knowledge of the holy literature," said the lord.

"Brother Alfred is the second youngest of our order," Abbot Henry continued. "A fine scholar, he has studied in Paris and is our most able scribe, as well as a most accomplished copyist. I would call him an artist in words and designs. Each letter in his manuscripts often tells a story in itself. He will make it possible for every monk in your abbey to be well read and knowledgeable in sacred and secular writings. His scripts and illuminations are highly prized even by kings."

"I am anxious to observe your well-known craft on my first visit to Tintern Abbey. I will be grateful if you can find time to make a copy of the Gospel of John for Chepstow's chapel," said Lord Clare.

Alfred nodded with a smile.

The Abbot and the lord moved on. "Hugh of Flaxley is highly dedicated to the art of Lectio Divina. He is a monk of many talents and has been used by our Blessed Virgin in secular and holy under-takings," stated Abbot Henry.

"I hope Abbot Henry will make you available for some of our important contacts and needs," replied the lord.

"Lord Clare, now meet our youngest, Brother Galandas. His father, Baldwin, the Count of Flanders and Artois, was killed on the way to the Holy Land. Galandas made his way back with the aid of a dedicated knight. He showed up one day on our doorstep and we took him in. Although small, he has become a hardworking and ded-icated monk. And he is wise beyond his years," added the Abbot.

Lord Clare looked puzzled for a moment, then nodded at the young monk and said, "I did not know Lord Baldwin was blessed with a son. I had the pleasure of meeting your father on one occasion.

I was impressed by his size and kindly manners. I knew he was destined to go on a Crusade. His death has left a gap in our fight with the heathen."

Galandas bowed his head and did not look at Lord Clare during this exchange.

"Next, we have found Brother Leofric to be an able translator of Latin, German, French, and English. The brother has attended schools at the Sorbonne in Paris and at Bologna in Italy."

Lord Clare was clearly impressed. He turned to the Abbot and said, "Outside of Rome, I have never seen such a gathering of scholars, monks, and dedicated brothers with such fine records and accomplishments. All Christendom admires the Cistercians. It is not an easy order to join."

"Our next monk is Brother Roger. He is one of our own who has experience in setting up new monasteries at Citeaux, Clairvaux, and L'Aumone. Roger is equally competent in wood, stone, and spiritual building," said the Abbot.

Lord Clare reached for Brother Roger's hand saying, "We shall certainly be calling on your experience here at Chepstow. We have a wall or two that needs mending!"

Abbot Henry said, "Here is the last of your choir monks, but not the least. Brother Ceolfred is an ordained priest who comes to us through the Canterbury Cathedral. He is bold in action, experienced in judgment, and zealous in religion. He is most noted for performing the impossible with few resources."

"Welcome, Brother Ceolfred. I have heard of your homilies. Perhaps the Chepstow chapel will be privileged to hear from you soon."

Abbot Henry next turned his attention to the conversi. "Here are ten lay brothers who are tried and experienced. All have volunteered. They have been with Brother Roger for many years. They all have taken the modified Rule. Our lay brothers are noted as much for their prayer and spiritual work as for their labor in dirt, sand, wood, and stone. These brothers are not hired help; they are dedicated men of God. The bulk of the heavy and agricultural work will be their tasks. Conversi wear the brown habit and, I say again, have earned a high reputation for their spiritual life," the Abbot said with a hint of pride in his voice.

Lord Clare reached out to touch each of their hands, welcoming each by name. Then he turned and addressed the entire group. "Your abbey will be a place of prayer and spiritual devotion. Our people cannot attend Mass daily and at times find it difficult even on the Lord's Day to be present. They will take comfort in knowing that God is praised and the Virgin is being honored by their holy men. They will feel better knowing your prayers will advance their deceased relatives' passage into heaven. They know that through me, they have a part in building Tintern Abbey. Before long, they will be making pilgrimages to Tintern Abbey where they can feel cleansed, healed, refreshed and absolved."

Overcome by admiration of Lord Clare, Alfred blurted out for all to hear, "By God, I would gladly die for a man like that!"

Personal introductions with the holy men appeared to have pleased the nobleman as well. "Rest and have nourishment, brothers. Soon the day will close. After our meal I will join you in Compline," Lord Clare said, referring to the end-of-the-day prayers. "For tomorrow we will journey to your new home. With God's blessing, where we go will soon be Tintern Abbey!"

2

Spiritual and Physical Foundations

FOLLOWING MORNING PRIME, the colony of monks gathered at the dock on the northeastern side of Chepstow Castle. Four boats had been prepared to provide transportation to the Tintern site, about four miles up the Wye Valley.

The group was in high spirits as the armada for God moved to the center of the River Wye, rowed by the strong-armed soldiers of Lord Clare. Moment by moment the night fog lifted. In the lead boat were Lord Clare, Abbot Henry, and Prior Geoffrey. The remainder of the choir monks filled the first and second boats. Lay brothers packed into the third boat, with supplies in the fourth. After their long days of walking, the company was delighted to be carried for the final leg of their journey.

The monks' usual posture involved holding their heads down. Today, their heads were up and alert, taking in every sound: the rustling of springtime ash leaves, the strange croaking of the Welsh frogs, the rapid assonance of the chatterer bird perched on a beech limb, and the steady hum of a dragonfly trying to alight on the tip of the swaying marsh grass. Galandas nudged Hugh of Flaxley and pointed to a handsome pheasant in a small meadow nearly surrounded by beech trees. Ahead, near the edge of the shallows on the west side of the Wye, stood a common heron. For those with sharp eyes, two rabbits could be seen, one grazing on spring roots, the other looking squarely at the slow-moving boats. The lay brothers noticed the bluebells, buttercups, daffodils, and wild strawberry plants along the water's edge.

The tree-covered hills on each bank seemed to rise higher as the River Wye became deeper. Lord Clare tapped the Abbot on the shoulder and pointed to one of three giant hogweeds at the river's edge. "You need to keep your distance from those big bunches of white flowers. Most of them are here in the Wye Valley. Their leaves carry a poisonous sap. Just brushing against this plant can leave you with large and painful blisters. They can grow as high as a man's shoulder."

"Thank you for the warning," the Abbot replied.

"Just ahead of us," the lord continued, "there on the left, you'll see some handsome white flowers with leaves that resemble ferns, with purple spotted stems that are about head high. Do you recognize them?"

"Hemlock!" answered Abbot Henry. "They say Socrates ended his life with a potion made from hemlock."

"Indeed." Lord Clare noted that this learned man was no ordinary monk—or Abbot for that matter.

Glancing up, the Abbot noticed a golden eagle circling overhead. The first eagle had brought them the storm on the plain of the giant stones. Could this be another omen?

"Take heed, brothers," Lord Clare called out to the trailing boats as he lifted his left hand and gestured outwardly. "There is your Tintern!"

Abbot Henry took in a deep breath. The landscape was stunning. He saw before him a majestic valley backed by a semicircle of rich wooded hills.

This is our destiny, my destiny, he thought. *Here we will do God's work. A great abbey will rise from this land to serve the Almighty and His people. I pray that I will lead this undertaking with wisdom and grace.*

As the husky soldiers pulled the boats high up out of the water, several monks whispered their relief in seeing that several buildings had already been erected. Others slowly turned their heads this way and that to observe the scene before them. Standing in awe of their new surroundings, they became quiet and still. Only the sounds of nature—the sparrows, the Welsh frogs—filled the air until Lord Clare broke the silence.

"Abbot, would you lead us in prayer?" he asked.

"Lord, there will be time later for us to memorialize this day with appropriate liturgy. For now, we feel that it was for this day that all of us were born. For this day You sent us into the world. Here on the banks of the River Wye and in this valley, an abbey to Your glory shall rise. Here we will ponder the mystery of the Cross, the mystery of the Blessed Virgin, and the mystery of Creation. In these walls the poor will be fed, and the homeless will find a bed. Here the sick will be succored, the wise will be counseled, and the gift of salvation will be contemplated. In the name of the Father and of the Son and of the Holy Spirit, Amen."

Well pleased with this prayer, Lord Clare knew Abbot Henry was indeed the man for the task. Lord Clare may even have somehow known that here in this amphitheater of a free-flowing quiet river, amid stately hills and stones of grandeur, monks, kings, noblemen, lay brothers, peasants, craftsmen, and pilgrims would spend hundreds of years praising God and singing of His grace.

"I will be leaving some of my craftsmen with you during construction," Lord Clare said as they approached the buildings and laborers. "They will be working under the direction of Brother Roger. If you have any needs we may fulfill, notify one of my soldiers to send a message."

Lord Clare pointed out that plenty of wood and timbers were available. Permission had been given to take whatever was needed from the forests and the quarry beyond the Wye.

"Come, let us examine the buildings," the lord said as he led the monks over to the dormitories. "You must realize that all these structures are but temporary until the finer structures of stone are built. Nevertheless, they are well built and will serve for the time being. May I give you a report on their construction?"

"Please do," replied Abbot Henry. "We wish to learn about this vast progress that preceded our arrival."

"The timbers for these buildings were carefully selected to follow the natural shape of the tree. First, we built two dormitories, one for the choir brothers and the other for the conversi. Each building is twenty feet wide and forty feet long. Using the latest construction techniques, a one-foot pit was dug and filled with good-quality straw. As this straw decays, it will give off some heat and provide a warm floor in winter. Both dormitories have heavy wooden floors that extend out one foot beyond the straw in the pits. Poles have been placed in the ground with one set of higher center poles allowing the beams to connect with the side structure."

The group walked slowly by the dormitories as Lord Clare pointed to the buildings' roof line. "The thatched roof extends out over the side walls, which allows the walls to support the eves of the roof. Branches have been woven to form walls, and thick clay has been used to fill in the gaps, to make the building draft-proof. Doors have iron hinges and bronze latches. Notice that three windows in each building are covered with vellum; by winter we plan to have all the windows shuttered. Candles will give you light. Materials are provided for each of you to make your own mattress."

Before moving on Lord Clare introduced some of his construction workers. Brother Roger knew several of the lead carpenters and plumbers, for they had worked together on other construction projects.

One of the carpenters approached Lord Clare with a question, and when that matter was settled, the lord suggested that the brothers pause briefly from their tour and partake of some refreshment. Lord Clare furnished bread and wine for all. After the rest, which lasted a little longer than he had expected, the nobleman gathered the new community together and escorted them to the dining facility.

"This refectory is built like the dormitories," he told them, "except it is twenty feet longer, with a kitchen built in the center to make it easier to serve the choir monks and the lay brothers. Outside the refectory, a latrine has been built over running water troughs. Its small size makes it possible to have a wooden roof made of green timber, which will swell, making it a rainproof roof."

After a pause for the monks who needed to try out the new facility, Lord Clare led the monks to the chapter house, the chamber designed for their daily meetings.

"A twenty-by-forty chapter room has been built, using the same construction methods as the other buildings. It has benches around three sides and a speaker's stand that can be moved around according to the need. Notice a four-by-eight-foot board has been attached to one wall for reminders, posters, small paintings, and notices to be attached by a pin or nail. This was a clever idea from one of our carpenters."

As the monks filed out of the chapter room, Lord Clare gestured to the building at the river's edge. "Over there is the porter house with a guest house nearer the river. These are fifteen by fifteen feet, and are put up like the other buildings."

Lord Clare had clearly saved his favorite building for last. "Please follow me to the southernmost building," he told them. His eyes sparkled with excitement and pride as they arrived at the chapel.

"Finally, a chapel has been erected in accordance with Cistercian standards. It is the only building with a finished floor and seating tables with benches facing each other. Step into the chapel for all to hear." Once inside, Lord Clare stepped to the front of the chapel near the altar. He modified his voice to a lower tone, respecting the reverence of the place of worship. "There is a finished oak wood altar with a tapestry of the Blessed Virgin hung above it. This tapestry was woven by Lady Clare and her maids. It speaks to us without words. And here, behind the altar, with the help of Father Gilbert, my workers have created, from walnut, a tabernacle for the Eucharist. As you can see, it is shaped with a pointed steeple and crowned by a small crucifix carved by one of my most trusted artisans, Alexander. The tabernacle has two doors in the front, both equipped with bronze hinges. These doors open from the center and when closed completely cover the Host, which is their only purpose."

As the crowd moved out of the chapel, Lord Clare singled out the monk who would be the keeper of the chapel supplies needed for the sacrament. "Brother Ordric, I assume that you have brought with you a chalice, paten, pall, ciborium, flagon, fair linen, a cruet, vail, and parament. Brother Ordric, if you have any need of these, Father Gilbert will help supply you with whatever you may need for your Eucharist." Turning to his castle priest, the lord laughed, "See, I did remember all of the necessary items from my altar boy days!"

Father Gilbert smiled and most of the monks nodded their heads in approval and amusement.

Several carpenters walked past the group while the monks mingled near the front of the chapel. Their unexpected presence reminded Lord Clare to acknowledge Raymond, who had made the missal stand for the top of the altar, and Alexander, the skilled wood carver. Lord Clare whispered a private request to Raymond, who nodded and slipped away behind the chapel. Alexander waited with the group as the lord continued describing the chapel, pointing out the three shuttered windows on each of the longer sides.

"I've asked Alexander to stay a moment as I share information about his exquisite carpentry work on our chapel door. The chapel door hangs on wooden hinges and can be latched. This door was made of finished oak with a carved cross in the center. I have been most gratified by his talents."

Pausing now for effect, Lord Clare asked everyone to be very quiet. Suddenly, from behind the chapel there rang the resounding gong of an iron bell.

"A bell!" exclaimed Alfred.

"We have a bell!" cried Roger.

The normally sedate group of celibate men looked at one another and smiled in amazement. "The bell has been rigged to be rung from the back of the chapel with a wooden shoot passing through a small hole in the wall," Lord Clare told them.

Brother Roger scurried around to the back of the chapel to admire the clever engineering and returned with a pleased look on his face.

"Father Gilbert, my soldiers, and fourteen young Welshmen have worked exceedingly hard and fast to prepare Tintern for your arrival," stated Lord Clare. "I'm also happy to say the weather has been most cooperative this spring."

"We are most pleased, Your Lordship," Abbot Henry replied. "God has blessed us with your faith, support, and commitment."

Lord Clare scanned the stunning landscape before them and felt compelled to relate a piece of history. "This part of Wales is called Gwent or sometimes Glamorgan or even Morganuck. Glamorgan was ruled by a king who fought gallantly against the Saxons. I will tell you more of him when you have your dedication ceremony on the ninth of May. At that time I will present the charter from King Henry, giving all the lands of Tintern and certain other properties to the Cistercian Order and to Tintern Abbey.

"There is much work yet to be done," Lord Clare continued. "My men will work for you or with you. I have confidence that Brother Roger and the Abbot already have ideas and some preliminary plans for the permanent locations of the stone buildings yet to be built. We have placed our temporary structures in areas that should not interfere with any proposed stone buildings."

Brother Roger gave a firm nod of approval. He was indeed bursting with architectural ideas.

"I also understand the veneration of relics is most important. I will work with your Abbot, bishops, and the Vatican to procure such. You are choice servants of God, and I know that many more will follow you here. Some may be Welsh; others may come from Scotland or Ireland. Monasteries are not unknown or new in these places."

Lord Clare became aware of a bit of restlessness floating through the crowd.

"You are surely anxious to get back to your monk's day schedule," he said. "The Abbot tells me regular hours will begin with Compline today. Between now and then, take time to gaze at the giant amphitheater in which you find yourselves and the huge stage on which you will each play your role before God, as will others, for centuries to come."

Lord Clare, Abbot Henry, and Brother Roger paced out measurements projecting where each stone structure might be placed. Brother Ordric reexamined the chapel and mentally rehearsed Prime, the first hour of the canonical day. Prior Geoffrey, Father William, and William the Templar stood on the bank of the River Wye and traded Crusade stories. Brother Galandas stood by himself on the river bank, mulling over in his head Lord Clare's comment about not knowing that Count Baldwin had had a son. Tears came to Galandas's eyes. Noticing Galandas alone, William the Templar walked over and invited the young monk join him for a short walk along the river bank.

On the ninth of May, 1131, the fair weather that had blessed the monks since their stormy night under the monoliths appeared to be coming to an end. By Prime, heavy clouds had given the whole valley a brown tinge. The Normans looked with wonder at this strange overcast. No rain had fallen, but everyone was sure it was on the way.

Abbot Henry wondered if this was the meaning of the golden eagle, or could something more sinister be in the offing?

The ceremonies had been set for Terce, the third canonical hour of the monk's schedule. They were to be followed by a Mass dedicated to the Virgin Mary. By virtue of his position, Abbot Henry would lead the major part of the service.

Abbot Henry called upon all to chant Psalm Forty-four.

Abbot:	*O God, we have heard with our ears,*
	Our fathers have told us,
Monks:	*The work that You did in their days,*
	In the times of old.
Abbot:	*You with Your own hand drove out the nations;*
	Then You planted them;
Monks:	*You afflicted the peoples,*
	Then You spread them abroad.
Abbot:	*For by their own sword they did not posses the land,*
	And their own arm did not save them,
Monks:	*But Your right hand and Your arm and the light of Your*
	presence, For You favored them. . . .
Abbot:	*For our soul has sunk down into the dust;*
	Our body cleaves to the earth.
Monks:	*Rise up be our help,*
	And redeem us for the sake of Your lovingkindness.

Following the chanting, Brother Ordric, the Sacrist stepped forward and announced, "From First Corinthians chapter three, beginning with verse five."

What then is Apollos? And what is Paul? Servants through whom you believed, even as the Lord gave opportunity to each one. I planted, Apollos watered, but God was causing the growth. So then neither the one who plants nor the one who waters is anything, but God who causes the growth. Now he who plants and he who waters are one; but each will receive his own reward according to his own labor. For we are God's fellow workers; you are God's field, God's building.

"This is God's word," Brother Ordric concluded.

To which the assembled monks responded, "Thanks be to God!"

Abbot Henry felt humbled as he called forth the nobleman, their patron who would soon announce the official declaration.

Lord Clare paused for a moment, then began. "Some of you have inquired about the origin of Tintern and why is this place called Tintern Abbey? I will answer the question this way.

"This is the tradition I have heard, and I am passing it on to you and for generations to come. Many years ago this land of Glamorgan was ruled by a devoted king named Tewdrig, or Theoderick. He was fair and just, and he never lost a battle, always holding the Saxons at bay. We have been told that one day an angel of the Lord said to King Theoderick, 'Go tomorrow to assist the people of God against the enemies of the Church, and your enemies will turn in flight when they see your face. But you will be wounded by a single arrow and in three days die in peace.' King Theoderick met the pagan Saxons near a forging place on the banks of the River Wye, this place. The Saxon army was routed and never again threatened Glamorgan. King Theoderick lived another three days and died at this forge of the river with his son, Maurice, holding his hands.

"In his will Maurice provided for a church to be built at this exact location, specifying that the church be named after his father's last battle. In the Welsh language, *din* means fortress or 'place of battle' and *teyrn* means 'chief' or 'sovereign.' In Welsh *D* is often pronounced *T*, and so the name celebrating the last battle of this mighty sovereign is pronounced 'Tintern.' Theoderick's tombstone, located near Chepstow Castle, reads, 'Martyrdom of Theoderick, who because he perished in a Battle against enemies of the Christian name, is esteemed a Martyr.'

"What grander memorial can come to this place than to have it forever named Tintern Abbey?"

Lord Clare's demeanor shifted to one of formality. He turned to Abbot Henry and said in a most solemn voice, "On behalf of his Majesty, King Henry, I present to you, Abbot Henry, representing the Order of Cistercians, the charter for this, Tintern Abbey and for all of the grounds, for certain properties at Porthcaseg, Penterry, Welcrick, Modesgate, a grange at Trellech, and Merthyrgern, and for the lands belonging to the church at Llandaff, as well as, for the benefit of Tintern Abbey, certain rock quarries across the River Wye. In all, this charter is for properties amounting to about four thousand acres."

Abbot Henry stepped forward with his response. "On behalf of the Cistercian Monastery of Tintern Abbey, the Cistercian Order accepts these generous gifts. With the help of God and the Virgin Mary, we shall devote ourselves to being worthy recipients of these bestowments. I can foresee this generation of Tintern Abbey's lay brothers vigorously preparing fields for cultivation, putting up grange buildings, felling woods, and draining swamps areas to extend available plough lands. I can see this pattern extending, with God's help, for many years into the future.

"And at this forge of the River Wye, about four miles from Chepstow Castle, where a mighty king fought and died, it will forever be known as Tintern Abbey!"

With that, the rains poured down, with lightning flashing and thunder echoing down the valley. It was if the Almighty God were closing the proceedings with a resounding, thundering *Amen!*

3

Religious Duties and Temporal Obligations

To those outside the cloistered halls of a twelfth-century monastery, the day-by-day, month-by-month, year-by-year routine may well have seemed pointless, dull, and even uninspired, as if the endless repetition of the liturgy could sap enthusiasm and make worship automatic, with flat, chanted words losing or even changing their meaning. It was commonly believed that the world outside the cloister was engaged in doing, while the monks inside the monastery, so thoroughly engaged in the ancient art of Lectio Divina, were totally unproductive. To the outsider a monk's life appeared hopelessly easy, with very little productive hard work.

The monks, however, believed the divine Word was brought to life by praising, praying, chanting, reading, meditations, individual soul-searching, posturing, Mass, studying, creative writing, blessing the holy water, honoring the monastic ritual schedule, and purifying the monastery to make it ready for holy work. Contemplation and making oneself a conduit of grace was hard work. This was the monk's work, which they called Opus Dei. And the monks believed, knew, that it was productive work.

What were the goals of the individual monks as they began their new life in a new place? Without knowing the inner divine spirit of each monk, we cannot know, but we can suppose that some of them saw Tintern Abbey as a new beginning, a transcendent opportunity to reach higher levels of blessedness, a chance to leave behind unpleasant events of the past, or an opportunity to prove their abilities to the Abbot or their fellow monks. Could some be playing out their lives with the goal of earning a place in the monastery graveyard? This might have been a worthy or an unworthy goal.

LIFE AT TINTERN began with inclement weather. It rained for nine consecutive days, although the air was warmer than usual for this time of the year in southern Wales.

On the tenth day the sun rose over the eastern mountains. Tintern Valley began to dry out slowly. It was still the rainy season and the lay brothers were unable to accomplish much physical work. The monks continued their divine liturgy, always being careful to dedicate the appropriate number of Masses to Lord and Lady Clare, and to King Henry, in addition to the Holy Virgin.

Abbot Henry met with a few hand-picked abbey members to seek guidance in formulating plans and preparations for the upcoming month. Prior Geoffrey, Hugh of Flaxley, William the Templar, and Brother Roger shared ideas about what needed to be completed at the abbey. They also discussed the need for several excursions outside the abbey lands to gather information about their neighbors.

Prior Geoffrey suggested that the entire membership be briefed on the abbey's responsibilities with respect to the community, adding that the briefing should include relevant background history. The Abbot agreed. Geoffrey believed the abbey members must learn the foundation of and the reasons for their new duties. The next day the entire membership family was called together. Following a devotion to the Blessed Virgin, Abbot Henry began.

"When William the Conqueror appointed himself Landlord of England, he deputized a number of his relatives and faithful follow-ers as tenants-in-chief to hold and administer all conquest lands and people for him. This system has survived, so that our Lord Clare is now King Henry's tenant-in-chief. You were all here, just a few days ago, when the Charter from King Henry was read.

"Although we of Tintern Abbey are of the Order of Cistercian, dedicated to worshiping and praising God night and day forever, we have been given the added duty to carry out the King's and our Lord Clare's work of being tenant-in-chief of all we have been given.

"We must now carry out both the spiritual and the temporal work with which we have been entrusted. We must look upon both of these obligations as holy, for we shall be held responsible for both. Let me say this clearly and slowly. For want of a better term, we are ecclesiastical lords. In other words, Tintern Abbey is the lord of all the lands, occupants, and properties given by Lord Clare for us to administer. Please let me explain.

"We will be the consumers of all of these lands' surplus. Coming to Tintern Abbey will be grain, beef, mutton, flour, bread, malt for ale, fodder, lard, beans, butter, corn, honey, lambs, wool, poultry, eggs, herrings, cheese, and more. By nature, we have become dedicated consumers. Our surplus will be used by us to build and maintain this abbey, to meet our current and future needs, and, certainly, to dispense charity to those in need."

Abbot Henry went on to discuss the relationship between religious duties and temporal obligations. Their religious duties were of course already well known to them. The Abbot suggested the importance of their new temporal obligations and what they had to know in order to fill this important role successfully.

"To perform our temporal duties, we must know what assets, means, resources, holdings, demesne, manors, churches, and assarts we have. Assarted land refers to recovered land, such as drained swamps; we will probably recover much land over the years. Also, we must determine which of our lands are fiefs and which free, which of the peasants are free and which are slaves, and we must know all about the tenants and their rents. We need to account for ackermen, lunatics, and frenzied ill persons, as well as the mills, granges, beehives, and ovens. Our records need also to include sheep, horses, oxen, cattle, pigs, ducks, and chickens that exist in our demesne, by which I mean the land owned by the monastery or reserved for our use as Lords of Tintern."

The Abbot noticed a stirring in his audience. Several monks looked unsettled. He felt prompted to give them assurances yet still be clear about the vastness of their mission. "Many of you may feel surprised at the enormity of our undertakings, but we do have experience on our side. Brother Ralf handled his father's lands in Burgundy, totaling over twenty thousand acres. Being a lord over so much may be a bit difficult at first," Abbot Henry continued. "The people under our control are peasants, called villeins. Some are free. These we will call free peasants. They hold this land directly from the Lord Clare, who in turn holds the land and is responsible to Tintern Abbey. The villein pays rent in cash quarterly and has certain other obligations, like working on roads, and giving the lord a hen at Christmas and a basket of eggs on Easter. The free peasant is obligated to have some weapon, such as a sword, and to come to the aid of his lord if the lord calls him. This lord is us!

"Much of this information concerning our lands and holdings was collected in the Domesday Book, in 1086, but we do not have access to these records and the details have surely changed much since that record was created.

"We will need to discover if any stewards, bailiffs, and reeves still exist. If not, we will need to create these from our tenants, merchants, or soldiers who have been granted lands by the King. Perhaps Lord Clare can be helpful in these matters. If we still have these officials, we must determine their abilities and whether they will be allowed to stay in power."

Abbot Henry took a deep breath and a sip of water before continuing. "Included in the bailiff's and reeve's responsibilities will be the courts. Lord Clare will be responsible for the Royal Courts. Royal Courts will deal with matters of high justice, such as homicide, rape, larceny, burglary, treason, and arson. We will be responsible for the Hallmote or Manoral Courts. The custom here will be to hold Hallmote's Court sessions two times a year. There are certain behaviors that will need to be handled in Church Court, such as adultery, divorce, oath-breaking, and so forth. I hope we have some time before there is a need for Church Court. Yet we must have a court ready when it may be needed. Prior Geoffrey has consented to do this for us."

Prior Geoffrey raised his hand and requested, "I seek two brothers to assist me in the Church Court. Please speak with me of your interest when we conclude this meeting."

"I realize that all of these additional responsibilities are what many of you left behind in order to spend your time glorifying God," stated the Abbot. "Now we must be in prayer, asking our Lord Jesus Christ to guide us in order that all of these works will be accomplished in a spiritual and physical manner. We must look to our Lady's divine leading. I have noted your hard work, which you have performed with little rest. Now, can it be said that we shall carry Christ's Cross yet another mile, maybe two? Will you help me?"

The monks were becoming used to Abbot Henry's ways. Instead of commanding or ordering, like some of the Abbots they had known, this Abbot asked them to carry the added load with him. A fluent communicator, the Abbot did not order his monks about, but calmly explained the reasons why certain activities needed to be done.

After the meeting, Hugh of Flaxley approached the Abbot with another recommendation concerning the upcoming excursions. Since Lord Clare had left three boats and six soldiers to help at Tintern, two expeditions could be divided, one group of three men to explore the properties north of Tintern and a second party to go south to locate the church and village at Llandaff. "My old maps indicate there may be more than one Llandaff," he added. "We will discover the exact location."

Abbot Henry complimented Hugh and assigned him the responsibility of locating and evaluating the Llandaff Church. Brother Hugh selected Brothers Ordric and Ralf to accompany him. William the Templar was assigned to go on both trips because of his extensive military background and powerful build. Few people would want to trifle with that giant.

The Abbot chose not to voice his concerns about the potential dangers of the fact-finding missions. He decided to send out the southbound group first and wait for their return before launching the northbound trip.

The following morning Abbot Henry stood at the river's edge, where he blessed the travelers, then lingered for a moment to watch soldiers Blaidd and Mawer guiding the vessel into the strong current. Blaidd and Mawer had been born on Lord Clare's estate in Normandy. Both were over six feet tall with powerful arms. Both were equally qualified to fight with sword, bow, and javelin.

The southern fact-finding group was to consult Lord Clare about the location of the Llandaff Church. Traveling with the current, they soon reached Chepstow Castle. As they neared shore, Mawer, the larger of the soldiers, leapt into water and pulled the boat and its inhabitants ashore. Blaidd stepped from the boat, signaling for Brother Hugh to follow the soldiers into the castle.

After a brief meeting, Lord Clare, Father Gilbert, Blaidd, Mawer, and Brother Hugh emerged from the massive castle door protecting the east entrance on the River Wye. Both soldiers were now more heavily armed.

Lord Clare assigned Father Gilbert to lead the south group to Llandaff Church. By either boat or land, Llandaff Church and Manor were about thirty miles southwest of Chepstow Castle. Brother Hugh felt it would be to their benefit to go by land. The remains of an old Roman road were picked up just west of Chepstow. Walking on the road was fairly easy.

Forests and low hill terrain lay to the north. The holy men crossed a primeval flood plain created by the Usk and Wye Rivers. Occasionally, breaking waves could be heard from the Bristol Channel. Except for a few observations of the scenery, there was little conversation. About halfway to their destination Father Gilbert broke the silence. "Just ahead of us in that clump of trees is a spring where we can rest and take nourishment."

Cool clear water refreshed the holy men. Dipping his cupped hands into the clear water, Father Gilbert said, "This ancient spring was one of the reasons why the Romans connected this spot to their road. However, the spring has a more ancient past. Notice how the spring water has cut a path all the way to the Bristol Channel."

With a sweeping gesture the priest continued, "All of the area you now see was once dark and heavily wooded. Wherever there was a spring, the area around it was considered sacred by the Celts. Their priests or holy men thought these areas to be natural holy places and made them into sanctuaries. They never erected holy buildings, choosing rather to worship in dark thick woods. Such pagans considered all things of nature to be holy, the dwelling places of their gods. This spring and others like it were places where the Druids and Celts thought they could reach into the earth, through the spring water, and connect with their gods. The goddess Sequana, for instance, was a spring nymph who they believed could bring about the healing of many deformities and ailments."

Father Gilbert was clearly fascinated by the ancient peoples and their beliefs. "In Chepstow Castle we have some offerings that were made here by the Celts. These include a carved wooden foot with some smashed toes, a pathetic carved stone head of a child evidently born blind, and a gold torque or arm bracelet. The Celts believed that these waters had magical healing powers. It was their strong belief that their gods would help them if they made an image of their ailment and placed it in the water, accompanied by votive offerings. Then, the pagans prayed intently, waiting, hoping."

The priest scanned his captivated audience, saving the most gruesome detail for that moment. "There is a legend that human sacrifices were held over there, where the place is dark with thick trees," Father Gilbert said, his arm stretched out. "Some of the large trees have ledges cut in them. We are told that such ledges originally held human heads."

"Do you think such devils still live here?" Brother Ordric asked. He grimaced as he poured out the cool water that had filled his cup.

"No, it is just a superstition," responded Brother Hugh.

"I would not be so certain," Father Gilbert whispered.

Mawer and Blaidd had heard many stories and Celtic legends about this place. They knew that most travelers went around or hurried through this area, if they could. Brother Ordric suggested they hasten on to the Llandaff Church. He had no wish to stay the night by this Druid Celtic spring and grove.

As they traveled on, Father Gilbert pointed toward a stone structure standing alone in a nearby green meadow. "Over there is an ancient chambered tomb. It is called Saint Lythan's Tomb, but it is much older than the saint, probably even older than the Celts. The two portal stones stand over six feet high. You'll notice that there is also a back stone with a portal hole. The massive capstone is over fifteen feet long and about ten feet wide, with a thickness of almost three feet. The whole tomb was once thought to be covered with soil.

Tradition says the tomb was uncovered by Romans hoping to find gold or other treasures. The Welsh name is Maes-y-Felin, which translated means 'The Mill in the Meadow.' The wedge-shaped capstone is believed by some to spin around three times on Midsummer's Eve. It is said the Druids cursed the spot and nothing ever grows there."

For a second time Brother Ordric urged the band to move on quickly.

Through an opening in the low-hanging tree limbs, Brother Hugh caught the first glimpse of the Llandaff Church. As they approached the building, Father Gilbert told them about the place they were visiting. "The structure is located on flat lands that were drained much better than the areas around the church. The church is a little longer than square, about thirty feet long and twenty feet wide, and is made of stone blocks about six inches cubed. A typical Anglo-Saxon building, the walls stand two rows deep. Four small windows grace the side walls, about the size of two stone blocks. An apse was added to the rear of the building. This addition is two stone blocks narrower on both sides, with the apse roof also a foot lower than the main church. Side walls are about thirty feet high." Father Gilbert smiled broadly. It was clear that he shared Lord Clare's enthusiasm for building details.

The visitors reached the building and looked it over. The thatched roof appeared to be in good condition. Newer patches could be recognized, indicating the building had been in use either as a church or community gathering place.

The church was a part of an Anglo-Saxon settlement. The Saxons had been noted for taking most of the best flat land and driving the native Celts into the higher, more rocky hills. The church stood two hundred yards north of the manor. Seventeen better-than-average cottages were scattered randomly inside a stoc, the partially stockaded village. Two longhouses stood south of the manor house. The enclosure was split by a burn, or a free-flowing stream, which was fed by three springs in the nearby hills to the north. The water was clear as it flowed south.

"The Anglo-Saxons took this land from the Celts and the depleted Roman legions, who were called home to bolster Rome's defenses from the barbarians. The Celts had done much the same to the Iron Age people from six hundred years before the birth of Christ to the coming of the Romans in the year of Our Lord fifty-eight," Father Gilbert said. He continued relating the history of the land they were traveling through. He described how the Romans' departure occurred in 409. By 500 most of the Celtic groups and tribes had been Christianized. Anglo-Saxons who invaded southeast Britain were pagan. This was quietly changed. By the time the Saxons invaded Scotland and Wales they had been converted. Most Saxons established churches and monasteries in their new lands. Built mostly of wood, but some of stone, these churches had exceptionally bright colors decorating their interiors. There were early significant Church divisions, but the Roman version of the Church prevailed over the Celtic after the Synod of Whitby in 664.

BROTHER HUGH WAS not leading a war party as they approached Llandaff village. All were monks except for Mawer and Blaidd. Lord Clare's soldiers were not dressed in military garb, but they were discreetly armed with swords and other weapons in their packs. It had been over sixty years since the Battle of Hastings. Peace had largely come to this part of Wales. But this was the first time that the authority of King Henry had extended this far west.

A distant bell warned the people of Llandaff that strangers were approaching. About half a mile from the village, William the Templar first noticed more than a dozen men coming toward them. Some had swords, but none of the swords were drawn. Two men were in front of the others, walking slowly. One was the Sheriff of Llandaff and the other was believed to be an Anglo-Saxon priest, Father Gascone.

The sheriff was tall with a thin suntanned Mediterranean face. His sword was sheathed. In his twenties, the sheriff's mannerisms and poise indicated a strong will. He appeared to be a man who would think first before using force.

Father Gascone was a person much harder to evaluate. A man of average height, his heart-shaped reddish brown face and close-set eyes hid his vast intellect. His belted black robe was of rough material that was somewhat different than those worn by priests. His hair was not tonsured, which left some doubt about his identity.

William the Templar and Brother Hugh stepped forward. At about ten paces separation, all stopped and stared at one another.

4

The Perfect Ones

THE SHERIFF OF Llandaff was the first to speak. "Brothers, what business brings you to our village?"

"I am Brother Hugh from Tintern Abbey. Our company is on a quest to learn about our neighbors. The Lord of Chepstow Castle, Walter Fitz Richard of Clare, has given to Tintern Abbey certain properties and responsibilities to administer. Among these properties is Llandaff Church. We come in peace. We mean no harm. Only two of us are armed, both of whom are servants of Lord Clare. We simply seek information. Upon my return, I shall render my report to Abbot Henry of Tintern Abbey, who will report to Lord Clare, who will report to King Henry."

"We are a small village," the sheriff replied. "Our accommodations are limited to the people of Llandaff. This has not been a good food producing year for us. We would like to be hospitable, but we are lacking."

This unexpected answer came as a surprise to Brother Hugh and the others. They looked hesitatingly at one another. Hospitality was customary and to be expected, especially since the monks considered themselves the lords of this village.

"Do you have Dominican priests among you?" the sheriff asked with a hint of caution.

Brother Hugh stepped forward. "No Dominicans, for we are Cistercians. We do have with us Lord Clare's household priest. Are you in need of a priest?"

"Not at this time. But we may have need of one later," answered the sheriff.

William the Templar felt suspicious. He motioned to Hugh,

bidding him to come back a few paces where they could speak in whispers.

William said softly, "I feel uneasy here. I have a hunch that Llandaff is not what we expect it to be. I sense real danger. Their priest is wearing a strange black robe and his hair is not tonsured. How can that be? Clipping and shaving the crown of the head is expected of all monks of the Roman Catholic faith. We may be in peril. Furthermore, the sheriff appears to fear Dominicans. Why might that be?

"I have a suggestion. Let us ask if you and I may go into the village, leaving the rest here in safety. With luck, we can do our work there. If you wish, I shall alert Blaidd and he can tell the others."

Hugh nodded approval to William. Then he smiled as he approached the sheriff and Father Gascone. "We do not wish to be a burden on Llandaff Village people," he said. "We have brought pro-visions and a tent in case of bad weather, so we need not impose. Could William and I come into your village where we can talk? That would give us a chance to meet some of your people, like your bailiff. If you would lead, we will follow."

The sheriff and Father Gascone looked startled. They stepped away a few paces and began talk in low tones to one another. Watching their vigorous gestures, Brothers Hugh and William could only suspect that strong feelings were being expressed.

Father Gascone remained silent while the sheriff continued the conversation with the visitors. "Many of our people are in the fields or the woods. We have a few old and infirm, perhaps too sick to be seen. But we will permit your visit. Please follow us into our village."

Father Gascone and the sheriff led the monks into Llandaff. As they approached the village, each step brought more anxiety and alertness to the Templar. He thought, *Where are the chickens? I do not see cattle, pigs, or sheep. And there are no children. Are these people Welsh, Saxon, Celts, or what?*

William's mind churned over the possibilities. As they passed the cemetery, he noticed two different kinds of markers for the people buried there. *There is something strange about that cemetery,* he thought. *It seems as if there are two different kind of people buried there.* Slowly, it all began to add up. The Templar was developing strong suspicions, but he knew he must keep them to himself until he could be sure. It was time for a little trickery.

William the Templar spoke directly to the priest. "It appears you have a fine Anglo-Saxon Church. I am from France and I have never seen the inside of a Saxon Church. Would you allow me to enter the church and have prayer?"

Both Father Gascone and the sheriff seemed alarmed. For the second time the pair stepped away, whispered to one another, and made more strong gestures. Even though spoken to directly, Gascone remained mum. The sheriff finally said hesitantly, "Why yes. I do not believe anyone is worshiping in the church now. The door is always unfastened. Be my guest."

The sheriff and Hugh walked a short ways to the edge of the little running creek while William entered the Saxon Church. Although there were six very small windows and the door was left open, it took several moments for the Templar's eyes to adjust. His first observation was that the walls had been whitewashed. Moving to the northeast corner, he took his index finger and scraped a tiny spot. It was as he had suspected. Under the whitewash lay a brilliant red. The Templar knew the Saxons always decorated even their small churches in bright colors.

William looked for other evidence. What kind of people worshiped here now? He turned toward the front of the church's interior, where he found a small table, perhaps an altar. Whether a plain table or altar, it had only one object on it, a manuscript of the Gospel of John, printed in Latin with Occitan notes in the margins. Because Occitan was a romance language spoken in southern France at that time, this Gospel of John had special meaning for William. During his journeys as a crusader, he had witnessed the Gospel of John lifted, read, and honored by the Bogomils. Surely these people are not Bogomils all the way here from Bulgaria?

He had seen enough of the church. Now for the cemetery.

Upon going out the door, the Templar turned left into the cemetery. The sheriff saw William walk toward the cemetery, but his only action was to take a deep breath and continue talking to Brother Hugh.

The cemetery was plotted north of the church and displayed two styles of markers. Next to the church were several rows of Anglo-Saxon tombstones. Most had straight shafts ranging in height from six feet down to three feet. All these had square crowns. All marked stones were about eighteen inches wide. The largest marker showed a crucifixion scene where the figure of Christ had been carved into the stone. Christ stood with arms outstretched, His thumbs and fingers extended. His face was damaged, but the halo was still visible. Next to His face on the left side an inverted "V" had been chiseled. Next to His face on the right side the image of a moon had been embossed. The inverted "V" and the moon appeared to have been much more recently carved. On the back side of the larger marker there were panes of interlace dividing some still visible writing. The inscriptions were "SAV" and "VIK," which William interpreted as "Save us from the Vikings." These inscriptions must have been made in the eighth or ninth century, when the Vikings were the terror from the north.

Next to the tall marker was a stone about three feet high with two interlaced panels divided by Anglo-Saxon capitals and runes: "MYREDAH MEH WORHSATE." The Templar translated the old Irish marking to mean "MYREDAH MADE ME." The Irish engraver had wanted whoever read this carving to know who carved it. The unusual writing brought a smile to Brother William.

Farther to the north, beyond a low stone wall, were some newer stones which were much different from any one might find in a Celt or Saxon graveyard. William was finding clues that could prove dangerous to the monks. This was, indeed, a strange cemetery. The northern markers were from two to four feet high. Three of the higher markers had three bordered circular lobes on the tops of the pedestals, one lobe positioned on top of two other lobes of the same size. The top bordered lobe was centered by an inverted "V." On the left side, underneath, the lobe contained a plain cross in its center. The right side bordered lobe was centered with a flying dove. All of the circled lobes were touching one another.

Taking a deep breath, the Templar silently exclaimed, "These look like...but how can they be...here?"

Many other stone markers were only a couple feet tall. Each of these had a base stone topped by a single bordered lobed marker. None of the strange stones had a name on the markers except a few which had the word "Parfaits" inscribed on them. One look at these markers took the Templar back to another cemetery he had seen in Languedoc, France. "Parfaits" is translated "Perfect." His hunches were all coming together. Then he saw the irrefutable proof: scrolled across one of the smaller stones was the word "Consolamentum." These letters spelled out the only sacrament of the hated Cathars!

William the Templar had traveled to the Holy Land through Béziers, Languedoc, northern Italy, and the Balkans on his way to and from the conquest of Jerusalem. The Balkans' mountainous area was home to the Bogomils, a strong group of early Christians that were influenced by the Gnostics, Donatism, Arianism, Pelagianism, and Manichaeism. These groups did extensive missionary work in Southern Europe from the seventh through the thirteenth centuries.

While traveling through the Basilica Pliska north of Greece, he heard many strange stories of their religion. He learned, for example, that Mary was truly worshiped there, but not the Blessed Virgin. Many churches were dedicated to Mary of Magdalene. One merchant in Pliska told the Templar that Jesus had had three children by the Magdalene and that there were several descendants of the union of Jesus and the Magdalene living in Languedoc in Southern France. In fact, the Cathars had had as many as five bishops at one time in that region.

And now here was evidence of a gathering, a whole village, of Cathars in Britain. For who else would mark graves with the words "Parfaits" and "Consolamentum"?

The Consolamentum was a Cathar sacrament that combined baptism, confirmation, ordination, and even, if received at death's door, Extreme Unction all rolled into one. This Cathar sacrament transformed an ordinary believer into one of the Perfect, who in turn could "console" others who were ready to live out their last days without food or water. It was performed by the laying on of hands with repeated instructions to live a chaste, sinless and ascetic life. The standing orders required the Perfect to pray at all times, fast frequently, and abstain from all sexual intimacy. They were to avoid all meat and any byproduct of copulation, such as cheese, milk, butter, and eggs. In this sense, the Cathars may have been the earliest vegetarians. However, they could drink wine; and they could eat fish, since fish were not the result of intercourse, but of spontaneous regeneration in water. One little slip, a stolen kiss, or sip of beef stew and the Consolamentum had to be done all over again.

Just before leaving the cemetery, Brother William noticed a recently dug grave. At the head of the grave was a stone base. On this base was one bordered lobe with the word "Parfaits" carved on its face.

Leaving the graveyard, William looked around again. There were no chickens, no pigs, no cattle in sight. There might have been sheep in the mountains, but these would be kept for their wool, not meat.

The Templar rushed to join the sheriff and Brother Hugh at the water's edge. Although he really did not need additional proof, he had one test that would undoubtedly seal his conclusions.

Suddenly a villager called out to the sheriff. The two talked together for a little while. This gave William an opportunity to relate some of his findings to Brother Hugh. He told him his suspicions that the people of Llandaff were Cathars, and concluded, "No wonder the sheriff and priest were so concerned that we might be Dominicans."

"Why is that?" Brother Hugh asked.

"These Perfects, as they are called, may be survivors of the butchery of Béziers by French knights. If not the same survivors, then at least they know of what happened. In the besieged city of Béziers, several thousand Christians and Cathars sought sanctuary in the cathedral. When the French soldiers complained that they could not distinguish between the Cathars and Christians, legend says that Lord Arnold Amaury of the French Army gave the astonishing order, 'Kill them all; God will know his own.' Regrettably, the French soldiers were aided by Dominican priests. Ever since that bloody event, the Cathars have had a morbid fear of Dominicans, and with reason."

When the sheriff returned, Father Gascone at his side, William was ready to spring his final test. "I understand you have several very sick people," said the Templar.

Father Gascone spoke for the first time. "Yes, one of the women is in a coma," he said.

"We have Lord Clare's priest with us and I understand he is also somewhat of a herbalist," Hugh suggested. "I'm sure he can be of benefit to your sick ones. The one in the coma may need Extreme Unction."

The sheriff and Father Gascone both shuddered. "Thank you for your kind interest in our ladies. Their spiritual and medical needs are being met," said Father Gascone.

The Templar wondered if these persons were undergoing the endura, a ritualistic fast resulting in death because not even water was allowed. The endura, unique to the Cathars, was a cruel mockery of the hospice work done by the Cathars in good times and bad. It was based on their interpretation of the Gospel of John and the traditions of the mystical Gnostics.

Neither Brothers Hugh nor William gave the slightest indication that they thought they had stumbled upon a Cathar cell. If they were correct, here at this Llandaff Church a deity was worshiped who was the god of light, the ruler of the invisible, the ethereal and the spiritual domain. This god did not care much about whom a person went to bed with before or after marriage, for all sexual union was considered evil. The Cathars were dualists who believed all of the material world was evil because it was created by Satan. They believed the soul, which had its origins in a good God, was trapped within a bad material body. In order to liberate the soul, thereby achieving salvation, it was necessary to undergo a ceremony called Consolamentum. After a probationary period of testing and instruction the new believer would be baptized by persons who had already received the Consolamentum. The person would then be required to take vows to remain celibate the rest of his or her life, never own property, never go to war, never eat any food that resulted from coition, and never sleep without breeches and a shirt covering the body. Following the Consolamentum the new believer would acquire the title of Perfect and was given permission to say the Lord's Prayer.

The Cathar doctrines made necessary a reinterpretation of the Bible. Much of the Old Testament was discarded. The God of the

Old Testament was believed to be an evil God who had created an evil world. The doctrine of the incarnation of Christ was rejected because the Son of God could not dwell in an evil body. Instead, Jesus was believed to be an angel whose sufferings and death were only apparent and not real. They believed that Jesus had existed as a shadowy appearance. Thus the Cathars believed in two equally powerful Gods; they were dualists, and theirs was an entirely different church from Christianity.

Brother Hugh and William the Templar, having applied the final test, were convinced they had happened upon a community of Cathars—in Britain, and in fact in the demesne of Tintern Abbey!

Brother Hugh wanted to leave as soon as possible, perhaps even before sundown. However, their business had not been completed. "Do you have a steward and a bailiff?" he inquired. William the Conqueror had directed that every person and every piece of land should have a lord. The steward, bailiff, and reeve constituted the lord's presence in a village, and Hugh was interested to know how these offices were filled in Llandaff.

The steward was the lord's executive officer whose duty it was to guard and increase the lord's property and livestock in an honest way and defend his rights and franchises. The wise lord appointed only a man "ripe in years," who had never been caught or convicted of treachery or any wrongdoing. The bailiff was chosen from village people and had a number of duties which included presiding at the manor court, preparing writs, managing the demesne, and protecting the villagers against another lord. The reeve, also known as the sheriff, was also a member of the village. He assisted the bailiff in maintaining law and order, executing writs, and overseeing the villagers who owed labor service; he also assisted the steward in making a total and detailed account of all the lord's properties.

"As you can see, I serve as Sheriff of the Llandaff Village and its environs," stated the sheriff.

"Who appointed you Sheriff of Llandaff and how long have you been here?" Brother Hugh asked. "Your accent seems to indicate that you are not Anglo-Saxon, Norman, or Celtic."

"You are most perceptive, Brother Hugh. I am from Southern

France. I received my Sheriff's appointment from King Henry. I am not of noble blood and therefore could not be appointed a marsh or frontier lord. My mother, who was from Toulouse, was a close friend of Matilda of Flanders, whom I am sure you will recognize. It always helps to have a family acquainted with those in high ranks."

After a glance toward the priest, the sheriff continued his explanation.

"We here at Llandaff Village have not been sure whether we fall under the lordship of Chepstow, Cardiff, or another lord. As to your other questions, our bailiff was killed a week ago by some hill renegades. He had gone into those northern hills to try to number our sheep. This is a frontier. Safety is illusive," the sheriff said.

"It looks as if the future of Llandaff will be in the hands of the King, the Lord of Cardiff, and the Lord of Chepstow," Brother Hugh declared. "We will take leave of you now. If you see a fire to the east, it will be our campfire. Expect to receive more visitors in the future."

As the visitors from Tintern Abbey departed, anxiety was felt on both sides of the restrained confrontation that had just taken place. Both Father Gascone and the sheriff heard in Brother Hugh's departing words an ominous warning.

As for Brother Hugh and William the Templar, they were nervous as well. As the Templar said, "History has recorded that the Cathars have not been above disposing of strangers or messengers."

5

Welsh Tensions

ON THEIR TRIP back to Tintern, Brothers Hugh and William the Templar stopped at Chepstow to relay to Lord Clare the disturbing news about Llandaff Church and Village.

"There appears to be strong evidence of Cathars infesting the Llandaff community," William said gravely. "This is not an Anglo-Saxon village as believed. We saw no children. This is not like the Saxons. We saw no animals, not even sheep, although the Sheriff of Llandaff did tell us their sheep were in the mountains to the north. The Saxon Church had a recent whitewash inside. Saxon churches normally have bright-colored interiors. There were no icons—again, not consistent with Saxon places of worship—not even a painting or icon of Mary."

"I hesitate to break into such a well-ordered report, but can you tell me a bit more about the Cathars?" asked Lord Clare.

"Cathars are dualists," William the Templar explained. "They see Christ not as the Son of God, but as an angel or a mortal person who did not suffer. They also have the superstition that Jesus and Mary Magdalene married and had children and that Magdalene moved to southern France along with Joseph, Martha, and Lazarus."

"And what evidence did you find of their presence at Llandaff?"

"Some Saxon markers in the cemetery appeared to have been changed; an inverted 'V' had been recently chiseled on some Saxon stones. The face of Christ on one marker had been mutilated. The north part of the cemetery was all given over to only Cathar markers, with which I am familiar from my travels through the French province of Languedoc and through the Balkans. Also, I saw many markers in the Llandaff cemetery with the inscription 'Parfait,' a term given to baptized members of the Carthars. I became more than ever convinced after seeing some markers with the word 'Consolamentum,' which is the sole sacrament of the Cathars, which transforms a novice believer into one of the Perfect. The Perfect do not eat anything that is the product of reproduction. They do not marry."

"Another question. Did you find a Roman priest?" the lord interrupted.

"The village had a purported Anglo-Saxon priest," reported William the Templar. "A Father Gascone, but his head was not tonsured and his black robe was much different, resembling some garments I saw in Carcassonne. Even though they had two very sick old women, one in a coma, Father Gascone would not allow your priest to minister to them. We fear the situation is indeed serious."

"Yes, it sounds serious, I agree," Lord Clare said. "But how can we be certain that your suspicions are right, and that the people in this community are indeed Cathars?"

"There is a test that is sometimes used in southern France to identify Cathars," William the Templar answered. "The Cathars believe in reincarnation and that a dead person could come back to life as a human, or an animal, maybe even a chicken. Believing they might be harming an ancestor, Cathars refuse to kill any animal or fowl. Knowing this, officials in southern France have demanded that the Cathars kill a chicken. If they refuse then they are branded as heretics. Since we were so small a group, we hesitated to consider any kind of confrontation."

"Intriguing," his lordship said. "Anything else?"

"One final item," Brother Hugh responded, "The sheriff told us that they were unclear who their lord was, Chepstow or Cardiff."

"Where did this sheriff get his authority? I know of no such appointment," said Lord Clare.

Brother Hugh responded, "The Sheriff of Llandaff stated that he received his appointment as sheriff directly from King Henry. He intimated that his family was close to the King. We could not question the bailiff. It seems their bailiff was recently killed by northern Welshmen."

"A thorough report," said Lord Clare. "You have given to us

hard decisions that must be handled by me or King Henry, and the Archbishop of Canterbury. Please restate your detailed report to Abbot Henry and your Prior. I know that both of you will be of much help when the King and Archbishop calls upon us to act. Meanwhile, pass this message on to Abbot Henry: the Tintern monks are not to return to Llandaff Village until these matters are resolved."

WILLIAM THE TEMPLAR and Brother Hugh's party departed the next morning. Blaidd and Mawer rowed against the swift current caused by heavy rains upon Mount Plynllimmon. Reaching the abbey about noon, Blaidd and Mawer pulled the boat high onto the bank so the monks could step out onto dry ground.

The travelers immediately noticed many changes that had taken place in the short time they had been gone. Irrigation ditches for a late planting of vegetables had been dug west of the abbey buildings. Seeds were sown. A brick oven was under construction, as was a dovecote for pigeons. A dock on the River Wye was nearing completion. Brother Roger had laid out stakes for a foundation, marking the future location of the monks' stone dormitory. Most of this work had been accomplished by conversi under the direction of brothers Roger and Ceolfred.

Across the Wye and two miles south was a large quarry of fine stone. The day before, Brother Roger had taken three experienced stone workers from among the conversi to examine the quarry. The stone would have to be floated across the river—no easy task. Boats and barges would have to be built. Depending upon the weather, the manufacturing of the watercraft could be done during the first winter season.

LORD CLARE PROMISED to have grape plants brought in the spring for planting with the hope of making wine. He read a letter from Abbot Nicholas of L'Aumone Abbey describing exactly how to plan and care for the vineyard. Abbot Nicholas extolled the values of wine grapes, stating how the leaves, shoots, and bark could benefit the looseness of the bowels, relieve headaches, and even benefit those who "spit blood."

The monks and conversi of the abbey were quick to agree that wine had many valuable properties.

There appeared to be joy everywhere. Not given much to idle conversation, the brothers were doing an inordinate amount of smiling. Perhaps it was the fresh air of the valleys of Wales. Perhaps it was the adventure of it all. Or maybe they felt the Holy Spirit moving in their hearts. Whatever it was, Abbot Henry saw the enthusiasm in both his monks and the lay brothers. It helped that up to this point the monks had faced little danger, and life in their community was full of hope for the future.

Hearing of the safe return of the first fact-finding expedition, Abbot Henry was anxious to meet with brothers Hugh and William for their report. The following day he and a small band would head north up the River Wye Valley for the second exploration.

Looking overhead, Abbot Henry noticed a golden eagle gliding in a wide circle just above the wooded hills. Abbot Henry did not fail to note its circling. Was this an omen, a warning that they would face something dreadful on their journey?

Abbot Henry made an unusual change in the monks' schedule that day. Chapter would be moved from the customary morning time to mid-afternoon. Chapter was the time set aside daily for the reading of a chapter from writings of the Rule of Saint Benedict of Nursia. The meeting included discussions of abbey business. Presided over by the Abbot or the Prior, Chapter started with martyrology, a commemoration of one of the saints celebrated that day by story and prayer.

Prior Geoffrey began, "Today, on the ninth of June, in the year of our Lord eleven hundred and thirty-one, we will seek the voice of Saint Columba. 'Let the blessed Saint Columba intercede for us, O Lord. May his prayers win us your help, since our own actions cannot merit it. Through Christ our Lord, Amen.'"

Readings from the Rule of Saint Benedict followed. Brother Ordric began: "Today we will hear from the Rule of St. Benedict for June nine."

The eleventh degree of humility
is that when a monk speak

he do so gently and without laughter,
humbly and seriously,
in few and sensible words,
and that he be not noisy in his speech.
"A wise man is known by the fewness
of his words."

This reading was followed by a passage from the Cistercian Book of Usages or statutes from the past General Chapter. Disciplinary matters followed, with the confessing monk prostrated on the floor, asking for pardon, the awaited judgment, and expected correction. While the whole community of monks might watch the proceedings, no one was to disclose what had transpired. After this, business matters were discussed. Today, the main item of business was the report of Brothers Hugh and William the Templar.

Brother Hugh and William the Templar related the story of their trip to Llandaff Church by way of Chepstow Castle. William gave his personal background concerning his knowledge of the Cathars and his conclusion that Cathars had infested the Llandaff Village. He recited his evidence along with a description of the Cathar's beliefs, beliefs that shocked the brothers.

"How could they be a church and not believe that Christ is real, in the flesh, and that he died and rose from the dead! Not to believe these things is heresy!" exclaimed Brother Alfred. "I learned about the Cathars in my studies in Paris, under Peter Abelard. The Cathars are connected to the dualist faith called Bogomilism. Do you mean that we have Cathars here in Wales?"

"Are these the people that can be identified by challenging them to kill chickens?" asked Brother Leofric. "Do they really believe that after we die, we can be reborn as chickens?"

"Yes, that appears to be true," responded William.

With no other questions from the assembly, the Abbot gave his final remarks before concluding the meeting. "We are all indebted to Brother Hugh of Flaxley and William the Templar for their work and the fine report given to us. They also bring us a message from Lord

Clare that Tintern monks are to stay away from Llandaff Village until the matter of the Cathars can be solved.

"I changed the time of our Chapter meeting in order to give everyone an opportunity to hear these reports. I will be leaving early in the morning for a search and inquiry mission up the Wye Valley. Going with me will be Ralf the Cellarer, William of Coventry, William the Templar, and Galandas. In addition, Lord Clare has consented to allow Blaidd and Mawer to go with us as protection. Both Blaidd and Mawer know what dangers lie north of us in the valley."

THE FOLLOWING MORNING, just after Lauds, the daily prayer time at daybreak, the explorers pushed out to the middle of the River Wye. The swift river taxed the strength of Blaidd and Mawer but when they steered out of the midstream flow, the boat moved at a good pace.

I would like to have Father Gilbert with us, thought Abbot Henry, *but he is needed at Chepstow because of the death in the family of one of Lord Clare's soldiers.* Before they parted, Lord Clare had told Abbot Henry in private that one must be always alert in dealing with the Welsh, because there had been some recent troubles at the Grange and elsewhere.

Father Gilbert had warned the Abbot about the Devil's Stones located not far from the Village of Trellech. These huge stones appeared sometimes to be turning around without help. Could the stones be a bad omen?

As the water became deeper, rowing upstream became a little easier. Steep and lofty cliffs now lined both sides of the river. Some conifers clung precariously to little patches of earth. As the valley widened, beech and oak trees shaded the river banks. The Abbot and his company were now passing through the middle of the Forest of Dean, fifteen thousand acres of forest, much of it occupying the hilly slopes around the river itself.

"There is much timber here for building long houses, barns, and churches," remarked Galandas.

Although spring was giving way to summer, the air was still

saturated with the fresh scent of generously bursting buds. William the Templar noticed a badger and an otter on the far side bank and pointed them out to his companions. An occasional salmon broke the water's surface.

Behind a single row of common alder trees, the land gave way to a wide plain. Galandas was fascinated by the tall trees, the high ridges, and the long-necked common herons near the bank with those strange-sounding frogs. Old trees falling and giving shelter to rodents and new saplings growing in their place created a balance in nature's harmony. Galandas pointed out the coppicing a hundred yards or so from the beach. He remembered what he had learned about coppicing from Abbot Henry as they had journeyed though the New Forest.

There was something unusual about Galandas. Smaller than the other monks, he also was fairer, with nearly blonde hair. Like many others of the nobility, Galandas's father, Count Baldwin of Flanders and Artois, had mortgaged his land and castles to join the First Crusade. Count Baldwin was killed in the Balkans while protecting some pilgrims from bandits. One of the king's knights was instructed to return Galandas to his home in France. But the knight was unable to fulfill his charge and chose to leave the orphaned lad at the Cistercian Abbey of L'Aumone. Fortunately, Galandas spoke French, English, and Latin fluently. Taken for a novice, the frail young man became an excellent translator from the very beginning and was considered an asset to the Cistercians. His quiet manners and keen wisdom for one so young won favor from all the holy men.

Rounding the bend of the River Wye, it was Galandas who first saw the old Anglo-Saxon Church through a small gap in the trees.

"Is that Llandogo?" he asked excitedly.

"Yes," answered Blaidd.

Abbot Henry said, as they reached shore, "We will spend the night here. From Llandogo to Trellech Grange is about a half-day's journey. Llandogo would have made a fine addition to Tintern Abbey, but it falls under the jurisdiction of the Bishop of Monmouth. Please look around, and if you find anyone, tell them we mean them no harm. Tell them we are monks from Tintern Abbey and we are only passing through on our way to the Trellech Grange. Point out to them that we have plenty of food, and that we will not be a burden. Ask if there is anyone in need, for we will gladly serve them. If you do find anyone in need, alert me so we can attend to them."

"Llandogo is a very ancient site," said Blaidd. "Those four circles of stone mark off family dwellings and date back to before the coming of the Celts. That same group of people probably erected the huge stones you passed by before your arrival at Chepstow. Lord Clare told us that last year some children playing around these circles turned over a stone and found underneath it a gold brooch that was probably used as a hair or clothing adornment. The children were given a reward, and the brooch was passed on to Saint Dogmaels Abbey. That large stone with the flat top is said to have been an altar which the Druids used for human sacrifices. The rock was closer to the river than it is now and may have been at the edge of a bog. The Celts sometimes sacrificed humans in such bogs and often flung gold and silver ornaments there as a gift to their water gods."

Galandas shuddered at the thought of human sacrifices.

At sundown the group gathered for Compline. The monks then had individual prayers until all except Abbot Henry and Brother Galandas had retired.

Talking in a low voice near the fire, Galandas asked the Abbot if he was superstitious.

"I believe everyone is a bit superstitious," Abbot Henry answered.

Galandas asked, "What is superstition, in your view?"

The Abbot thought a moment. "Superstition is more of a pagan or primitive way of looking at things, rather than a Christian way. To read the stars to find our destiny is to give to the stars more power than we give to God. To personify ideas such as victory, peace, fame, or concord is to worship abstractions rather than God. Finding the future by examining the entrails of a slain animal is a form of nature worship. Making a model of one of our organs that is ailing and putting it into a spring or pool of water is worshiping that god believed to be in the water. To rely too much on one's own abilities, or one's virtues can make a person to become a worshiper of one's self.

The Greeks had a myth about a man named Narcissus, who did just that, so much so that he fell in love with his own image reflected in a pool. When we give such power to things, ideas, or people, we are behaving superstitiously. I believe the source of superstition begins with ignorance of God's role in natural causes."

Abbot Henry did not want to admit his own fears about the golden eagle's recent appearance. But his own personal uncertainties needed to be put aside. This young monk seemed worried, as though there was more hidden beneath the surface than he would reveal. The Abbot paused, then looked more closely at Galandas. "Is there something bothering you?" he asked.

"I have a sense of uneasiness. I feel a sense of doom," said Galandas.

"I feel you are leaving something out. Will you tell me more?" the Abbot gently requested.

"I am unable to tell you more. I wish I could. A monk who keeps secrets from his Abbot should not be a monk," said Galandas. "I must retire for the night. Please pray for me."

The Abbot paused a moment before speaking. "My prayers will be with you." He raised his right hand and waved his blessing upon Galandas.

The holy men were silent under the stars of a midspring night in the River Wye Valley. The glow of their fire and some fireflies made the only earthly light.

6

Death of a Monk

DAY WAS JUST beginning to break when the first words of Lauds were spoken by Abbot Henry. A superstitious person would probably have felt the spirits of the Iron Age and era of the Celts lingering around this place, which had been holy to both. Immediately following Lauds, William of Coventry led the group in the Eucharist.

A breakfast of hard bread and wine was eagerly eaten. Walking west over an old Roman trail, each of the men experienced his own thoughts. The Abbot contemplated his conversation with Galandas the night before. Blaidd led the group as scout and watched for any danger that might occur. Mawer brought up the caravan's rear, with an eye on both sides and behind the trail.

William of Coventry silently practiced "cutting the Bible," letting the Bible fall open and reading the first passage his eyes fell upon. He did not even need to hold a Bible in his hand to do this. William would close his eyes for a second or two. Then he would open his eyes. Perhaps he saw a rock. This would cause him to think of the book of Ruth or for that matter any thing or person in the Bible that started with an R. He would go over in his mind any information he knew about Ruth as a woman, or anyone she knew. He believed that St. Augustine's conversion came from such a practice. William concentrated so intently that he did not hear the cry of the sparrow hawk on the highest branch of a nearby common oak.

William the Templar could not shake off his warrior days. He was alert and keenly aware of his hidden weapon, which he carried concealed at all times.

Galandas wavered between prayer and superstition. *Is my fear a sign from God or is it the devil punishing me?* wondered the young monk.

Should I tell the Abbot or let things continue as they are? After all, God got me into this situation. He will understand. I must put this out of my mind. Pray! That is what I shall do, pray. Walking slowly, Galandas closed his eyes and silently pleaded: *Lord, you know I have not neglected any of my responsibilities. Each duty given to me I have performed. I have not missed a single calling. I have revered all that is holy. You know how many nights I have spent in prayer to You and to the Holy Mother. Lord give me patience and the meaning of all of this.* Galandas also did not hear the cry of the sparrow hawk.

THE RIDGE THEY crossed was heavily forested with wild cherry, silver birch, and the common alder. If Lord Clare's directions were correct, they would soon reach the low plateau, where slow rolling hills were crisscrossed by streams fed by the Black Hills and spotty springs. Iron Age and Celtic farmers had cleared this plateau of trees long ago. Although the topsoil was shallow, it was good for gardens, sheep, and cattle grazing. According to Lord Clare, they should soon see a large, long building and some cottages. Some of these cottages were stone, others wood-walled. All had thatched roofs.

The occupants were Welsh who had obligations to their Welsh lord as well as to the new conquerors. All of the men, young or old, were excellent fighters. Most had Celtic blood in them. Abbot Henry was their new under-lord, carrying the authority from the King and Lord Clare to decide the best use of the land. His mind was not yet made up on this matter. At the moment, he was more concerned with whether or not he had enough lay brothers. Several of the conversi, although not of noble blood, had extensive experience in farming and in handling both sheep and cattle. Since the Cistercians ate little meat, the land would probably be used for sheep pasture. This plan would provide wool for the monks' garments and bedding, with enough left over to sell for needed cash.

Trellech Manor reportedly covered about two thousand acres. Trellech would be an immense operation needing close supervision. A sheriff, a bailiff, and a steward would have to be appointed by the Abbot. Two of these would come from the Welsh. Abbot Henry and the new steward would have to consider issues that could profoundly influence the villagers' way of life. Many peasants, villagers, or tenants would be expected to remain, while others would have to leave; but which would stay and which would go, and who would make that decision? How much would the local people have to change to their customs under the new regime? Were the Norman and Welsh customs similar, or would great changes be required?

Would the Abbot and the steward keep the same medieval work schedule, expecting tenants to work two or three days per week on the lord's land? Would they keep the old cleavage custom, which required a payment to the lord if a person wished to leave the grange? Would they require the villagers to pay for the use of the lord's common mill to grind their grain? Would they continue to require payment for the use of the lord's common oven to bake their bread or for the use of the lord's common pasture to graze their animals? Certainly the charges would be enforced for the use of the manorial court to settle disputes and fines.

Many other payments to the lord would very likely be continued or established, such as merchet, a payment to the lord when a villager's daughter married, or heriot, the payment of a dead man's best animal or movable property to the lord. The second-best animal went to the priest. Such ancient practices could hardly be stopped. *We will surely continue the gersum,* Abbot Henry thought, referring to a payment the lord received when a villein inherits or is given property or money. Then, there was the tithe. A penny was given to the priest or monastic lord for each chicken or goose, as well as one tenth of the milk, wool, or garden produce. One sheep in seven went to the lord. But by far the most hated of all taxes was the tallage, the tax which could be exacted on a peasant by his lord at any time, for any reason, and for any amount.

How strict would Tintern Abbey be in imposing the old bans? Abbot Henry wondered. Except for household use, a woman was banned from making wine. One tenth of what she made went to the lord. What could be done about bans prohibiting villagers from making windmills, water mills, dovecots, and private ovens? There was a ban against hunting wild animals, cutting down trees, and building fish ponds.

The ban against unmarried sex must continue. This was a Church Court matter. Unmarried sex resulted in a fine to be paid by the girl's father or living relatives. The intent was one of social control, requiring the girl's family to be responsible for her behavior.

There was so much at stake running a grange and being an abbey lord. If any changes were made in these customary ways, a wholesale upset of their entire way of life might occur. One idea Abbot Henry had been considering for a long time was to lease the land and let the lessee make it profitable. But he realized this idea was too new and revolutionary; it was perhaps an idea for the future.

IT WAS EARLY afternoon when Blaidd and Mawer caught a glimpse of the Trellech Grange about a mile to the northwest.

Trellech had been an Iron Age encampment, dating back to three thousand years before Christ. The Celts overran the inhabitants, followed by the Romans, with the Vikings and Celts in turn being overrun by the Saxons. Each new wave of population left its mark on the land and its own collection of relics, reminders of past eras. The Iron Age people left the C-shaped rock foundations, henges, dolmens, cairns, and sarsens. The Celts left silver cauldrons decorated with bulls, horned men's heads, gold and silver warriors dead and alive riding on bronze or silver horses, interlacing decorations, and their famous open-ended circles. The Romans left roads, walls, baths, villas, a written language, gold and silver hoards, and the beginnings of Christianity. The Vikings left fear in the memory of all who lived at that time, grave sites with boat-shaped plots, long ships and hoards of treasures. The Anglo-Saxons left church buildings, monastic orders, powerful kings or bretwalda, overlordship, and the overpowering English language.

The old Roman trail led to the edge of Trellech Grange. Blaidd approached the grange buildings alone, as a scout. There he came face to face with Owain ap Gruffudd, son of Gruffudd ap Rys ap Tewdwr. Owain was an oversized Welshman of both Celtic and Viking ancestry. Like many young Welshmen, Owain was a warrior, but he was also practical. He was a Welshman who was trying to project what Wales would look like in five, ten, and even fifteen years.

He knew nearly all the peasants living in the grange by name. Some of their sons had already died fighting for would-be Welsh kings. To avoid useless slaughter as much as possible, Owain was willing make any pact that would benefit Wales or Trellech in the long run.

Blaidd was the first to speak. "I am Blaidd. I am one of Lord Clare's soldiers. As you know, Lord Clare is one of the Marcher lords. He is the Lord of Chepstow. As you may have heard, Lord Clare has established a monastery at Tintern Crossing, known as Tintern Abbey. He has assigned certain of his properties to the overlordship of Tintern Abbey, and among these is Trellech Grange."

Blaidd turned and signaled Abbot Henry to come out from the group and meet Owain. As Abbot Henry was stepping forward, Owain noticed the powerful build and the size of this monk. The Abbot's blue eyes and his stature told Owain that the Abbot had Saxon ancestry and that he probably had been a soldier or at least a strong leader of men before donning the robe.

"I am Abbot Henry of Tintern Abbey," the monk announced. "You must be Owain. Lord Clare told me to deal with you in all things. I am most happy to meet you. My colleagues and I are here to learn about Trellech Manor, how it is organized, what facilities it has, and any needs it may have. Except for two of Lord Clare's soldiers, we are unarmed. We come in peace. We wish to bring no harm to anyone at Trellech. No one in your manor should be alarmed by our presence.

"We knew you would be coming," Owain replied, looking at the small group. "I am glad you are not a large body of soldiers coming to take charge of the land. Our peasants have been on this land for many generations. They are fearful that they may be evicted, made slaves, or lose their status. A few hold their land as a fief from my grandfather."

"I have heard of your father. He was a brave and fearless warrior," replied the Abbot.

A hint of a smile passed over Owain's lips. *It is good that this monk has heard of my father and is able to pay a tribute to him,* Owain thought.

Owain welcomed the party. "Thanks to our scouts, we have known you were coming for over two hours and have prepared food and lodging for you. We have an ancient church built by the Celts.

You will be welcome to hold any of your liturgical hours there. You will not be bothered in that place."

Pausing and again to observe the party, Owain observed, "Your white cloaks tell me you are Cistercians. Your piety is well known in Wales. Gerald of Wales has stated that you bring prosperity and plenty wherever you go. I have heard you are builders, not destroyers."

Are these words of welcome or deception? Abbot Henry wondered.

This reception is certainly a different from the one we received at Llandaff Village, thought William the Templar.

Following None held in the manor church, all of the Tintern Abbey company took a tour of Trellech Manor and the close-by grange. The huge manor house was over seventy feet long, with stone walls and a thatched roof. East of the manor house was a mill for grinding grain, and farther east was a large oven. Near the oven and shaded by several trees stood the blacksmith shop. Two dovecotes were made of brick. There were two spring-fed streams; one provided water to drink, and the other carried away wastewater. Three large barns with stone walls were west of the church. There was enough room under their cover for many animals during bad weather. The graveyard separated the oven from the Celtic church. Both of these were a few hundred feet from a pond which still carried the Celtic name of Sequana. Sequana was fed by springs which the Romans named after Sulis, their god of water. Both Celts and Romans believed such springs were the dwelling place of gods, and as such had healing properties.

Farther east, between the church and the road, was a gallows. A relic from Roman times, it was in good repair, which meant that it was probably still in use. Orchards and grape vines could be seen from the manor house.

The monks met the head keeper of the animals, a free peasant named Rhys. Blaidd had heard of Rhys' competence as a rider and breeder of large, fast, and strong horses.

Known only to a few, Owain kept a stable of fast horses on the far western section of the shire. Caring for the horses were over twenty youthful riders, led by one of Owain's brothers. These riders were skilled at letting an arrow fly from their bow with great accuracy while their horse was at a full gallop. For this reason, rebels all over Wales made every effort to find favor with Owain.

The village included three houses with stone walls and thatch roofs. Thirty-one timber houses covered with wattle and daub stood together on the east side. On three sides of the village were fields divided into strips. Owain's strips separated the village plots, apparently to ensure the worker's equal attention to all crops.

Following supper and Vespers, Owain, his brother Cymru, Abbot Henry, and William the Templar met together by the fireplace in the manor house. After introductions, Abbot Henry opened the conversation.

"Cymru, I see that you have the same name as Wales."

"Yes," replied Cymru. "My father had great ambitions to make Wales a sovereign state. Maybe he thought I would be the one to bring it about. But the Saxons and the Normans have had other ideas for Wales."

Abbot Henry would have liked to learn more of Cymru's historical and personal perspectives, but it was time to present his own business.

"This is what we have concluded about the grange. There are about two thousand acres, at least one village and numerous isolated homes, great timbers, and marsh lands, perhaps affording opportunities for assarting. By assarting I mean reclaiming marsh or wooded land for more productive use. I understand you have already done this to large areas. You are to be commended. There could be enough land for two hundred free or bonded peasants to better themselves.

"Owain, you have done a splendid job at Trellech Manor," the Abbot continued. "On behalf of Lord Clare and Tintern Abbey, I would like to offer you the highly responsible position of Sheriff of Trellech and its environs. Along with my offer will come a commission from King Henry. And to you Cymru, if you will accept it, I offer an important appointment as bailiff."

Owain and Cymru looked at one another. This was obviously a surprise. Both took a deep breath and looked back at Henry.

"Now before you answer, let me say that Tintern Abbey will send two of our conversi as advisors, to give assistance and to maintain a communication link with Tintern Abbey. Conversi are lay brothers of our order. These are men who have helped us to manage land and animals. They are experienced in building, assarting, caring for animals, and other duties. They are devoted men who wear a brown garb, pray daily, and have taken vows of obedience to their Abbot. They know the Cistercian ways and can be of help to you."

After a pause, Abbot Henry continued, "Please think over these offers. I will need your answer in the morning. It is our intention to return to Tintern Abbey tomorrow."

AFTER THE MONKS left the manor house, Cymru shot an angry look at his brother. Owain put another log on the fire and stirred the embers.

"I am against it!" Cymru stated firmly. "We have a small army and horses not far away. They can be here in the morning."

"That is true," Owain replied. "Yes, we could kill them or take them hostage. We could do all these things tomorrow. But, within a month or sooner, Lord Clare and the king would be here to ravage this place and all our people in it. Brother, we are not powerful enough yet to do what our father hoped to do. We are too fractured politically and have too many divided families to stand up against the Normans and the English."

"But—"

"I do not want to see Trellech devastated," Owain said. "I am going to accept the position offered me as sheriff. With the position of sheriff, I can be in esteemed places and learn much. We will have our day, but not now."

THE FOLLOWING MORNING, the monks observed Lauds and celebrated the Eucharist in the ancient Celtic church. Owain made a point of being present.

Looking over the pond of fresh water, Abbot Henry asked for Owain's decision. "I am going to accept your offer," the Welshman replied. "I believe I can work with you. I have admired the way Lord Clare has restrained his army and sought in a number of ways to help a defeated people. I have known the situation in the Llandaff Village for some time. I do not envy this lord," Owain said.

"Where is Cymru?" asked Abbot Henry. "Will he take the offer of bailiff?"

"Cymru had business in the next shire. He declined to be bailiff," answered Owain. "I pray you will have a good trip back to Tintern Abbey."

THE HOLY MEN set out on their return journey. Just as they reached the trees, Abbot Henry gazed skyward. The now familiar golden eagle circled above the party. This time it glided much closer than it had on its previous appearances.

Suddenly William the Templar shouted out! There were human shadows moving among the trees. A fast whistling sound abruptly ended with a thud.

Galandas dropped on the old Roman path. An arrow had pierced his back on the left side and its point was sticking out of the front of his chest. The lad was not breathing. No movement. No pulse.

Galandas was dead.

William of Coventry, their only priest, responded quickly and administered Extreme Unction. Forming a shield around the holy men, Blaidd and Mawer drew their swords, ready for any attack. William the Templar dashed through the edge of the woods but found no one. He thought, *If I could only get my hands on that culprit, I would separate his soul from his body in quick order.*

The monks were in shock, crouching low and scanning the trees for more hidden assassins. Privately, Henry was as outraged as the Templar that anyone would attack men of God. Publicly, the Abbot spoke to bring order and direction in the face of chaos.

"We do not know who is out there or how many there are. Our attackers appear to have fled for now. We are a long way from home. We must gather ourselves together and push on. It is only a few miles to Llandogo. When we reach our boat, we will move swiftly downstream. We should reach Tintern Abbey by sundown. Brothers, pray for our safe return. And pray for our fallen brother, Galandas."

William the Templar broke off both ends of the arrow, leaving the shaft in Galandas. He saved the point and feathers, hoping the markings would offer some clue as to the shooter's identity. Blaidd already had one definite clue; he knew the arrow was Welsh.

A stretcher was quickly created. William the Templar and Mawer carried Galandas's lifeless body. There were tears in the eyes of the Templar.

All hurried. All were alert. Who might be next?

They reached Llandogo. After laying the body of Galandas tenderly in the boat, the rest boarded. Silence and sadness traveled with them on the final phase of their journey. Mawer's and Blaidd's powerful rowing added speed to the fast-flowing current. All watched the shores alertly, watching…praying.…

7

A Deep Secret Revealed

NOT A WORD was spoken. There would be plenty of time later for talk.

Abbot Henry was deeply moved by the loss of Brother Galandas. He had known something—maybe something dreadful—was disturbing his young monk, but for some reason he had been unable to reach this young man who had had so much promise. Now Galandas lay dead in the middle of the boat, the shaft of an arrow piercing his heart. There was no chance for Galandas to speak, to reach out, to understand, to ask for help. One moment here, the next in eternity.

As the party rounded the last bend of the River Wye, Tintern Abbey came into view. Blaidd and Mawer pulled the side of the boat against the wooden dock, which had been completed in their absence.

William the Templar leaped out and began to relate the bad news. All who heard crossed themselves, uttering a brief prayer. Grief spread quickly throughout the Cistercian community.

This was the first time the abbey had needed to make arrangements for the burial of one of their own. Brother Roger saw to it that the grave was dug. He also prepared the plain wooden coffin, which would hold the body only during the service. This work had to be done quickly, as they were unprepared for the event. In the future, it would be Tintern Abbey's custom to have burial graves already dug for monks who required them.

Abbot Henry asked William the Templar and Ordric the Sacrist to prepare Galandas's body for burial. William the Templar picked up the dead monk, carried him into the chapter room, and laid him on the table for preparation. Grabbing hold of the arrow, the Templar pulled it through Galandas's chest and gently placed it on a nearby chair. Since Galandas's habit was covered with blood, it would need to be replaced. With his knife the Templar cut the blood stained habit from Galandas's chest.

"Heaven preserve us!" Ordric muttered in amazement.

They were not prepared for the sight of the frail body before them. The Templar and Ordric could neither believe nor accept what their eyes beheld. This dead young monk had breasts! The left breast had been mutilated by the arrow, but the right was was perfectly formed, definitely not the breast of a young man. The Sacrist and the Templar both stepped back in fear, then moved forward again for a closer look. Then, to be sure their eyes had not deceived them, they removed the rest of Galandas's garments, held their breaths and examined the body, then looked at each other in wonder.

Galandas was a young woman. A girl! Galandas was a female. No! Impossible! What were they to do?

"We can't just pass this over," the Templar said.

Ordric said, "Perhaps we should do just that. No one would know this secret but ourselves. Do we want to bring shame to our order?"

"We must inform the Abbot and Prior Geoffrey," the Templar insisted.

"Very well. I shall go get them," Ordic said hurriedly.

"I shall cover him, I mean her body until you return."

Ordric ran from the chapter house. He found the Abbot and Prior near the church. "Both of you must come now to the chapter house!" Ordric cried. "Your presence is urgently needed!"

The Abbot and Prior nodded at each other and followed the alarmed brother.

Entering the chapter house the Abbot calmly asked, "How can we help? Do you need assistance in preparing Galandas?"

The Templar moved his hand to the top of the cover, hesitated, and whispered, "In our task, we have discovered a secret." He slowly uncovered the right side of the naked form, revealing one of the breasts. "He is a young woman. She is a girl."

The Abbot and Prior moved closer. "Are you sure? What about—"

"That too," Ordric said. "Galandas is most certainly female."

"Are you sure he has not been castrated?" asked Prior Geoffrey.

"I am sure," said the Templar. "I have seen men who have been castrated. There is significant scarring, and there is no such scarring on this body. And look at her uninjured breast. I have never seen a slim man with a breast this size."

Abbot Henry nodded. "Continue preparing the body for burial. The Prior and I will discuss this matter and get back with you shortly." The Abbot and the Prior turned and left the room.

Galandas's body was washed and lightly oiled, then covered in a white sheet. An incense candle was lit. The Templar and the Sacrist spoke softly in hushed tones as they waited for the Abbot's decision.

ABBOT HENRY AND Prior Geoffrey entered the chapel to discuss this startling turn of events. "The night we spent at Llandogo on our way to Trellech Manor, Galandas asked me if I was superstitious," the Abbot recalled. "I responded by saying most of us are superstitious in one way or another and went on to tell him what I thought about superstition; but somehow that didn't seem to satisfy him. He spoke of a sense of uneasiness and doom, but would not explain when I asked him to tell me more. I spent part of that night praying for the young man—for that's what he was to me—trying to understand. And now he—or she—is dead. I feel as if I failed him somehow, as if he died with unanswered questions and fears.

"And now we face serious questions. What kind of alternatives ought we consider?" Abbot Henry requested. "I seek your council. How shall we bury this person whom we loved but knew so little about?"

The Prior shook his head. "This is a difficult decision. We can choose to say nothing, bury Galandas as the first member of our Abbey to die, and remain silent the rest of our days. Or we can admit to her condition and bury Galandas at edge of our new cemetery or just outside of it."

Abbot Henry agonized over the choices. He believed that Galandas had been on the verge of confiding with him shortly before the young monk's death. The Abbot struggled with his indecisiveness. He contemplated the question how best to honor God, the abbey, and this devoted follower.

Prior Geoffrey continued his advice. "We can blame Galandas, this girl, and cast her out of Tintern Abbey as one unworthy to be here in the first place."

"Go on," Abbot Henry softly urged.

"We could hold our Mother Abbey responsible for making this mistake and putting us in this dilemma. But monasteries do not physically examine new candidates or even oblates, if they accept them. We could even blame ourselves," the Prior said, "but we do not take baths with other monks, nor do we allow anyone else to see our nakedness."

"And God forbid," the Abbot added, "that we would blame God for our present situation. But what if God is testing us? Giving us a challenge? I expect He's watching to see how we respond to the crisis."

Prior Geoffrey nodded in agreement. "I suppose at this point it's useless to try to decide whom to blame for all this. In some sense it has to be a part of God's plan, and I feel we should try to embrace patience and understanding. I still have trouble with the understanding. How could this have happened?"

"I can imagine how this could have happened," the Abbot responded. "She was with her father, the Count of Flanders and Artois, on his crusade journey."

Brother Geoffrey looked surprised at this comment.

"Yes, brother," the Abbot said, nodding. "Despite the decree from Pope Urban that no women, old people, or children take part in the crusades, a number of them chose to join the forces to free Jerusalem. William the Templar has told me stories of young boys accompanying their fathers, and of women also participating in the crusades.

"Sadly, Galandas's father was killed in the Balkans defending some Christians who were being attacked by outlaws. A gallant knight brought her back to France, but failed to give any information about her to the abbey where he left her. Then perhaps monks, knowing only that the child was of noble blood, was small, and in need of help, mistook her for a boy and admitted her. She did not complain, because if she had she would have been turned out with no dowry to enter a convent or no dowry for a husband."

"It sounds like a fantastic story, but from all I have heard, this could very well have happened," Geoffrey said.

"But now we're back to the question at hand. What do you advise concerning Galandas's burial?" the Abbot asked.

Prior Geoffrey paused to contemplate all the information they had. What was to be done of Galandas's body? If he could think of Galandas as a monk and try to ignore gender, then what would he recommend? He sighed and said, "I know she was not completely honest, but I am not yet ready to cast stones at her. This monk was one of the finest I have known. I never heard Galandas complain about any task. It may sound Pharisaic, but I know of no time when Galandas was corrected for any transgression. And if I may ask a rhetorical question, would not Tintern Abbey be more harmed by casting out this child, rather than giving her a proper monk's burial?"

The Prior sighed and continued, "If we had learned of this while Galandas was living, what would we have done? Obviously she would have had to go. But with her proper contrition, would we not have provided her a dowry to enter a convent? Our problem remains: how are we going to render justice in this situation? We cannot cast what is left of her to the dogs. I know the decision is ultimately in your hands, Abbot Henry, but has she not earned something from us? Are we like the Pharisee who stood in the Temple saying, 'I thank God that I am not like other men, sinners, evil doers, robbers, adulterers,' or are we like the man who beats his chest, saying, 'God be merciful to me, forgive me, for I have sinned'?"

"I am grateful to have a trusted brother with whom to discuss these delicate and private matters," the Abbot answered. "And your thoroughness has helped me broaden my views of the choices I must consider. If I am ever called before any council or court, I would like to have you as my counsel."

"I am honored," Prior Geoffrey replied. "Are we any closer to a decision?"

Abbot Henry answered. "I do not think that this is the kind of decision that should be put to a vote," he began. "Abbot Nicholas of

L'Aumone Abbey chose me, and I and the other monks have chosen you, to lead this new abbey. Humble though we are, we were also both chosen by God—not to make easy decisions, but to make hard ones, sometimes even decisions of life or death. Our twelve monks, including Galandas, vowed that they would follow and obey in all things, spiritual and otherwise. I only wish that the two of us, alone, could have known of this situation. I have made a decision, and after hearing your arguments, I believe you agree with me in the matter. I will also tell William the Templar and Ordric the Sacrist. I pray they will be in accord with me. You stay here and pray. I will go to speak to Brothers William and Ordric now."

WILLIAM AND ORDRIC were waiting beside the preparation table when Abbot Henry entered the room. The young girl's body was completely covered.

The Abbot spoke softly. "I have made a decision, and I believe it is a moral decision. I do not make decisions because they will be liked or disliked. I make decisions because I have been chosen to do so. When each of you becomes an Abbot, as I know you both will some day, you will be called upon to make hard decisions, not easy ones. My decision is that we shall bury Galandas as we would any other monk; Galandas labored as we all have in the Lord's vineyard, and we shall bury Galandas tomorrow according to the customs of Cistercians. Since we do not have headstones, our actions will be known only to God and the four of us. I pray that you will honor this monk with your silence on this matter."

William and Ordric agreed. Their bodies relaxed as they learned news they had hoped for their fallen fellow monk.

ABOUT HALFWAY BETWEEN midnight and daybreak the next morning, the monks of Tintern Abbey rose to observe Vigils—the canonical hour reminding them to be watchful for the coming of the Lord. They arose again about daybreak for Lauds. Lauds was followed by a requiem Mass for Galandas.

The funeral began at the church and was attended by the whole Tintern Abbey community. Also attending were Lord and Lady Clare of Chepstow. The corpse was in the wooden box made by Brother Roger.

With incense waved over the corpse at the end of each collect, the body was carried to the grave site by the same four monks who had carried the dead monk into the church. They were followed by all the other monks, the lay brothers, and Lord and Lady Clare. Father William of Coventry blessed the grave site. The body was lifted from the coffin and held over the grave while holy water and incense were waved over the grave and the grave diggers. Wrapped in the new habit, Galandas was lowered into the warm, soft and caressing ground without a coffin or a shroud. The infirmarer climbed into the grave so he could arrange the body appropriately.

There was no marker.

When the burial was completed the entire community, led by lay brothers, proceeded back to the church where all recited the Seven Penitential Psalms. Abbot Henry prostrated himself in front of the altar. Near the end of the ceremonies, the gathering of monks participated in the requiem aeternam, a responsory funeral song where the choir speaks for the dead person.

"Libera me, Domine, de morte æternam," they vocalized.

Deliver me, O Lord, from eternal death on that fearful day, when the heavens and the earth are moved, when you will come to judge the world through fire. I am made to tremble and I fear, when the desolation shall come, and also the coming wrath, that day, day of wrath, calamity, and misery, day of terror and exceeding bitterness. Grant them eternal rest, O Lord, and let perpetual light shine upon them.

A final prayer, a collect, concluded the service.

THE BONDS BETWEEN the monks and Galandas would not end until thirty days had passed, during which time they believed the person's soul passed through purgatory. Throughout this time extra collects were offered for the monk at the canonical offices and Masses were celebrated to help secure the soul a swift passage to salvation. Abbot

Henry celebrated in the chapter house on the thirtieth day, marking the soul's release from purgatory.

Tintern Abbey was now without the services of one monk. This may not sound like a large difference, but every monk had his place and function in the workings of the church, and especially in the readings of the Scripture, which were expressions of the Divine reaching out to the monks. This was their way of knowing God. The church was the medium through which the Bible grew, was nourished, and kept. Offices, periods of prayer, sacred readings, and intercessions were all communal, and each monk had a role. Every significant part of this keeping of Scripture was done by monks, some named, most nameless. That was why the loss of a monk was felt so strongly by the tight-knit community.

PART II

The Church and the Castle

8

Troubles in the Valley

FOR OVER THIRTY years Abbot Henry watched, prayed, and labored in the vineyard of Tintern. Austerity marked those early days in this truly enchanted place.

Time brought many changes during his time as the Abbot. The wooden dormitories of the monks and lay brothers were replaced by a long two-story stone building. The lower story housed monks, while the upper story was devoted to the conversi. A dovecote emerged, providing meat for the brothers. A stone kitchen arose between the monks' and the lay brothers' dining halls. An Abbot's house and a visitor's house expanded near the river. A large fish pond was built close to the River Wye to keep fish alive and fresh for meals. Fresh flowing water from the Wye was diverted into the fish pond, from whence it overflowed back into the river. A net at the south end allowed small fish to return to the big stream. The cloister was complete when the chapter house became connected to the north end of the dormitory building. Tintern had taken on the appearance of an abbey, although the wooden chapel remained unchanged.

Led by William the Templar, Lord Clare's soldiers had resolved the situation of the Cathars in Llandaff Village. Blaidd and Mawer played prominent roles, as did Owain of Trellech Manor. In order to prevent escapes, Owain's capable horsemen guarded the passes into the mountains north of Llandaff. Half of the mountain guards were led by his brother Cymru. Although suspicion had brewed among Tintern's monks, blaming Cymru for the killing of Galandas, nothing could be proven.

Lord Clare's militia attacked the Cathars' camp before dawn, catching the Llandaff inhabitants by complete surprise. The action was so swift that the Cathars' warning bell did not sound, and the Sheriff of Llandaff was killed by an arrow through his chest before any resistance could be organized. It was thought that in the turmoil Father Gascone and a few others escaped to the Bristol Channel, where they were picked up by merchant vessels bringing supplies to the Cathars.

Saxons, who had fled north into the mountains to escape the Cathars, trickled back to the Llandaff environs. In time, the Saxons restored the village to its original condition and customs, even repainting the interior of the church with the bright colors it had had before the Cathars occupied it. Except for some strange cemetery markers without names, history became blind to this place ever having been a Cathar village.

For the cleansing of the area Lord Clare was awarded the land between Llandaff Village and Chepstow Castle. Owain was given the Cathars' sheep as a reward for his military efforts in guarding the north passes. He was now sheriff over two thousand acres of fine pasture land in the vicinity of Trellech. An older and more mature Cymru was now bailiff. The two oversaw more than three thousand sheep for Tintern Abbey.

TOWARD THE END of Abbot Henry's thirty-year tenure, more and more graves filled the Tintern Abbey cemetery. These were remembered in the daily prayers of monks at the abbey. One place on the burial ground was especially noted by the monks in their daily walk. Only the older monks knew which one it was. When they came to this grave, these older monks often crossed themselves and offered a brief prayer. Since their prayers were silent, no one else knew why they paused.

During his tenure, Abbot Henry made two extensive trips. One was to Clairvaux, where he spent several months being tutored by Bernard of Clairvaux. While there he assisted Bernard in producing *The Consideratione*. In this work, which was eventually published, Bernard reflected on his efforts to promote steps leading to a more spiritual life and his efforts in promoting the Second Crusade. As the Abbott walked with Bernard they discussed how the spiritual steps strengthened a monk's devotion.

Abbot Henry's second trip was to Rome where he assisted Pope Blessed Eugene III in calming the people of Rome, who had been agitated by the rabble-rousing Arnold of Brescia. Arnold had been exiled from Italy by the Roman Council of 1139. Many in Rome had been convinced by Arnold to sever their relationship with the Vatican. Abbot Henry was able to convince the ruling families of Rome that without the Pope their city would have no distinction and undoubtedly would become a third-rate city. Abbot Henry was offered a post at the Vatican, but he refused. Instead, he returned to Wales by way of the abbeys of Citeaux, L'Aumone, and Waverley. Abbot Henry was warmly greeted at Tintern by his faithful monks and lay brothers.

Tintern monks knew that they had one of the finest and most spiritual Abbots in Christendom, a man of increasing wisdom, devotion, and influence. They also knew that nothing on earth is permanent, and not long after returning to his beloved Tintern Abbey, Abbot Henry died. He had tirelessly borne the burdens of the heat of the day, kept the observance of Holy Rule, and toiled even to his last gasp. Having laid aside the burden of the flesh, he went to his rest, and his body was placed next to that grave where so many of the older monks often paused to pray. Now they had two reasons for these brief devotions. One was to honor Abbot Henry, and the other was for Galandas.

Abbot Henry was succeeded by his friend and colleague, Prior Geoffrey, who became Abbot Geoffrey of Tintern Abbey, until he, too, died and was placed in the ground beside his old friend.

A BARGE MOVED slowly up River Wye. Approaching the dock the two rowing soldiers reached out to grab the rope tossed by a lay brother. Younger Blaidd grabbed the rope while younger Mawer pulled the boat against the dock. These two young men were the sons of the soldiers by the same name, who had served Lord Clare in the early years of Tintern Abbey. The boat also carried two monks unknown to the abbey members and the new Lord Clare. With the loss of the honored nobleman who had first welcomed the Cistercians to the Wye Valley, the title of Lord Clare had passed on to his son, Gilbert.

Edward, the lay brother, greeted the nobleman. "If we had have known of your coming, we would have had a proper reception, Your Grace."

"No need for that. Your help with the boat is sufficient and greatly appreciated, Brother Edward," replied Lord Clare. "There, I see your Sacrist Ordric coming to meet us. It seems each time I see Ordric, he appears to be moving more slowly. I am concerned about his health. Maybe there is something we can do."

Ordric had spent most of his life at this abbey. His knowledge and wisdom of Cistercian customs and rules made him highly respected by Tintern's brothers and the Welsh leaders who knew him.

"Brother Ordric, it is so good to see you," said Lord Clare. "How are your new sacristy and scriptorium? I certainly hope they meet your needs."

"I am most pleased with them, especially the windows and lighting. I cannot see as well as I used to," responded the aging monk.

"Brother Ordric, you are the first person of Tintern to be introduced to your new Abbot. He has just arrived from the Cistercian General Chapter, where he was chosen for the position. Ordric, this is Abbot Mark. Brother Ordric is one of the founding monks of Tintern Abbey. Nearly all of those founding brothers are in their eternal rest," continued the lord, "a rest that they certainly deserved. They did not get much rest while they were living."

"Abbot Mark," said Ordric.

"Brother Ordric," the Abbot replied. The two monks seemed unsure of one another, and relied on formality to carry the moment.

"Lord Clare, I shall call all members of our abbey to meet in the cloister following supper," Ordric said.

Lord Clare noticed that Brother Ordric had taken charge of things here, since there has not been an Abbot or Prior recently. *If it were not for his age, he would make a fine Abbot himself,* the lord thought.

LORD CLARE ATE supper with the monks, while young Blaidd and young Mawer were fed with the conversi. There was no complaint from young Blaidd or young Mawer, since both knew they would have a much heartier meal eating with the lay brothers. "I would rather be eating with you tonight," Lord Clare whispered to young Blaidd. Young Blaidd and young Mawer grinned back.

Following supper, all gathered in the cloister.

Standing straight, with unfolded hands, Brother Ordric spoke: "We are always cheered to have Lord Clare visiting Tintern Abbey. It was the Clare family—our patrons—who planned, launched, and financed the beginnings of Tintern Abbey, protecting it with all their resources. As you know, some abbeys in north Wales have been raided and even burned. We thank the Virgin Mother and Lord Clare for keeping us safe. Many times Lord Clare has visited us just to see if all is going well, and we are most happy for these visits. But today's visit is something different. Tintern Abbey brothers and friends, I present Lord Clare."

LORD CLARE STEPPED forward, looking slowly about, as if he were catching the eye of all, monks and lay brothers, alike. "You all know that I do not deal too much with formalities, except on rare occasions," he began. "This is a most rare occasion. Since our beloved Abbot Henry and Abbot Geoffrey died, you have been without an Abbot, although as anyone can see, you have not been leaderless. I want to extend my gratitude to Brothers Ordric, Roger, and all of you for sustaining this abbey, in a spiritual and a temporal manner. Two days ago, Brother Mark arrived from your General Chapter, held in France, with outstanding news. His letter from the Cistercian General Chapter introduced him as the new Abbot of Tintern Abbey. He was accompanied by Prior James of Citeaux, who will assist in his installation. Now, I want to introduce Prior James of Citeaux Abbey."

Prior James rose. With only a hint of gray in his hair, a hint that went well with his white robe, he looked every bit a leader from Citeaux, the mother abbey of all Cistercians. Indeed, the Cistercians looked more to Citeaux than they did to Rome, and it was an honor now to be hosting the influential Prior of that abbey. Prior James and Abbot Bernard had been almost equally responsible for the founding of over six hundred abbeys and the close organization that tied them together.

The Prior stepped forward and began his presentation. "Like

Lord Clare, I do not embrace formalities or, being a Cistercian, small talk either. However, will you please grant me just a few formal words? When Abbots Henry and Geoffrey died, we all, Abbots and Priors alike, began to ask: 'Who will go for us? Whom can we send to Tintern Abbey?' We were not looking for another Abbot Henry, whose work did so much to make Tintern Abbey a great abbey, nearly complete in every respect. As far as we could determine, spiritually, the only thing now needed was a stone chapel worthy of the Blessed Virgin, which will certainly happen in its own proper time. But an abbey needs an Abbot, so in that sense we were faced with the task of choosing a monk to replace Abbot Henry and Abbot Geoffrey. We went so far as to contact Bernard of Clairvaux for his advice. And we feel we've found a fine leader for this fine abbey. Just as Abbot Henry was the right monk when Tintern was nothing more than a prayer in the heart of Lord Clare's father, we now feel that your new Abbot is the right monk for this humble and yet mighty Tintern Abbey.

"Abbot Mark is an Englishman. He has studied in Paris and at Oxford. He has attended our General Chapter meetings four times and has been the recorder of those gatherings. He has been to Rome and has spent a year at Clairvaux. The past four years Mark has served as Prior at Waverley Abbey. He is a scholar and a writer. His parents are of high standing. Tintern Abbey, brothers, conversi, and guests, I present to you your new Abbot, Abbot Mark."

Brother Ordric was so moved by the introductions that he almost applauded, but thought better of it. All men present nodded their approval.

Abbot Mark stood, stepped forward, and addressed the group in a strong, distinctive voice. "I marveled as we traveled up the River Wye. This is truly a land of beauty, a fair wilderness of glory. It is a heaven in miniature. Now I know why your record shows that no one has ever wanted to leave here and go to another abbey. All of us want to be proud. I should not use that word, but I shall. We want to be proud and satisfied with our location and our abbey. You have found a garden and improved upon it. By the observance of the Rule, this place has become what it is. I know that your prayers reach right into the presence of Mary and to the Throne of God. I feel most honored to be here, with you, in this place, at this time."

Abbot Mark paused for a moment, then continued. "There is something I desire you to mention in your private prayers during the coming week. We shall have the honor of choosing a Prior. Will you be in prayer with me about this?"

Ordric felt a sense of familiarity. *I feel Abbot Henry has come back to us,* he thought. *Our first Abbot often asked us to work with him, not for him!*

THE MONKS AND lay brothers crossed themselves, then proceeded to their next meetings; Prior James of Citeaux accompanied them. Lord Clare, Abbot Mark, Brother Ordric, and Brother Roger stayed behind. Ordric was anxious to alert them to recent weighty developments.

"Lord Clare and Abbot Mark, we do have a serious problem that came to our attention three days ago," Ordric began. "About three miles west of us, over the mountain and on the ridge, lives one of our free tenant families—a man named Thomas, his wife, two boys about fourteen, and a twelve-year-old daughter. They live in a large long house and have two barns for cows and sheep. They are descendants of both Celts and Saxons. They are prosperous, have never failed to pay their rent, and have been most generous at Michaelmas. Thomas and some of our lay brothers have been building a road to his place. Two weeks ago, one of his younger sheep was found mutilated. A week later, the same happened to one of his young heifers. These were disturbing events, but only the beginning.

"A few days ago Thomas came down to us greatly grieved. One of his sons was found dead; he too had been badly mutilated. As feeble as he was, our priest, William of Coventry, climbed the mountain and helped bury the child. The tenant, Thomas, believes these terrible deeds were the work of some Welshmen who want to run him off of the land."

"This is distressing news," said Lord Clare. "The Wye Valley has been most peaceful, and I am alarmed to learn of such atrocities. I have heard of no uprisings in the area. It could be that strangers are involved. I shall send a messenger to Owain of Trellech. He served my father and Tintern Abbey for many years, and his health is still strong despite his age. He will inform us of any renegades fomenting trouble. If there are some rebels in our area he will know about them or can certainly find out about them, so we can know who is behind these dreadful calamities, and why they have been happening. I shall send some of my soldiers to the Thomas family's holdings to scout the area."

The new Abbot valued the decisive nature of Lord Clare and agreed with his directives.

"Will you stay and enjoy another meal with us, Lord Clare?" the Abbot asked.

"No, I shall take my leave," replied Lord Clare.

"But what of Prior James?" inquired the new Abbot. "Will he return to Chepstow with your party?"

"Prior James has requested to stay on until after Tintern Abbey's election of a Prior. His wisdom will be greatly regarded," the lord replied.

The two men walked to the boat moored at the dock where Lord Clare's party was beginning to board. "I shall also send back young Blaidd, young Mawer, and Santeurs," Lord Clare said. "Santeurs is the finest tracker in all of Normandy. He also has a fine dog, Darius, with a keen nose. If there are any trails left, Santeurs will find them. Abbot Mark, if you feel in need of any soldiers for protection, send me a note by boat or by runner and I shall immediately respond."

"Brother Roger has already spoken to me about safety," said Abbot Mark. "He has placed some of the lay brothers on duty as watchmen. Our bell will be rung in case we have any intruders. We appreciate your concern and willingness. There are times when we need the secular forces and we shall not be timid in calling upon you. Of course, we depend upon the forces of God for protection, but I consider your soldiers as a part of God's forces. Our prayers are with you and Lady Clare."

With a raised hand Abbot Mark extended his blessing upon the boat and its passengers.

THE NEXT DAY, young Blaidd, young Mawer, and Santeurs, with his dog, arrived at Tintern. The following day, they climbed the hills to the west until they were out of sight.

SEVEN DAYS LATER, the choir monks chose a quiet but energetic monk, Brother Francis, to be their Prior. Brother Francis had been born in London, the son of a knight who became a merchant and had the means to send his son to Paris for his education. Francis was blessed with an excellent memory and verbal skills, but was hardly a scholar. He remained faithful to his mother's ideals, and was devout and chaste.

Searching for ways to spend his life, Brother Francis joined the household of Theobald, the Archbishop of Canterbury. In the early morning hours in the Center Chapel of Canterbury, Francis experienced an epiphany, of which he seldom spoke. But that moment had a profound effect upon him. The Archbishop suggested to Francis that he join a new and intriguing order, the Cistercians. After the young man's novitiate, he asked to become a part of a wilderness abbey in Wales and was accepted. And now he was chosen by his fellow monks at Tintern Abbey to be their Prior.

THE NEXT DAY some shepherds brought another disturbing message to the abbey. One of their sheepherders had been killed and his body badly mutilated.

Young Blaidd, young Mawer, and Santeurs returned to Tintern Abbey for additional supplies. The three immediately went to Abbot Mark to give their report, an account of their investigation.

"We went directly to the Thomas house," young Blaidd reported. "He holds three hides, or a little over three hundred acres. He has five villeins, none of whom are married. They are young, but appear to be capable and loyal to Thomas. The five have individual houses, which means Thomas expects them to have families in the future. Thomas is Anglo-Saxon by birth. His wife appears to have some Celtic background. All appear to be devoted Christians. There was a small Christian altar in the Thomas house, but we noted mistletoe over the door and some green decorating the house interior. The mistletoe is perhaps explained by the wife's Celtic heritage. We investigated the location of the animals and the death of Thomas's son. Recent heavy rains had destroyed any scent the dog might follow."

Young Mawer continued the report. "We talked with the herdsmen about their loss. As you already have heard, they told us of the death of a young sheep boy as well as of several sheep. We noted that those persons who were killed were young and somewhat inexperienced. The animals were also young and relatively small. All had been mutilated, torn apart. At first, we considered wild animals. But we know of no animals in our area capable of such destruction. That left us with the conclusion that the killings could be related to some rebels of Welsh origin who may want Thomas off this land. We understand that Lord Clare has sent a messenger to Trellech to try to learn if there are any uprisings or revolts in our area."

Abbot Mark said, "These killings are a shock to all of us. The random slaying of innocent persons and animals is an abomination. These terrorists apparently have their motives, and I want to know what they are. Of course we have taken precautions to guard the abbey, because if this is an uprising, we may be next. As you know, some abbeys in the north have been raided and burned, with the loss of many lives. I have cautioned our brothers about leaving the safety of the abbey. In more peaceful times, I understand, a monk, feeling the need to be alone, would cross the river and climb the mountain east of the abbey to a scenic spot overlooking the River Wye. The place is called 'Devil's Pulpit,' and legend has it that the devil often stands up there and slings rocks or makes fun of Tintern's monks who are praying. In spite of the legend, I'm told it was a favorite place to find a bit of solitude for contemplation. However, because of present circumstances—"

"Abbot Mark!" Prior Francis said, rushing into the hall. "Brother Anselm is missing! He may have wandered to Devil's Pulpit. We fear for his safety. Ordric went in search of him."

"What? Brother Ordric? Why did you not stop our aged brother?" the Abbot asked.

"I tried, but he insisted. Ordric knows Anselm's family well, and

Ordric promised to help the young man in his transition into our abbey."

Before Abbot Mark could dispatch the soldiers to begin their search, Ordric stumbled into the room. "It's Anselm! Across the river. At the Devil's Pulpit. He is dead! Dreadfully torn apart! Mangled!"

Ordric's face suddenly twisted in agony. His body stiffened, and his voice cracked. "I gave him last rites," the old monk whispered as he crumpled to the floor. His eyes rolled up into his head, his entire body jerked, twitched, and then was still.

Abbot Mark bent down to Ordric and felt his throat for a pulse. There was none. Ordric was gone.

The Abbot made the sign of the cross. He asked young Blaidd and young Mawer to assist in moving Ordric's body for funeral preparations. Then, for the safety of his other brothers, the Abbot instructed the soldiers to retrieve the remains of Anselm. Santeurs was dispatched to Lord Clare with a plea for help.

THE NEXT MORNING one hundred soldiers arrived from Chepstow in ten boats. Among these was Santeurs with his dog, Darius. A thorough search of the area west of Tintern Abbey was planned. Messengers were sent on their way to secure the help of Owain at the Trellech Grange. Owain and his riders were requested to comb the area from the north. Lord Clare offered a reward to whoever found the killer—dead or alive.

Although up in years, William the Templar was recruited by young Blaidd because of his vast experience. William had voiced his opinion that all of these catastrophes were connected, since they had all taken place within twenty miles of the Thomas farmstead. They were all bloody and violent. The killing of the animals was not done for either their meat or their pelts. True, they were torn apart, but the pieces were all there. No one carried them off or skinned the animal carcasses. The mutilation of humans was inexplicable. People were killed and then mutilated, but to what purpose? Were two or more persons involved? No one had seen the grisly killings. Indeed, there was no evidence that the murders and killings had been done by men. No one had found any arrows, knives, or broken weapons. As

William the Templar repeated, tucking his hidden weapon under his cloak as he prepared to leave, the matter was most puzzling.

Responses among the people in the vicinity were vigilant and varied. Those with large herds of sheep placed more men on guard. The number of trained dogs increased twofold around the sheep. Women especially expressed fear for themselves and their children. Men showed anger and stress. It was not a good time for strangers to be traveling through the Tintern or Trellech regions.

Four additional boatloads of soldiers docked at Tintern the next morning. Ten bowmen supported the well-equipped footmen. Landing ready to go into the field, the soldiers were divided into three groups. Leading the three different bands were young Blaidd, young Mawer, and Santeurs. Two of the groups took old paths over the hills, while Santeurs cut a new path to the north. William the Templar accompanied Santeurs.

Autumn had come to the River Wye valley and adjoining hills, the trees were clad in lovely golden and bronze colors. But Lord Clare's soldiers hardly noticed the beauty around them. Nor did the hunting parties pause to remark on the irony that such gruesome events had occurred in such serene-looking lands.

"I need to caution all the bowmen and spearmen to be on the alert," Santeurs stated. "With so many pounding the bushes, we may see some deer, which Lord Clare tells me are plentiful. We must not kill any of these. They belong to the King, and he would take unkindly toward anyone who killed a Welsh deer."

Knowing Santeurs was new to Wales, William the Templar told him a bit about the surrounding countryside. "There, just ahead of us in the clearing of the woods, is an ancient cairn marking a burial place. The three upright stones are covered by a single much larger capstone. This was probably erected by Iron Age people before the coming of the Celts. It offers some shelter from the rain if one is caught in a storm. The name of the cairn is Gwal-y-Filiast. Nearly every-where you put your feet down in Wales, you will find such graves of Iron Age people or Celts. Not long after the Saxons reached the island they were converted and began burying their dead in church cemeteries. Even some of those churches and graveyards have been covered over with time."

Santeurs abruptly raised his hand to interrupt the Templar. "Wait!" he called out to the band of soldiers. "Quiet!"

The Templar listened. Then, he too, heard the sounds of distress. A bowman shouted out, "It sounds like the cry of a sheep! And there is another cry, above the cry of a sheep. That one is the cry of man or a boy. Listen! Hear him? He is calling for help!"

Breaking through the trees into the meadow they could see clearly. A sheep had fallen on the ground, and a small shepherd boy was trying to fend off two wild boars, one larger than the other.

The bowmen did not wait for a command to charge the boars. As they approached, the startled boars turned to face the bowmen. Moving quickly, the small boy separated himself from the ferocious boars, giving the bowmen a clear shot. Three arrows quickly flew. Two struck the larger boar, and one struck the smaller. In an instant the footmen were finishing off the vicious animals with their spears.

"What do you make of this, Brother William?" Santeurs asked.

William the Templar shook his head. "Boars can be vicious," he said. "Ferocious and cunning beasts. They're also intelligent, fast, and agile, and difficult to track down and kill. Difficult, and dangerous. So it's quite possible these two were the villains we've been looking for; it would be quite possible for them to have killed and mutilated the sheep and people who have died recently. What I don't understand is why they did not eat their kill. I suppose that will always remain a mystery."

SANTEURS AND HIS bowmen received their reward from Lord Clare. The head of the boar was displayed in the lord's trophy room, along with his battle keepsakes. No more mutilation deaths were recorded. William the Templar was praised in the chapter house for bravery against unholy demonic forces.

THE OPENING OF the thirteenth century found the abbey at the height of its fortunes. A new stone Abbot's house arose. Two guest houses had been built near the river. The building projects all complete, the abbey stopped growing but continued to prosper.

John Oswaine, a Welshmen who supported the English efforts in Gwent, purchased a lifetime of keep at the abbey. He gave his fortune, over five hundred acres west of the abbey and the church of Lydd in Kent, to Tintern Abbey. He and his wife moved into a room at the north end of the monk's dormitory. Oswaine was popular among some of the monks because he held classes teaching the Welsh language. Oswaine and his wife were granted one gallon of the better beer daily, as well as the same fish portions given daily to the monks. Master Oswaine usually saved at least half of his wife's beer portion as a nightcap. As Christmas time drew near, he would drink generous helpings of his nightcap, then stroll into the monk's cloister, where he would sing at the top of his voice his favorite Christmas carols and a few old Welsh drinking songs.

One evening, Prior Francis, his Vigils interrupted by the loud singing, hurried to the cloister. He found Oswaine standing out in the light of the full moon.

Smiling as he approached, Prior Francis said, "You need to teach some of the Welsh carols to us. I note they are very vivid and have a sprightly tune to them."

"Yes and it takes a lifetime to know them all. I have just started! Will you join me, Prior Francis?" Oswaine stumbled as he spoke.

"Perhaps at a later time. Vigils are closing and we need to return to our beds. Can I help you?"

The two walked quietly to Oswaine's room. All of the commotion had not awakened his wife, who was snoring loudly.

All appeared to be going well until about an hour before Lauds. Again, from the middle of the cloister, a booming voice was heard all over the abbey.

Some are gaming, some are drinking,
Some are living without thinking;
And of those who make a racket,
Some are stripped out of cloak and jacket;
Some get clothes of finer feather,

Some are cleaned out altogether;
No one there dreads invasion,
But all drink in emulation.

This time it was Abbot Mark who rushed through the doorway leading to the cloister. Approaching Oswaine, the Abbot was not smiling. "Have you finished all of your ale and beer?" he inquired sternly.

"Yes, I just drank the last," replied Oswaine. "I am sorry that I do not have a drink to offer you. Maybe we could make some. I have the know-how, and I know you have the ingredients to make a better beer. What do you say?"

"Thank you for your offer. I know you must be tired and sleepy. Let me take you to your room. We can discuss making a better beer tomorrow," said Abbot Mark.

The two walked slowly to Oswaine's room. His wife was still snoring. Abbot Mark bade Oswaine goodnight and left.

Day was breaking. Abbot Mark whispered some psalms and, without returning to bed, rang the bell for Lauds.

9

Fulfilling a Promise

WHEN THE CISTERCIANS came to the River Wye in 1131, they found wooden structures erected with great care and love, paid for by Walter Fitz Richard de Clare. By 1200, the only original wooden structure still standing at Tintern Abbey was the wooden chapel, with its plain exterior and its finished wooden floors. The bell at the back of the chapel was still rung by a wooden shoot passing through a small hole in the eastern wall. The finished oak altar still stood in its place of honor, as it had for nearly seventy years. Worn and scratched by years of use, the missal rested on the altar. The tapestry honoring the Virgin, woven by the original Lady Clare and her maids, had faded somewhat, but anyone would recognize the image of Mary and know what the tapestry symbolized.

Attached to the eastern wall, the walnut tabernacle, shaped like a steeple and crowned by a small crucifix, still held and hid from view the chalice and the paten. It was the first work carved by Lord Clare's chief craftsman, Alexander, who had been laid tenderly to rest just outside the abbey grounds. One of the two bronze hinges had to be replaced, but the beauty and the meaning of the tabernacle had not diminished.

FROM THE BEGINNING, Tintern Abbey had been blessed with support from the lords of Chepstow Castle, a fortress of great tactical importance to the English Crown. In 1067, one year after the Norman Invasion, William the Conqueror sent William Fitz Osbern, one of his most trusted lords, to the junction of the River Wye and the Bristol Channel, instructing him to build the formidable castle, which was to become the launching point for expeditions into Wales in order to subdue the rebellious population.

Once the castle had been erected, King William placed it in the hands of another loyal Norman supporter and distant relative, Lord Walter Fitz Richard of Clare, who was responsible for welcoming the Cistercians to the Wye Valley in 1131. The powerful Clare family produced the famous Richard "Strongbow," who helped the Normans in their campaign to partially subdue Ireland. Strongbow was buried in a crypt in the wooden chapel floor at Tintern Abbey in 1147. Chepstow was passed on to the powerful William Marshal in 1189. William Marshal's sons held the castle from 1219 until 1266, when it was passed by King Edward to Roger Bigod, the fifth Earl of Norfolk and the son of William Marshal's daughter, Maud.

BROTHER WALLACE, THE Cellarer, a choir monk from the abbey, was the first member of the Cistercian community to hear that King Edward had appointed Roger Bigod as Lord of Chepstow and its environs. He learned this news while he was checking accounts at Chepstow Castle, and he was quick to tell Abbot Mark as soon as he returned to the abbey.

The Abbot convened a chapter meeting to announce the appointment and to discuss what it might foretell about the abbey's future. How would it change the abbey and its work? History had shown that an abbey without the support of its lord often declined and in some cases closed its doors.

Abbot Mark was an old man by this time, but he remained vigorous and alert. He began by telling the brothers what he knew about the new Lord of Chepstow Castle. "I have heard he served as marshal at King Edward's coronation," he began. "His mother, Maud, or Matilda, as she was sometimes called, is buried in a crypt below the floor of our chapel. As you know, Maud was the daughter of Lord William Marshal, who gave so much to our abbey, including a second stone quarry. I met Lord Roger Bigod on one of my trips to Parliament in London. I was impressed by him, and I feel his appointment will be favorable to our abbey. I ask all of you to pray about this matter, and I now invite you to join in an open discussion about our changing of lords."

Brother Lock, the Sacrist, had a long face, a dark scowl, and a reputation among his colleagues for being skeptical. He stood up and commanded their attention. "I feel there is something sinister happening here," he grumbled. "Our way of life at Tintern could be in danger of changing. And from my experience, I feel most changes are bad." He paused, looked around to all, and continued. "For a long time, I have felt uneasy about Tintern's enterprises, and being lords over so much land, having many more sheep than we need for our clothing, accepting tithes from peasants, and eating too much broth and meat. I think the nobility has too much influence over us already. And now the lords will make their influence even more oppressive. Our most important task is the salvation of our souls and the souls of those whom we serve with our intercessions. Anything that interferes with these obligations will lead us to damnation. Souls will be lost—maybe even our own!" With these strong words, Lock finished his outburst and sat down, slowly folded his hands, and bowed his head.

Brother Wallace asked for recognition from Abbot Mark. The Abbot nodded and said, "I want all of us to have our say in this matter. Tell us how you feel, Brother Wallace."

Strong and husky, Wallace tended to see things in a practical and positive way. He saw the prosperity of Tintern Abbey as a part of God's overall plan for Wales and for its monks. Tending to view problems as opportunities, others had marveled at his fresh approach to crisis situations.

He stood and addressed the chapter meeting. "I share some of the views of Brother Lock, and I praise him for his continual fasting, and his devotion to prayer is clear. I have noted that Brother Lock has been extending our time in liturgy for months by quietly adding psalms, praises, and prayers. But we all need to be reminded that prayers alone are not enough, and without the money and support of our patron lords and even the King, Tintern Abbey would not exist. These men hold their positions of power from God. Although some wealthy and powerful nobles have tried to impose their wills on other monasteries, at Tintern we have been fortunate enough to be spared these interferences. Besides, it is too early for us to be predicting future strife." Brother Wallace finished his statement with a tinge of anger in voice.

"Are there others who wish to speak?" asked the Abbot. "I see Brother Giotto's hand."

Brother Giotto was among the well educated and was the first master mason to don the habit. A distant relative of William Fitz Osbern, Giotto had directed the repair of his cousin's castle in Normandy. Small, yet powerfully built, he had often been called upon by other abbeys to shore up aging buildings and castles. A month earlier, Giotto had been summoned to Chepstow Castle to advise on the strengthening of the stone outer walls.

"Maybe I can ease the fears of some about the future of Tintern under Lord Roger Bigod. It is my opinion that we have much to be grateful for in this situation."

There was a murmur among the monks, and when it quieted down, Giotto continued. "On my recent trip to Chepstow Castle, I was made privy to some information about our new lord. Lord Roger Bigod is the Fifth Earl of Norfolk. This family has been very close to our Kings. He is a direct descendant of the First Earl of Norfolk, who came to England in the Norman Conquest. We must remember that Lord Hugh Bigod lost his lands and his life defending the King against an uprising, and he is buried here at Tintern Abbey. Hugh's title was passed to his son Roger, and now Roger has been made Lord of Chepstow Castle. Lord Roger Bigod has been married twice, but has no children."

Brother Giotto paused and cleared his throat. "I realize that many of you already know this background information, but I think you'll be excited by what I tell you next." He looked around, smiled, and continued. "It seems that King Edward, the Archbishop of Canterbury, and Lord Roger Bigod met in London some time ago to talk about many things. One of the items discussed was Tintern Abbey. As I understand it, before his death, Lord Hugh Bigod had made a vow to build a great stone church at Tintern Abbey, worthy of the Blessed Virgin. Later, Lord Hugh's son, our Lord Roger Bigod, promised his father that a worthy church would be erected at Tintern Abbey. The Archbishop, the King, and our new Lord Bigod agreed to sponsor this project!"

Brother Giotto sat. All around him an excited murmur rose from the monks, until Abbot Mark called for their attention.

"We should all thank Brother Giotto for this valuable insight," he said. "I feel we have sufficient information to believe that this new church is clearly the will of God and will go forward to the glory of the Virgin. Yes, Brother Lock? Do you have something to add?"

The dour Brother Lock rose to his feet. "I agree that it is the will of God that we should have a chapel in which to pray. We already have a chapel. But a huge and expensive church—do we really need that in order to worship?"

Brother Wallace responded, "I feel that this is a gift from God, from King Edward, from the Archbishop, and from the Lord of Chepstow Castle. Who are we to say the gift is anything but a blessing?"

But Brother Lock shook his head. "I know that many of our abbeys, like Waverley, Fountains, Rievaulx, Strata Florida, and others, have built magnificent chapels, trying to imitate grand cathedrals. Perhaps there is value in this extravagance, a value I cannot see because I think humbly. But I do want to say that except for patching and replacing the thatched roof from time to time, and redoing some floor work, the chapel we have now has served our brothers for well over a hundred years. Brothers, we need to guard against making unnecessary and extravagant changes to Tintern Abbey, and especially to this chapel."

LORD ROGER BIGOD lost no time establishing his relationship with his new fief. The week after arriving at Chepstow Castle, he journeyed up the River Wye. Like many others, Bigod was amazed by the breathtaking beauty of the panorama surrounding Tintern Abbey.

When Lord Roger Bigod's boat floated to the wooden dock, he was greeted warmly by Brother Wallace, who extended his hand to assist the nobleman onto the dock.

"Welcome, Lord Bigod! Your coming to Tintern Abbey has excited all of us here at the abbey. Some wine and hot bread have been prepared for your soldiers in the lay brothers' refectory. Abbot Mark has planned to include you in the chapter meeting later today. There, I see Prior Francis just rounding the corner of the lay refectory. He looks forward to taking you on a tour of Tintern Abbey."

When the elderly Prior reached the dock, Brother Wallace said to him, "Prior Francis, I have the honor of presenting to you Lord Roger Bigod, the new Lord of Chepstow Castle."

"According to the people of Chepstow Castle, Prior Francis, you have an enviable reputation," said Lord Bigod. "It is an honor to meet you."

"The honor is all mine, Lord Bigod," responded the Prior. "Since this is a rather warm day for fall in Wales, we have cool water in the choir brothers' refectory. We also have wine, if you prefer."

"First, take me on the tour," the nobleman responded. "There will be time later for wine. I have heard so many fine things about the setting of Tintern Abbey. From what I have seen, the description does not begin to equal its reality. Framed by your rolling green hills on all sides, I can feel an atmosphere of seclusion so different from that of any other abbey I have ever visited—and I have seen many of them. Truly, here you have not run away from world; you have run into the glory of God. Surely, many years ago, an angel inspired Lord Clare to choose this place for an abbey. It is obvious that the finger of God shaped this valley just for you Cistercians. The Eternal One knew some day a Cistercian monk would kneel to praise Him in this holy valley."

Brother Wallace remarked to himself that the new lord was skillful in the way he treated people.

On his tour Lord Bigod met nearly all of the choir monks and lay brothers. Like the previous lords of Chepstow, he offered the unexpected gesture of repeating each brother's name and reaching for his hand in acknowledgment.

"I hope that God will be as friendly and caring as Lord Bigod," Simeon disclosed to a fellow lay brother after his personal introduction to the nobleman. Simeon was a serious-minded lay brother known for his strong commitment and dedication to the abbey. *This is the man I had a dream about last month,* Simeon thought. *This is the man who will finance the building of our new stone church with a lead roof. I know that our new church will be for the glory of God, but I shall take great pride in it, even if pride is a sin.*

IN THE EARLY evening, following Vespers and supper, a meeting was held in the chapter room. All the brothers of Tintern Abbey gathered to hear Lord Bigod's presentation.

Abbot Mark opened the evening proceedings by calling upon the Blessed Virgin to bless the gathering. Since Compline would be observed following their meeting, no other rituals were observed, and the Abbot moved on to the business at hand. "Choir brothers and lay brothers," he said, "I have the great honor to present to you our new patron, Lord Roger Bigod, the Fifth Earl of Norfolk and Lord of Chepstow. And I might add, the man who so generously provided the extra-large portions of meat and wine to the lay brothers for their supper this evening."

Lord Bigod stood before the gathering, pausing to acknowledge the attentive nods and smiles he saw before him.

"Abbot Mark, Prior Francis, and Tintern brothers, I feel humbled and grateful that God has allowed me to be a part of Tintern Abbey," Lord Bigod began. "With the free-flowing River Wye running behind the abbey, and with green hills and mountains on two sides, one does not have to go very far to sense the glory of God and His handiwork. Your past brothers and you have taken a wilderness and made it into a garden, and dare I say, one almost as beautiful as the Garden of Eden."

He stopped to sip some cool water, then continued. "Almost six months ago, King Edward, the Archbishop of Canterbury, and I talked together in London about Tintern Abbey. We have heard encouraging reports of granges, sheep, cattle, grain, and buildings being built. Fortunately, you have been spared the bitter fighting in northern Wales, for the most part. It is my opinion that the northern Welsh see the Benedictines as a religious arm of English conquest, and therefore an enemy, while the Cistercians are viewed as French and therefore less to be feared.

"I was also happy to learn that there is no record of a single complaint having been recorded concerning your chapel. It was well built and has served your every need. My family has entered Tintern Abbey in several ways. First, my mother Maud, whom some of you may know as Matilda, is buried in a crypt in your chapel. Another relative of mine, Strongbow, is buried beside her. As you may know, my family is closely related to William Marshal, who, as I understand, was most generous to Tintern Abbey.

"Then, there is my father Lord Hugh Bigod, who had a very special relationship with the abbey. Shortly before his death, he revealed that he had made a vow to build a large stone church to take the place of Lord Clare's chapel, which you are now using. I loved my father and I have taken a vow, also, to build his church here at Tintern. Naturally, as are all Cistercian chapels, it will be dedicated to the Blessed Virgin.

"I make this gift freely, to show you my good will and to honor my father's wishes. There are just three requests I have of you, concerning the building of this church. First, I request that a stained glass window carry the crest of the Bigod family. The second requirement is that you remember the Bigod family in your prayers, so that we may spend as little time as possible in purgatory. And the third is that my father's remains, which are buried here in the grounds of Tintern Abbey, be interred inside this new church."

Lord Roger's voice revealed a hint of emotion. He cleared his throat and composed himself. "Finally, I want you to know that the Archbishop of Canterbury has authenticated a relic that I shall give to the new Tintern Abbey church. According to the Archbishop, the relic has miraculous powers."

Excited whispers filled the room. Many of the monks had prayed that God would bestow a relic upon them. Relics—physical remains or artifacts associated with a saint, martyr, or holy person, such as a bone or a cloth or effigy—were highly regarded throughout Christendom, since they were believed to hold great spiritual and healing powers. The presence of a relic at Tintern Abbey would increase the number of pilgrims to its location and offerings to its church. What would this relic be?

Lord Bigod waited patiently for the murmuring to subside. He had predicted the monks would respond like this. When the assembly began to quiet down, it was time to return to the subject of the new church.

"I shall tell you more about your relic in due time. For now, let me provide you with information about the exciting building project ahead of us.

"The master mason, who will be in charge of the project, will join you in early winter, with construction work scheduled to begin in the spring," Lord Bigod told them. "His name is Master Ralf, and he has been helping me at Chepstow and in my properties in Normandy. I do not wish to steal his thunder, but I don't think he'll object if I share with you some of the plans and specifications. The overall plan is to build the church in the traditional form of a cross. The new church will be about ten times larger than your present chapel. It will have a lead roof and will be erected of stone in the modern Gothic style. From the measurements on file in your mother abbey I can roughly predict a nave of about two hundred thirty feet, with a transept of about one hundred fifty feet. Each wing will have two eastern chapels. With these measurements I can predict a central crossing to be about seventy feet high. The nave will have clerestories, which will allow much light to enter the church. The high altar will be under the tower. The church will be connected to both the choir monks' and lay brothers' dormitories, making it unnecessary for any brothers to go outside to enter their own portions of the church," the lord explained.

"A pulpitum screen will separate the monks' portion of the chapel from the lay brothers' portion," he continued. "During their own services they will not be able to see or hear one another. Monks' choir stalls will be facing each other."

Lord Bigod paused, allowing the crowd to absorb the extraordinary details of their new church. The lord discerned a look of confusion on the face of Brother Wallace, the monk who had greeted him at the dock.

"Brother Wallace, do you have a question?" the nobleman asked.

"Yes, my lord. What will happen to our original chapel?" Brother Wallace knew he was not alone in seeking an answer to the future of this sturdy old edifice. Many of the monks had been curious and concerned about the fate of the wooden chapel.

"Nothing for quite a while," Lord Roger answered. "Master Ralf has informed me that the Tintern Abbey church will be built right around and over the present chapel, the one built by Lord Clare. The chapel will continue to be used. In time, when the wooden chapel is completely engulfed, it will be taken down. The present crypt will be left untouched, except where the markers cannot be read. Where necessary, new markers will be made."

Brother Lock raised his hand in forceful manner.

Lord Bigod acknowledged him. "Yes, Brother Lock, I remember your name from our introductions. Please state your question or comment."

Brother Lock stepped forward. The rest of the gathering felt uneasy, knowing of Lock's opposition to any kind of change—other than an increase of liturgy, of course. What would he say? Would he confront Lord Bigod? Would he embarrass the abbey? Even Abbot Mark seemed to be holding his breath.

Brother Lock began softly, but his words were filled with emotion. "This must be a miracle!" he said. "I never dreamed that we could ever have such an edifice as you have described, a worthy church erected to glory of God and dedicated to Mary, the Blessed Virgin. Surely, God must be working His will here on the floor of the River Wye Valley. I have a vision that people will come not as much to observe our glorious setting, as to praise God in the new church and to enjoy the healing of spirit and body because of their pilgrimage to honor the Mother of God at Tintern Abbey!"

Abbot Mark said a silent prayer of gratitude. *The monks are all of one mind again,* he thought.

The meeting concluded and the day ended with Compline.

MASTER RALF ARRIVED in early winter, after he had notified his colleagues, laborers, and craftsmen of the upcoming construction project. Plans were already under way in the abbey and the nearby village to provide food and shelter for the many people who would be needed during construction.

Master Ralf began his on-site planning by assessing the lay brothers and training some of them in the many skills needed to keep the construction work moving forward. He put them to work erecting temporary shelters, much like those built to house early-day monks. They also built a storage building with a wooden floor to keep perishables from mold and rats, as well as a corral and a shelter for horses and oxen.

Many meetings were held with the lay brothers. Even those who had never worked on a church began to feel comfortable in their duties and tasks.

News of the building of this future church spread quickly throughout Wales and beyond. Before the last spring frost, workers—some skilled, others unskilled—began arriving nearly every day. While a few came from France, Ireland, and Wales, most were Englishmen and Scots.

Master Ralf knew many of these new arrivals. Some had worked with him on construction and repairs at the abbey church in Waverley, Canterbury Cathedral, Winchester Cathedral, Westminster Abbey, and a few castles. Others he knew from projects in London: stone masons, both master and rough, wood carvers, carpenters, hewers, wallers, marblers, tool carriers, hod carriers, pulley workers, cooks, bakers, forest wood workmen, tile makers and layers, and canters, who work on floors and roofing.

Lord Bigod also appointed Gratian, one of his own knights who had served as his bodyguard, to keep order in the land surrounding the abbey and to report to him any unruliness during the influx of workers. Although he probably would not need it, the knight brought his full battle armor and horse armor with him. Tall and slender, with blue eyes and a light complexion, Gratian was descended from Vikings who had settled in Normandy in the tenth century. His father was a minor Norman lord. Gratian spoke French, English, and Welsh, and he had earned the reputation of acting quickly in any incident affecting his lord. His accomplishments and talents, however, were not the only remarkable things about this knight. Gratian had six fingers on each hand.

Accompanying Gratian was his squire, Roland, who was a direct descendent of William the Conqueror. A little shorter than Gratian, Roland had a powerful build. He too was blond, with blue eyes. As a squire, Roland had learned to ride war horses and was allowed to carry his own sword and shield, which showed the rank he had attained. His armor was like a second skin to him. He ably fulfilled the squire's responsibilities of caring for his knight's horse and cleaning and polishing his armor, so that all would be ready for use at a moment's notice. Gratian respected Roland and treated his squire as almost an equal. Lord Bigod also had his eye on Roland, whom he expected to develop in time into a higher calling.

Arriving with Gratian and Roland were two riding horses, gifts from Lord Bigod to Abbot Mark. Contact with the outside world would now be easier.

BROTHER LOCK'S EYES scanned the growing number of scenes of activity on the abbey grounds before him. A conflict still brewed within. He praised God for the gift of the magnificent church that was manifesting itself before him. Yet he remembered his own warning, his original concerns and fears returning with each passing day. *Our way of life could be in danger,* he thought. *So many strangers arriving at our abbey. So many changes happening so quickly. For better or for worse, Tintern Abbey will never be the same again.*

10

Building the Abbey Church

LIKE ANY CATHEDRAL, or for that matter any place of Christian worship in the thirteenth century, Tintern Abby's church was to be built essentially as a stage for the reenactment of the Mass, the greatest drama of the Christian faith. The building itself, both inside and outside, would illustrate telling the story of those times when men and women encountered God in all His majesty and glory. The tale of the construction of any church was primarily a tale of faith. The church brought folk into this world and the church took mankind out of this world into the next. More than simply a construction project, a matter of piling one stone upon another spanning space, the building of a church was an expression of the thought, faith, hope, dreams, and devotion of its people. Mankind is the only creature to erect huge structures not to live in but to worship their gods.

The methods used for building the church at Tintern Abbey in the thirteenth century were very much the same as those used in the building of earlier churches, such as the cathedrals at Canterbury and Chartres. The builders relied on three major tools: a measuring stick, a square, and a caliper. Other tools included a pickax with an iron head, an auger, a mallet, a hammer, a leveler, two kinds of saws, and a wedge. How well these and still other tools were used depended upon the skill, experience, and reputation of the master craftsmen. The master mason worked in stone. The master carpenter worked in wood. The rough-cut master masons worked in the quarry to provide the stone to build the abbey. The master builder, and sometimes the master mason, were in charge of the total project. There were no architects.

Four major temporary buildings were created west of the abbey:

a stone workshop, a carpenter's workshop, a glass maker's workshop, and a blacksmith's workshop. The master blacksmith made and repaired all the tools necessary for the building of the abbey church. The master carpenter sculpted wood and crafted all the handles, wedges, and templates.

With the arrival of all of the construction workmen, a small village emerged west and north of the abbey. As wealth accumulated around this village, it became known as Parva, or Tintern Parva. Lord Bigod decided to give this village to Gratian as a payment for the knight's service. Thus Gratian became the lord of Tintern Parva and its environs. A warrant from King Edward making Gratian a sheriff of all Lord Bigod's properties had arrived the week before at Chepstow Castle, and so Gratian became the sheriff of Tintern Parva as well as its lord. As sheriff, his primary duty was to the King, but he also served Lord Bigod and Abbot Mark.

Gratian's responsibilities also included sorting out which tenants were serfs, and who were free. Serfs were bound to one another by feudal and personal obligations, and they would toil for Gratian without pay. In return, the knight would be accountable for their upkeep. Over the years, Gratian was slowly becoming lord of a manor. Tintern Parva grew and was eventually rich enough to support the knight and his household as well as pay rent to Abbot Mark.

Since Cistercians did not become pastors of their nearby flocks, Tintern Parva would need a church of its own for its growing community. Lord Bigod was attempting to enlist the services of a friar from the newly formed Franciscan Order to look after Parva's spiritual needs. In doing so, Bigod was running the risk of angering the Archbishop of Canterbury, because such a move would rob the bishop of some of his power and revenues.

EARLY ON A spring morning in 1269, Master Ralf, Brother Giotto, and the Head Lay Brother Villard met in the monks' day room, a large vaulted building located north of the chapter house and reached through a passageway connecting to the northeast corner of the monk's cloister. Four stone columns along the center line supported the vaults with pilasters at the walls. This eighty-by-thirty-five foot structure had been temporarily taken over by the master mason and master carpenter until their working sheds and buildings would be ready to be occupied. From this location would come all of the orders and directions for the construction of the new church. The next spring a temporary building for the master builder was also scheduled for erection.

Following the noon meal Master Ralf gathered all the headmen and laborers into the monks' day room. It was Ralf's strong reputation as a master mason that originally brought him to the attention of Lord Bigod. The nobleman had hired him for a wage of two shillings per week to guide the building of his century hall and block at Chepstow Castle.

Master Ralf was of medium height and almost completely bald. His crystal eyes made others feel he was in command of whatever was happening. The bushy eyebrows frequently needed trimming. Ralf's long face seemed to go well with his large nose and thin lips. Serious minded and never idle, he expected the same behavior from all his men, from highly skilled master craftsmen to menial laborers. At forty years of age, he had been always blessed with good health. Ralf never hesitated to demonstrate how and why tasks should be done. The master spoke fluently in French, Latin, and English. He was diligent in praising good work in front of others and chose to provide his criticism in private. He ate his first meal with supervisors and his middle meal with lay brothers and laborers, and he finished the day with a light snack with the monks in their warming room. Knowing every man's name encouraged harder work. His only vices, if they could be called vices, were a desire to ride fine horses and to drink fresh milk sweetened with honey.

Master Ralf opened the meeting with a call for prayer. "Let us pause here for a moment of meditation. We must never forget that God is the real Master Builder. None of us has the power to build these magnificent mountains and the stunning valley that enhance this site."

A moment of silence was honored as each privately gave thanks for the divine guidance that had brought them together for their holy mission. Master Ralf then officially greeted the assembly.

"It is good to see so many of my old friends here to build this glorious abbey church. I've just received a message from Abbot Mark, who will be joining us soon, and he insisted that we go ahead and begin our meeting. We have much information to cover. Today I shall summarize our overall plans and designs.

"First, let me share its form and style." With his right hand Master Ralf drew an imaginary cross and continued. "Naturally, the church will be built in the form of a cross, following the newly created decorative styles now famous in Paris. The nave, running approximately east to west, will be two hundred twenty-eight feet. My plans call for twenty-four center piers holding up the vaults, with twenty-two engaged columns supporting the outer walls. The ceiling will be vaulted. Counting the foundation stones, these piers and columns will be ninety feet high."

A murmur revealed that the assembled workers were excited by the enormity of the project they were embarking on.

"A clerestory will run the length of the church on each side," Ralf continued. "As you already know, the clerestory is the upper story of a building with colored glass windows above the adjacent roofs. These windows illuminate the nave and high altar portions with changing colors cascading the interior as the sun travels across the sky. It will be a most worshipful experience for all inside the church. You will all get to see it and marvel at such beauty.

"This church will be but one of God's palaces, but it must be a place of extraordinary beauty, one worthy of holding the treasured Blessed Mary icon, which I understand is nearly life-size."

Another murmur rose from the gathering. Could Ralf be talking about the holy relic Lord Bigod had promised to give the abbey? Master Ralf called for their attention, his face beet red. "Oh my, I fear I may have let the cat out of the bag," he said. "Please forget what I just said!"

"But Master Ralf," Brother Giotto protested, "you cannot blame us for being curious—"

"Indeed," Ralf responded. "But I must leave to Abbot Mark the honor of announcing the details of the icon. Please, my friends. I repeat, do not remember what I just said." He shifted uncomfortably until the room was silent once more.

"To go on, the great window in the east will have a round bar tracery, separating the panes of stained glass in a design that will contain the crest of the Bigod family. At the west end will be double doors with false doors on each side. False tracery will decorate these false doors. Doors and false doors will be framed in the gothic style. All the windows, too, will be of the Gothic design and will contain brilliantly colored glass. Afternoon sunlight will pass through a large window over the western doors, a beautiful stained glass window shaped by stone tracery. All of the tracery work will be in stone. Brother Giotto will supervise this delicate work. It may be another season before we can have a master glass maker here on site."

The faces of the craftsmen and laborers before him seemed to glow with pride, as if colored light were already shining upon them. Ralf smiled back at them and continued. "Turning to more practical matters, as you know, the foundation is critical for a building of this size. This valley floor has been filled in many times by floods, which means in order to have a firm foundation we must dig twenty feet down—perhaps more, perhaps less, but in any case until we run into firm rock. We shall be digging twenty-four large placements for the piers and twenty-two columns to assist the clerestory. Trenches will connect the pier and column placements. Pier, column, and trenches must be level with one another. Let me repeat, these placements must be absolutely level! For this reason each placement will be triple checked. The first will be done by Brother Giotto, who is a master mason. The brother has permission from his Abbot to work with us on this project. Lord Bigod will secure another master mason, who will do the second check, and I shall do the final check. Poor footings are a source of serious collapses. No amount of careful building higher up can correct for problems at the base!"

Master Ralf paused to be certain he had made his point. The men nodded to show they understood, or even that this was something they did not need to be told.

"The transept, or crossing, will be one hundred fifty feet in length, with the highest point reaching under the crossing at seventy-five feet," Master Builder Ralf went on. "Each wing will have two small chapels for private Masses by ordained monks.

"And now, I have a special announcement, so please listen carefully. If there are those here or among your workers who are unskilled and would like to become apprentices in masonry or wood carving or carpentry, or as lead workers for roofs and plumbing, please approach me after this meeting or after Sunday Mass. Those who express interest will be referred to the masters of these various skills for an interview. If you can read, it would be more helpful. One of the monks, Brother Warwick, has volunteered to hold reading classes after your working day. If you are interested, please speak to Prior Francis. As I have been told, the reading classes will not be open to conversi or lay brothers. However, they are open to all other laborers, including Welshmen."

This offer caused considerable excitement, not only because the chance to learn to read was so rare for most laborers, but also because it appeared to be a generous gesture to the Welsh, whom the English were accustomed to regard as barely civilized.

"Tomorrow Brother Giotto and rough-cut master stone mason Samsone will take one of the conversi with them to visit the stone quarry, which I understand is across the River Wye and about two to three miles southeast of us. While that is being done, I shall take the master woodman and some conversi with me to scour our forests, marking any trees that we may be able to use for construction, for scaffolding, workshops, and machines. I hope we can find the trees here, but an abbey renter, Thomas, who lives west of Tintern Abbey, tells me that we may have to go north, maybe even to the land of the Vandals, to find trees big enough and strong enough for our frames and trusses. Getting heavy materials to our building site will be difficult, of course. Fortunately, we have the ocean and the Bristol Channel leading right up to the River Wye. The River Wye will be of tremendous help in getting the cut stone from the quarry to our building site."

Master Ralf paused again, then said, "You are probably wondering when we shall actually break ground to get this construction under way. Brother Giotto and I have already staked out the ground that will be dug for the foundations. If all goes well, the first stone of the foundation will be blessed and lowered into the bed sometime before the snow and cold weather comes. I believe that Lord Bigod attempted to get the King and his chaplain to bless this work, but they will be unavailable this fall. However, the King volunteered the Archbishop of Canterbury for this special blessing and he has agreed. This is, indeed, a great honor that will come to Tintern Abbey. It is good to know that the abbey has such important and influential friends and allies."

Master Ralf rubbed his bald head and smiled. "I know this meeting is long, but I also know you are interested in knowing a bit more about what you may expect. Some of you have asked me what will constitute a working day for this project. In summer our working day will be about twelve hours long, as light allows. We shall begin work at sunrise. There will be a half-hour break at mid-morning, and an hour-and-a-half-long break at high noon to eat and nap. We'll stop the day's work at sundown. Days will be shortened in winter to about nine hours. Although some workers will be kept over the winter, most will be going home, after we prepare for winter by covering the open work with straw and dung to prevent freezing and wind damage. When we shut down sometime in November, I shall tell you when to report for work in the spring. If you would like to work through the winter and have the skills we need, please notify me of this. No work will be done on the Sabbath. One of Tintern's monks, Brother Godfrey, will preside at Mass on these holy days.

"Now, concerning wages, we shall follow the customary rate. Pay will be in English money. Master workmen have been recruited and you know what your pay will be. Of course, lay brothers or conversi will not be paid. They are a part of the abbey and have little time for our needs. They have their own work for the abbey, which must be done, as well as their daily prayers. But there are a few highly skilled conversi whom the Abbot has given us permission to use, and we'll be grateful for their time and work.

"Now hear this carefully, for I think you will be surprised and elated. All our Tintern workers have one great advantage working here. I have never heard of such generosity before. Your lodgings, such as they are, are a gift from Lord Bigod. Your meals—and I know they will be generous—will also be furnished by Lord Bigod as his gift to you. Now, are we not all obligated to work hard to be worthy of Lord Bigod's generosity?

"Friends, this has been a long meeting," Master Ralf concluded. "But if I am any reader of groups, you have remained alert through- out, for which I thank you. Are there any questions?"

One young man raised his hand and was quickly acknowledged. "I am Fulbert, a Welshman who works in wood. I am from Cardiff. Work here seems to be fulfilling and the pay is good. I can read and write. You stated a little while ago that lay brothers or conversi are not eligible to learn to read and write. One of my countrymen was accepted not long ago as a lay brother at Tintern Abbey. His name is Loder from Llandaff Village. He came to the abbey because of the partial destruction of his village, and no work was there for a young man. He is spiritually minded. Can you tell me why a Welsh lay brother is not allowed to better himself by learning to read and write? Is it because he is Welsh?"

Abbot Mark, who had just joined the meeting a few minutes earlier, stepped forward to answer the question.

"I know some things about Llandaff Village. It is now a peaceful village occupied by Anglo Saxons of long standing, although I gather there are some Welshmen there, like your friend. But whether a man is Saxon or Welsh that would make no difference as far as our reading policy is concerned. We do not have any lay brothers who can read, and there is a reason for this policy. Let me explain.

"In the beginning of our Cistercian Order, Brother Steven Harding of Citeaux Abbey established the standards that we practice today. These standards, which are approved by the Pope, are followed in all Cistercian abbeys.

"It is well known that God set the order of all things as well as our places and stations in life. This is as it should be, even if we some- times question the way God set up the world. In any case, in order for the abbeys to fulfill their missions, the choir monks are called upon daily and sometimes hourly to pray for our souls and keep themselves worthy, while the conversi are called to be holy agricul- tural workers who make possible the daily prayers of the monks," explained the Abbot.

"From the beginning, lay brothers normally have come from less exalted stock who could neither read nor write. The lay brothers take only partial vows. In exchange for their work, they are furnished clothing, food, and a roof over their heads. In order to be a choir monk, one must be of noble birth and be able to read and write in Latin as well as speak in English or French. One must also be chaste and be willing to dedicate his entire life to God, obeying his Abbot in all things.

"To prevent envy and strife, only volunteer men who cannot read and write, but are in good health, God-fearing, willing to work and perhaps to learn a trade, are chosen to the high office of the lay brotherhood. There is no promotion from the position of a lay brother to the office of a choir monk. This plan is God's order of things and will not change.

"I know Loder," the Abbot added. "He is a fine young man who is doing good things for the abbey and God. However, if he harbors envy to become a choir monk, he will lead a miserable life and find little contentment here at Tintern Abbey."

Dwindling questions signaled time to release the men to their labors. The meeting had lasted longer than Master Ralf expected. As the crowd filed out of the monks' room, he apologized to the Abbot for mentioning information about the relic to the assembly. Abbot Mark smiled with understanding. A nearly life-sized icon of the Virgin Mary with spiritual and healing powers soared above his hopes and expectations. The gift from God was too compelling for him to keep the secret as well. Now that the cat was out of the bag, it would surely be no time before everyone at the abbey knew.

THE NEXT DAY Brother Giotto, Master Builder Ralf, Master Stone Mason Samsone from Glastonbury, and lay brother Villard, along with some of Lord Bigod's soldiers, boarded a boat for the short ride south to the quarry. After rounding a bend in the river, they came ashore on a sandy beach and headed east along a marked path.

Walking east along a road narrowed by growth and packed by carts, the party came upon the quarry in less than an hour. Four old buildings were in disrepair. One still had the remains of a large stone forge. Rotting poles and pieces of broken stone littered the area.

Although it had been over twenty years since the quarry was last mined, its location was convenient for the new construction project, and the extensive digging done in the past made the task of extracting stone relatively easier.

A pit over seventy-five feet deep, one hundred sixty feet wide, and ninety feet across on the northern side had been cut from the old quarry. Grass and some small trees marked the edge of the quarry. Stone from this quarry had been tested and was found to be sound and easy to carve and shape as needed. In fact, stone from this quarry had been used in the building of Chepstow Castle and later some stone buildings at the abbey.

"This limestone is fascinating," Master Mason Samsone remarked. "I've seen stone like this from other quarries. Look, you can see here what looks like the image of a shell from the sea. God certainly is a creator of miracles!"

Master Mason Samsone estimated it would take about fifty workmen of various skills to begin to supply the builders at the abbey. He anticipated something over a half million stones would be needed. Samsone also estimated that it would take about twenty years to complete the abbey church.

THE WORKSHOPS FOR the stone cutters and the forge for the repair of broken tools were the first to be erected. Not long after this Master Blacksmith Melbourne arrived from Cardiff. Bellowing black smoke, the forge was soon in working order. Apprentice cutters quickly had pieces of stone ready for laborers to raise to the surface, where they would undergo the necessary chiseling and hammering by stone masons. These stones soon began to match the patterns or templates supplied by the Master Mason.

Samsone made sure that each stone was marked three times with an appropriate symbol. One was to show exactly where the stone would fit into the abbey church. Another was to show which mason had actually rough-finished the stone at the quarry for his payment, and the third marked the stone as belonging to the quarry owned by Lord Bigod. One more mark was made at the abbey showing which Master Mason laid or supervised the laying of each stone.

A WEEK LATER Abbot Mark, Sheriff Gratian, Prior Francis, and Brother Loder started their journey. Two Welsh laborers, one of whom was Brother Loder's friend Fulbert, were chosen to join the expedition because of their knowledge of the area and their expertise in working with lumber. The group's quest was to find oaks, yew, alder, beech, and other woods fit enough for the construction of the roof, rafters, and other needs. Trees in this region had been used by Romans and Celts before them, for building houses, barns, and military forts; and the Romans further decimated the forests in an attempt to clear the land for military purposes. Anglo-Saxons continued harvesting the forests after Roman times, and now the Normans were doing the same thing. These were times of ambitious construction, with the erection of enormous cathedrals in England requiring large pieces of wood, some sixty to eighty feet long. Canterbury Cathedral, Westminster Abbey Cathedral, Salisbury Cathedral, and Gloucester Cathedral, as well as many other large churches, all required great quantities of timber. As a result, England's forests were losing much of their hardwood resources. Would there be enough trees nearby to serve the building needs for Tintern Abbey's new church? Our searchers were attempting to answer this question.

Traveling west along a road built by lay brothers, the wood searching party soon reached the Thomases' demesne. Thomas showed them two areas near the southeast border of his land that he thought might furnish much of the wood necessary for the abbey. "I need to reclaim this land in any case," he said, "so I can use it for gardens, pastures, and farmland. Now that I've allowed two of my free tenants to marry, I need the new ground more than ever."

"This looks like a fine opportunity," Abbot Mark said. "One that will benefit us both. Assarting will provide you with the land you need, and in the process of clearing and draining your land, Tintern Abbey will get its building wood."

The company from the abbey wasted no time exploring the area and assessing the trees to be taken down. When their day's work was done, they were treated to a luscious and filling early evening meal by Mistress Thomas.

After the company was seated and served, and prayers of thanks were given, Mistress Thomas stood and said, "I am pleased, finally, to have an opportunity to thank the monks of Tintern Abbey for your brave and generous deed, when you rid our area of the boars that killed a member of my husband's family, as well as other people and farm animals nearby. My grandmother often told me of the elderly monk who put them down, and how he was so kind and helpful in that time of crisis. We also cannot ever repay those abbey lay brothers who built a road to our land and home. On a heavy, misty night we can just barely hear the bell calling your holy men to prayer. We are so far away from a chapel that we seldom get a chance to attend Mass. It is so comforting to know that God is being praised and prayer is being offered for us and others by monks of Tintern.

"I expect you have noticed that our little Virgin Mary icon has green plants around it. This comes from my grandmother's ancient Celtic background. The old ways are sometimes hard to leave behind. Everywhere I walk on our land, I see little bits and pieces of remembrance of the Celts. My little statue reminds me of the Blessed Virgin. The greenery around it reminds me of my ancestors' faith."

Abbot Mark walked across the room and, taking the wife's hand, spoke softly but loud enough for all to hear. "This, indeed, is a fine Christian home. I have known your husband for many years and have observed his kindness to strangers and his generosity to our abbey. I have often asked myself, where does this man get his spirit? Now I know. This spirit comes from his home and especially from his wife, who is truly a virtuous woman. The monks of Tintern Abbey could learn a lot here. We are daily engaged in attempting to be holy, when true holiness is just over our hill."

Sheriff Gratian added, "As Lord Bigod's knight and also the Sheriff of Tintern Parva, I too wish to express my gratitude to the Thomas family, and I am sure Lord Bigod is pleased that we have found a way and a reason to clear some of this land for the benefit of all concerned. It appears to me that you will have about forty to forty-five more acres to use for your purposes once the ground is cleared. It will take a few months to organize the necessary woodmen and wagons to start clearing your land. However, if we are able to secure the wagons and horses, we may send some small crews to cut lumber sooner, if the weather permits. We are in the process of building new working and bunking houses. It seems the number of our workers is beginning to outdistance our materials."

"Let me know if I can assist," Thomas offered. "We have four horses, two wagons, and three men."

"We may well be calling upon your generosity," said Prior Francis.

IT WAS PAST dark when the woodmen returned to the abbey. Abbot Mark was noticeably limping when he reached his own quarters. No one seemed to know exactly what had happened on the walk back from Thomas's land. Later in the night, when Abbot Mark failed to awaken the monks for Vigils, Prior Francis ran to the Abbot's quarters, where he found his friend to be sweating profusely with a high fever. The Prior called for help, and Abbot Mark was carried to the infirmary. By now he was unconscious, although his arms were flailing randomly. Prior Francis knelt by the Abbot's bed and wept, praying for his friend, knowing full well that God's will would be done.

AT LAUDS PRIOR Francis announced to the monks who had gathered to greet the new day with prayer that Abbot Mark was dead. Tears quickly came to some of the monks' eyes. Others sat stunned. If there could be more silence than silence, this was it. Prior Francis broke the silence by saying, "I'm sure many of us wonder why our beloved Abbot has been taken from the abbey's work. The only answer is that we must trust the will of God. Abbot Mark was a hard worker and exceptionally devout. Perhaps he was needed in heaven."

Eucharist was held a little later than customary. As usual, this love feast was dedicated to the Blessed Virgin. The ritual moved in a deliberate manner with each word and phrase spoken exactly and distinctly as written. The monks were going through the words mechanically.

Sheriff Gratian dispatched Roland on horseback to notify Lord Bigod of the Abbot's death. Roland knew how to pace his horse in order to get the sad message quickly to Chepstow Castle. By noon

Lord and Lady Bigod arrived at Tintern's dock, accompanied by their chaplain.

Two monks washed and anointed the Abbot's body. He was dressed in a new white cowl. A new grave was dug by the lay brothers.

Following a Mass, Abbot Mark's body was carried out the east door of the wooden chapel by four monks and placed among his deceased brothers. The ceremony was humble and called no special attention to the Abbot's status or achievements over his long life's service to the Cistercian Order. But all the choir monks and lay brothers present at the funeral knew that Abbot Mark had at last received the rest that eluded him during his days as an ordinary monk and his exalted time as an Abbot.

FOLLOWING THE RULES of the Cistercian Order, Prior Francis assumed the direction of Tintern Abbey, but not the title of Abbot. At the first chapter meeting following the death of their Abbot, Prior Francis spoke with a tone of reverence:

"These are moments of strain and joy. Strain because we have so many tasks before us that will demand the very best in all of us, in order to meet this challenge of our new abbey church, so much larger and grander than our present modest chapel. Joy, because our beloved Abbot Mark went to his heavenly peace while serving our tenants, and with the knowledge that a great stone church would rise out of our simple ground.

"Among the Cistercians, we do not ask, 'Whom can we find to replace our Abbot? Who can possibly take his place?' One Abbot does not replace another. We do not ask of our new Abbot that he be bigger, stronger, more saintly, wiser, or holier than the next man; nor do we require that he be as eloquent a speaker, or as understanding, as firm, as intelligent, as thrifty, or as bold as our past Abbot. No, we ask only that God will send us one who can be first among equals.

"For this reason I shall not be a candidate for Abbot of Tintern Abbey. When our new Abbot is installed, I shall relinquish my duties as Prior, and shall not be a candidate for that position either. These

are firm decisions I have made, and I ask that this matter never again
be raised in our chapter," said the Prior.

A LETTER WAS sent to Abbey L'Aumone, Tintern's mother abbey,
announcing that Abbot Mark had been mortally stricken. Other
letters were sent to the Archbishop of Canterbury, to the King, to
Waverley Abbey, and to Citeaux.

It took nearly two years for a new Abbot to be installed at Tintern.
In the interim, following the usual custom, Lord Bigod continued to
receive all the revenues from the abbey into his own treasury. Usually
a monastery without an Abbot would send all or most of its revenues
to the King. However, the Marcher lords were given very indepen-
dent and far-reaching rights, which were necessary to pacify the wilderness. As could be expected, there was some grumbling among the
Tintern monks, who noted that they did all of the work and Bigod
got all the revenue. They had to acknowledge, though, Lord Bigod
was paying for most of the costs of the new church, for which they
remained grateful.

The General Chapter at Citeaux was well aware of Lord Bigod's
involvement with Tintern Abbey, his assuming the income for himself,
and his financial support of the abbey's new church. Knowing that
Lord Bigod had a large responsibility for keeping the peace—continued unrest and rebellion in Wales had resulted in the death of some
monks, along with damages to the Strata Florida Abbey and some
damages to other abbeys—the governing body of the Cistercian
Order followed the policy that abbeys stay clear of dynastic and
political fights between lords. After all, it was likely that Lord Bigod's
protection had kept Tintern Abbey safe from violence and damage.

The Annual General Chapter Meeting was held at Citeaux in the
spring of 1271. The time had come to honor Abbot Mark of Tintern,
who had died suddenly of unusual circumstances, by selecting a
suitable replacement. Abbot Rynland of Waverley Abbey proposed
the name of John, one of their bright and aggressive brothers, to be
the new Abbot of Tintern Abbey. One of the Abbots asked why the
current Prior now in charge of Tintern was not being considered for
the position of Abbot. Abbot Rynland produced a letter stating that

Prior Francis had refused to be considered for the office of Abbot of Tintern Abbey.

"This may be for the best," responded another Chapter Meeting Abbot who was acquainted with the Prior. "Prior Francis is an old man, probably too old for the weight of the position of Abbot. But he will serve as a trusted advisor to Tintern's new leadership. Abbot Rynland, tell us more of Brother John, your choice. Why would he be an appropriate choice for Abbot?"

Abbot Rynland nodded. "You should know this about Brother John. He was left at the abbey of Bury Saint Edmunds as a child by his uncle, the Archbishop of York. A considerable gift was made to Bury by the Archbishop. The child was raised by the eminent Jouycelin of Brakelond. As some of you know, Jouycelin was the Chaplain of the late Abbot Samson of Bury Saint Edmunds. The child ran away and was taken in at Waverley Abbey. As a young boy, John had heard of Bernard of Clairvaux and knew much about the beliefs, rigor and personal sacrifices of the Cistercians when he arrived at Waverley. It seemed to us a miracle, for this lad knew so much about the White Monks. He could read and speak Latin. He was familiar with the Lectio Divina. We were amazed that he could also speak French and German. He was accepted as a novice at Waverley and has been an exemplary and sometimes a militant brother. His enthusiasm knows no end. With the tremendous monastic changes that are going on everywhere, and especially at Tintern Abbey, Waverley would strongly propose Brother John to be Abbot at Tintern Abbey."

Thus, with very little fanfare or discussion, Brother John of Waverley Abbey was appointed Abbot of Tintern Abbey.

By THE FALL of 1271, Abbot John had been installed as Abbot of Tintern Abbey. Abbot John's installation remarks came as a shock and created much unrest among the usually congenial Tintern monks.

"I have found discipline to be lax among the monks of Tintern Abbey," he began. "I have found some eating meat more than the three times per week as set at the General Chapter. This will stop!"

He paused to look over his notes, then continued, "I have noticed that you allow the sheriff to come and go as he pleases in the abbey.

This will also stop. The sheriff will seek permission from me to enter the abbey grounds.

"Following strict procedures, now that I have arrived to be your Abbot, no further money will be given to Lord Bigod. I shall be responsible for all funds and their disbursements until our new Cellarer is properly installed and instructed. I shall tell you more about the new Cellarer in a moment."

The monks shifted on their benches. No one dared utter a word of protest, but the feeling of protest was clear to all, including Abbot John, who glared back, then proceeded.

"I shall be drawing up a new set of regulations concerning the merchants of Tintern Parva. Our abbey is not getting its proper share of revenues from goods sold at the market, which is just outside the abbey gate. It is customary for the abbey to get one penny for every transaction. I have assigned Brother Giotto to open and close the market and to collect our revenues. Lord Bigod will be notified of this change.

"A new stall will be built for your new Abbot's horses. I do not want my horses put among the work horses and oxen. I also notice that the Abbot's fish pond is in disrepair and will hardly hold water. Some of my fish are actually dying! I direct that the abbey divert some of the water now going to Tintern Parva vegetable gardens and channel such water into the Abbot's fish pond. Moreover, I notice that this abbey does not have a fish catcher on the River Wye, but buys fish from local fishermen. This will stop! I have instructed Brother Giotto to take some of the lumber from the Thomas land and build a fish catcher. With this done, the abbey will have a monopoly on fish in the area. River Wye fish will add to the revenues of the abbey."

Monks looked at each other as if to ask themselves if this speech was to be believed.

"I have other concerns about the Thomas land," the new Abbot continued. "In going over the accounts, I see that Thomas demesne does not have an exaction. He gives twenty pounds each year at Michaelmas, but this is not what he should be paying. I have appointed my new Cellarer. He is Brother Morgan, and his first task will be to notify Thomas that thirty pounds will be expected at next Michaelmas. And Morgan," the Abbot called out, unconcerned with making eye contact, "during your visit you are to examine this Thomas's stables and select his most valuable horse to bring back for my personal use. We shall replace it with one of our old quarry horses."

The Abbot paused, glared, then went on. "As you know, a new church has been built in Tintern Parva. I shall be telling Lord Bigod and the sheriff that the Abbot of Tintern Abbey will be appointing the rector or vicar to any church in Tintern Abbey regions. The owner of Parva Church is the abbey and this abbey will be receiving all of the revenues, less a vicar's needs."

By now the monks had stopped shifting on their benches and had stopped glancing at one another. They had been stunned into submission, as if turned to stone.

The Abbot had another directive. "Also I want it known that any burial inside the abbey grounds will be up to me as Abbot and I shall set the standards and honorarium. It may be that we shall have to use the custom of distraint. I gather that Tintern has never used distraint, which is the seizing or detaining of someone's property until an obligation is met. It is most useful at burials, because until the family pays the honorarium the person cannot be properly buried in the new church or abbey grounds.

"Furthermore, I have noted that the River Wye is free-flowing. I have asked Brother Giotto to draw up plans for building a water mill. When erected, this mill will bring high revenues to this abbey. We shall require all peasants and free persons to use our mill for grinding their grain. Some places have fined people who grind their own or another's grain. For now, I shall not do this."

One quiet monk whispered to his neighbor, "How generous. How long do you think that will last?"

"I'm more concerned about how long this speech will last," the other monk whispered back.

"In addition, I have noticed that this abbey was purchasing its wine from local persons. After we have set up our own winemaking system, we shall stop purchasing wine from others. This new change will save the abbey money and will also be an income maker.

"Now, listen carefully to this: I do not see the abbey getting the most it can for its wool. Too much is going to the Welshmen in the Trellech Manor. The best way to sell our wool is to do it on contract. In the future, we shall be paid in advance for our wool. I shall talk more of this with Lord Bigod without consulting Trellech."

Abbot John smiled, and some of the monks noted that his smile was even grimmer, more disturbing, than his scowl. "As you can see," he said, "I believe that an abbey is more than a place to pray and make good little monks. Abbeys can be tremendous financial enterprises. There are so many ways an abbey can make more money. Little changes add up to big total revenues. I want to see Tintern Abbey as the biggest, largest, and most powerful abbey in Wales, maybe in all of England. I know all of you can be with me on this adventure. Under my leadership you will be surprised at the power our abbey can exert." He paused. "When you made your vows, you pledged to obey your Abbot in all things. I now claim that pledge.

"Coming soon to our new church will be a holy relic. Many pilgrims will come seeking healing, forgiveness, hope, and peace. In gratitude they will leave gold and silver or other valuables, all to the glory of God and the Blessed Virgin, of course.

"I have said what I have had to say. I am challenging you to perform well, and I am requiring your full support. We are embarking on a regime that will reward us all."

The chapter meeting was over, but the monks did not rise. They were too stunned to move. They had never considered their cloak as a symbol of power or wealth, or their abbey as a means for making money; for them in was a place to pray for souls entrusted to them to be kept pure from the stains of the world. Oh, yes, they had always accepted property and other valuables; and at times they received gifts when they offered Masses for the salvation of souls or petitioned for a soul to be released more early from the flames of purgatory. But the monks had prayed eagerly and sincerely for most of mankind, at times naming individuals, not primarily for money, but because of their belief that God, the Blessed Virgin, or the saints could and would intercede and bring salvation and relief.

THERE IS A saying that time is needed to heal wounds, both spiritual and physical. But in this case it appeared as if time had brought new wounds. As the years went by old-timers in the village were heard to say, "Yes, Tintern Abbey is certainly changing."

The greed of the new Abbot was also noticed by higher powers in London. In 1282 an overambitious Abbot John caused Tintern Abbey to be fined one hundred twelve pounds for felling two hundred acres of timber without authority to deal, selling the oaks for one hundred fifty pounds. Abbot John blamed the entire transaction on his Cellarer Morgan, with whom he had split the profit.

But time also brought the fulfillment of a dream.

On the third of October, 1288, the choir monks of Tintern Abbey at last filed into the presbytery of the completed Tintern Abbey church, to offer the first Mass at the high altar under the transept, flooded by brilliantly patterned colors from God's radiant sun.

TINTERN ABBEY'S ABBOT John, who had seen to the completion of the new stone church, was summoned shortly thereafter by the Archbishop of Canterbury to lead a fund-raising campaign for the repair of some of Canterbury's aging tombs. On the journey his stallion bolted, throwing John down an embankment and breaking his neck.

Because the accident happened far from Tintern Abbey, Abbot John was not buried in his own abbey, but was buried instead at Battle Abbey.

Upon hearing of the accident, some of Tintern Abbey's monks remarked, "God rest his soul." Others were glad to add Abbot John's name to their memorials; whether they were glad to do so out of loyalty to the Abbot or just glad to have the Abbot remembered and not seen was a question they were never expected to answer.

PART III
The Great Mortality

11

The Black Death

THE EARLY YEARS of the fourteenth century were a time of prosperity for southeastern Wales, and indeed for much of Europe. Population was increasing, and through assarting more and more land was being made available for agriculture. The ongoing war between England and France still flared up, but the turmoil of war scarcely affected the tranquil ongoing peace of the Wye Valley and Tintern Abbey.

It was during this time, early in the fourteenth century, that the abbey reached its zenith, with twenty-two gifts of land, approved by King Edward I shortly before his death in 1307. Because William the Conqueror had declared all of England, Wales, and Scotland his own property, all transfers of land to religious organizations had to be approved by the King. That Tintern Abbey received such generous gifts with the support of the Crown was an indication of the abbey's importance—politically, economically, strategically, and spiritually.

As an indication of their power and influence, Tintern Abbots received five different summons to Parliament in the first half of the fourteenth century to advise on state matters relating to the production of wool and to assarting.

Although smaller in size than many of the other Cistercian abbey churches, the Tintern Abbey church had become the envy of monks because of its innovations and its location. The visiting Abbot's lodgings had doubled in size and the dovecote was redone in stone, decorated with dove statues.

The three-quarter life-size icon of the Blessed Virgin continued to attract many pilgrims to Tintern Abbey, including sick and lame people in need of healing. Reported healings of sick pilgrims brought more income to the abbey. In the early fourteenth century the Pope granted dispensations to those journeying to Tintern Abbey, which significantly increased the number of visitors, and increased revenues. Considering conditions in most of Wales, Tintern Abbey was relatively prosperous, enjoying the financial security it had known since the abbey was founded in 1131.

ABBOT TURHOLD MADE his year-end report in December, 1347 to the choir monks and lay brothers assembled in the chapter room. Turhold had been the Abbot of Tintern Abbey for over a decade, and he was well admired by everyone in the community, as were his capable new administrator, Prior Frank, and the Abbot's Sacrist, Brother Araud.

"As you know we have sixteen choir monks and twenty-one lay brothers at Tintern Abbey" the Abbot began. "Our income from all sources this past year totaled one hundred eighty-six pounds, six shillings, and one penny. One hundred twenty-five pounds came from wool. Twenty-one pounds came from rents, Tintern Parva Merchant assessments, and burials on Abbey grounds. Ten pounds came from the Manor Court as fines for various kinds of infractions. Twelve pounds, six shillings, and one penny came from the sale of fish. Eighteen pounds came from pilgrims visiting the Blessed Virgin.

"Three of our brothers have gone to their final rest. These were Brother Nakin, Brother Easons, and Prior Rollins. Let us remember these brothers in our prayers in order to have their time in purgatory shortened. God rest their souls. At this time, four brothers are in feeble condition in the infirmary. These are Brother Godfrey, Brother Aelfwine, Brother Peter, and Brother Thomas. Only Brother Thomas is able to attend chapter and Mass on a somewhat regular basis.

"I need to report that we have had some short-time fund shortages that have been met by a few loans made to us by our generous wool merchants.

"During this past year Chepstow Castle was given to Lady Margaret, the Plantagenet Duchess of Norfolk," the Abbot continued. "Chepstow lords have always been kind to their abbey, and I believe we can count on their continued support. The future indeed looks bright for our beloved Tintern Abbey. Surely nothing but prosperous times lie ahead."

Abbot Turhold smiled at the monks and lay brothers, and some of them smiled back. He understood, as did they, that their smiles were not smiles of pride, but of gratitude.

IN THE MIDDLE of summer, 1348, an ordained Cistercian monk named Brother Gerome stopped at the abbey for lodgings on his way from L'Aumone to Whitland Abbey, which was located near the Welsh coast on the Irish Sea. Driven by recent torrential rains and storms in the Black Mountains, the River Wye was pushing its banks as slow-moving limbs floated by. Brother Gerome was properly impressed by the new and inviting abbey church.

After Lauds and Eucharist were completed on the first morning of his visit, the monks gathered at Chapter. Brother Araud, the Sacrist, presented a reading from Isung of Prufening titled "Dialogue Between a Cluniac and a Cistercian." This dialogue gave the monks a rare opportunity to express their opinions and to boast a bit about the superiority of Cistercian views.

Following a lively discussion, the guest of the abbey asked if he might speak. Brother Araud welcomed Brother Gerome formally and invited him to stand up and address the community.

Brother Gerome stood before them, a tall man with a solemn yet friendly face. "I am Gerome," he said simply. "I am on my way from your mother house, L'Aumone, to Whitland Abbey, where I will become their new Abbot. I must say that your new abbey church is splendid. It is in line with most of the recently built Cistercian chapels I have seen. I don't know what our ancestors would say about it, but I find it is most worshipful. For a few moments I watched the changing colors on the high altar as the sun's rays passed through the stained glass of the clerestory. I plan to take another look as I pray this afternoon."

Pausing to clear his throat, Gerome continued. "I thank you for your hospitality. It is good to greet old friends like Brother Araud. He reads Latin so well and clearly. I was not aware of this writing, but there have been many dialogues between Cistercians and Benedictine

Cluniacs. I am happy to know that some of these meetings are being recorded. Brothers Warden and Benedict, I know from my early days.

"It is always joyful when travelers bring good tidings," Brother Gerome said, in a soft but commanding voice. "But, in these days, news is not always good. It is my sad duty to relay to you some frightening events from southern Europe. What I am going to tell you comes from several reliable sources. If they were from one person I would dismiss them as the ravings of a maniac. Yet I have three reliable sources. I have also spoken with a physician from Oxford, who knew quite a bit about the phenomena involved.

"The story first comes from a Benedictine brother named Edmund, whom I knew from the city of Toulouse in Southern France. Both of us were spending a night at Bath Abbey. According to this brother, a frightening pestilence attacked some Genoese galleys that were docked in the port of Messina in Sicily. Some sailors aboard the ships were already dead. Others were delirious with a high fever, sweating, with large sores on their necks and arms. Within a few days many people from Messina became as ill as the sailors. The people of Messina were furious and drove the ships out of the port and back to sea. Brother Edmund said so many people died in Messina, the survivors reportedly pitched the dead into large pits and covered them, some without last rites."

Brother Gerome coughed. The visiting monk was obviously uncomfortable being the bearer of such distressing tidings. He cleared his throat several times, until Abbot Turhold offered him his own water flask.

"Thank you for your kindness." Brother Gerome nodded to the Abbot, then continued his news. "The time or sequence of this next story is uncertain. However, according to a merchant from Venice, three ships entered the ports of Genoa and Venice early this year carrying the same pestilence. The people of those cities, learning that many of the ships' sailors were dead or dying, ran the ships out of port with flaming arrows. Two of the ships caught fire, but the flames were quickly put out. Shortly afterward, people in Genoa and Venice started to die, suffering from high fever, a red and black complexion, plus boils under their armpits and in their groins. The cause was unknown, although some speculated that sin was to blame.

"Finally, we go to the illustrious city of Florence, where a group of sailors had traveled by land. They too were carrying the disease, and the people of Florence ran them off with arrows, because they did not want to get close enough to the diseased men to use their swords."

A tense murmur grew among the monks and lay brothers in the chapter room. Brother Gerome nodded with understanding. "I'm sure you are wondering what could cause these terrible events," he said. "I have wondered the same thing. At Bath, I met a physician of the church named Luke who lectures at Oxford. The physician was visiting his brother, the Bishop of Bath. While bathing in that huge pool he heard stories of the same pestilence, which he called a plague. It was Luke's belief that this pestilence occurred in more ancient times also.

"The Bishop of Bath believes the terrible fatalities were punishment from God for the faithlessness and sins of the people. To ward off similar punishment the Bishop has required the people of Bath to exhibit penitence by marching around their cathedral barefooted one time for each apostle while repeating holy songs and holy words.

"Another view of the cause was suggested by Physician Luke. The Oxford physician's view was astronomical. He told me an unfortunate conjunction of the planets Saturn, Jupiter, and Mars occurred only two years ago. According to some scholars, a conjunction of this sort would produce hot and moist conditions, inducing the earth to exhale poisonous vapors from the ground and lakes. Some witnesses claim to have seen a 'miasma,' or poisonous cloud, erupting from the earth near where the disease occurs. Others have speculated that this putrefaction may be caused by the planets or cracks in the earth or even the rotting of human flesh. The truth is we do not know what is the cause of this terrible pestilence. But whatever the causes, these scholars, not priests, have recommended certain steps be taken to avoid such pestilence."

Brother Gerome was still having trouble with his voice, which was beginning to sound rough. He coughed several times, then reached for the Abbot's flask again to soothe his throat. After he composed himself, he related the details of the scholars' remedies.

"They recommend that no one eat poultry or water fowl. They also advise no pig should be eaten, nor old beef, nor fatty meat. Olive oil with meat can be mortal. Absolutely no cooking should be done in rain water. They also say it is dangerous to take baths. As for positive advice, the scholars suggest meditation, and they say thinking about gold, silver, and precious stones may be helpful."

Brother Gerome paused, as if inviting the monks to comment. Brother Araud spoke up. "I'm not a physician, nor am I a scholar, and I'm certainly not a bishop," he said. "But in my role as Sacrist in this abbey, I will do what I can. We shall add more psalms and pleasant thoughts of the Blessed Virgin to our prayers for those poor afflicted persons."

"These are disturbing messages," added Prior Frank. "Brother Gerome, can you describe to us any signs or symptoms of this disease? We are far from these calamities. There is little or no chance of the plague coming our way, but we should be alert and prepared. Is it possible to diagnose the plague as, for instance, we are able to do with the pox?"

"Like Brother Araud, I am no physician. But I will tell you all I have heard. I gather there are several signs of the disease. Sometimes death can come overnight with little or no warning. A person goes to bed healthy and is found dead the next morning. On the other hand, most cases develop more slowly, with grotesque visible symptoms. I have been told that one fatal sign is the coughing up of blood or blood running from the nose. Other evidences are buboes or boils. These skin eruptions may be as big as an onion, a carbuncle, or an apple. They are often found in armpits and the groin area, but can also be anywhere, even on the face. Scholars also describe the stench of a plague victim as unbearable. The person loses all dignity. Their urine is often black or red. All of this is accompanied by high fever. Death usually comes in less than five days."

Now the visiting monk looked especially grave. "As the messenger of such disturbing tidings, I feel I must give you all a severe warning. I have been told that virtually any contact between an infected person and another could be fatal. Anyone who visits the sick person, has business with him, or carries him to the grave will quickly follow him there. I regret to report there are no known means of protection except, maybe, running away, and even this is uncertain. Many who have run away have succeeded only in spreading the pestilence to innocent persons."

Cough.

"I do not wish to alarm you, but your Abbot said you should know these things and I have told you all I know."

The meeting concluded with an undercurrent of murmurs. Several monks took pause to speak further with Brother Gerome. Others silently offered their private thanks to God for sparing Tintern Abbey from the awful fate described by the visiting monk.

BROTHER GEROME, ON his way to become the Abbot of Whitland Abbey, stayed overnight at Tintern. That evening he spent a few hours talking to those in the infirmary. Then Abbot Turhold and Brother Gerome exchanged a few stories and talked about the challenges facing new Abbots. Finally, they bade each other goodnight and retired.

At sunrise, with Whitland Abbey beckoning, Brother Gerome set off toward his new calling by way of the Thomas demesne. Seeing that the monk was not well, the Thomas family insisted he spend the night with them and prepared one of their houses for his stay. Mistress Thomas packed some hard tack for his journey and filled his canteen with the best wine. These items were placed at his front door. When Thomas awakened the following morning, Brother Gerome had already left.

BROTHER ARAUD, WHOSE zeal for the psalms was almost legendary, insisted that the number of psalms and the intensity of the prayers be immediately increased at Tintern Abbey. Masses and prayers continued daily to the Father and the Blessed Virgin on behalf of King Edward; Tintern's founding family, Walter Fitz Richard of Clare and Lady Clare; as well as other noble patrons, including Strongbow and lady Matilda; Tintern Abbots Henry, Mark, and John; Brothers

William the Templar and Galandas, and others that came before them who served the mission.

As time passed, the shocking stories of faraway lands told by Brother Gerome seemed to fade in the memories of the Tintern Abbey community. The monks appeared to have few cares in the world, except their rounds of services and appointed Masses, some of which had been repeated for over two hundred years.

ONE HOT AFTERNOON late in July, two members of the Tintern Abbey community, Brother Warden and the abbey's newest novice, Simon, returned from Bristol, where they had been arranging for the sale of wool. A barge had carried them across the Severn to Chepstow Castle, from whence they had hiked, as quickly as they could, the four miles north to the abbey. As soon as they reached the abbey, Brother Warden made a frightened gesture to Abbot Turhold. The Abbot took them into the shade of the cloister, where they found Prior Frank seated on a bench. The Prior rose and welcomed the monks home, and then Abbot Turhold addressed them urgently.

"Your faces are covered with sweat and you are out of breath. Settle down and tell us the reason for your haste."

"It's here! It's here!" cried Brother Warden. "I cannot believe what we discovered!"

"What is here? Where?" asked the Abbot.

"The plague is there—in Bristol! As you know, we went there to discuss a shipment of wool for this fall. But we did not stay long enough to conclude our business. We were afraid. We learned that a ship from Italy had docked there a week or so ago. The Bristol warehousemen thought it strange when only two of the sailors came ashore. They did some unloading and then carried a great amount of water on board.

"The sailors asked for Bristol's physician. But he was in Bath and did not return until the ship had been tied to Bristol's dock for six days. When he arrived, the physician climbed casually aboard, but in a matter of minutes he ran off the boat, screaming 'Plague! Plague! Plague!' Many of the workers did not know what he was talking about and continued unloading. Within the hour bowmen rushed to the dock and demanded that the ship leave Bristol harbor immediately. When the ship was slow in leaving, the bowmen volleyed flaming arrows toward the ship.

"The wind blew briskly. The ship moving out into the Severn was last seen approaching the Bristol Channel. The men on shore did see what they thought were bodies being tossed overboard from the fleeing ship. The physician claimed that half the sailors on the boat were dead and several others were infected with fever, boils, and black patches on their skin.

"Just before we left, we learned that many people in Bristol had already been infected and some had died. A black flag has been raised, warning boats to stay away from Bristol."

"It was a dreadful sight!" exclaimed Simon. "We did not know what to do! We wanted to leave there as soon as possible."

"This is most distressing," Abbot Turhold said, his head bowed as though in prayer.

"You have done well to warn us so quickly of this news," Prior Frank told the alarmed monks. "Go to the refectory for nourishment and then to your dormitory to rest. The Abbot and I must first discuss this information."

Warden and Simon accepted the Prior's direction. They stepped away, whispering to each other in hushed, urgent tones.

The Abbot shook his head and repeated, "Most distressing! The dreaded plague, the one Brother Gerome told us about. It's come to Bristol!"

Prior Frank turned intently to the Abbot, great concern showing in his countenance. "The pestilence may be even closer than that," he said. "Will you come with me to our infirmary? There is something I must show you."

"Yes, of course."

As the Abbot and the Prior walked, the Prior continued, "Remember how gracious Brother Gerome was in talking to all of our brothers and how he spent one whole afternoon in the infirmary with Brothers Thomas, Aelfwin, Peter, and Godfrey? They were so elated at having someone pay more attention to them. Will you have a look at Brother Thomas and give me your conclusions?" asked the Prior.

Thomas's bed was along the east wall of the infirmary. As the Abbot and Prior entered Brother Peter raised up from his nap and spoke. "You need to look at Brother Thomas! He is not well!"

"Thank you for telling us. We will have a look at him now," answered the Prior.

Moving toward Thomas's bed, they could see he was still and his breathing was shallow. Pulling his blanket down, they found the monk was dressed in his cowl. A strong, detestable odor emanated from his body. His usually clean-shaven face had one boil on his left cheek and another along his forehead hair line.

"How long has he been this way?" asked the Abbot.

"One day, maybe two," answered the Prior.

"Do you remember what Brother Gerome said about tumors? Did he not say that tumors in the groin or under the arms or armpits were signs?" asked the Abbot.

"Yes, I am sure it was in the armpits and the groin," Prior Frank answered. "We need to further examine him. Will you help me remove his cowl?"

At this moment Brother Thomas slowly opened his eyes. He stared at the ceiling and did not seem to recognize either monk beside his bed.

"We are going to help you, Brother Thomas," the Abbot told him. "Can you raise your arms or turn over?"

There was no response from ill monk. His glazed eyes stared at the ceiling. He did not raise his arms or attempt to roll over. Abbot Turhold and Prior Frank gently eased the ailing monk out of his cowl. The Prior placed a cover over Thomas to hide his nakedness from the other brothers.

"Do you smell the stench?" the Abbot whispered.

"Yes," answered Prior Frank. "This is not a good sign. See here, on both sides of his groin are knobby-looking nodes. There is also one under his left arm, as big as an egg." He touched Brother Thomas's forehead. "He feels hot."

Abbot Turhold closed his eyes. His emotional tribulation seemed unbearable. His prayer was brief and silent: *O merciful God, I do not know your plan for us. Be my holy guide as we enter this unknown world of despair. Give us all the strength to face this test of faith. Amen.*

"We need to keep this secret," the Abbot said as he opened his eyes. "But I do not know how long we can. We must move Thomas out of this infirmary so we can give him better care and treatment that will not disturb our other three brothers. The only place we have is the visiting Abbot's building, which has been unoccupied since Brother Gerome left. It's close to my lodging, but the two are not connected. There are two beds there and a fireplace. If Thomas becomes conscious, delirious, and restless, we need to have someone watch over him. He must be watered and fed. We have done this before when the abbey experienced an isolated pox."

"What can we tell the brothers?" asked Prior Frank.

"We will say Brother Thomas was delirious and kept the others from any peace and quiet. Get Brother Crispin to be in charge of moving Thomas. I think I know whom he will choose to assist him. I am sure it will be Lay Brother Evan. You see, I happen to know Crispin is teaching Evan to read, which is against our policy, but I'm looking the other way." The Abbot rubbed his eyes and brow, as if to erase the anxiety from his soul. "I pray this pestilence is not just the beginning of evil times," he said.

ALTHOUGH CRISPIN AND Evan took excellent care of Brother Thomas, in five days he was dead. All the brothers thought it was strange that Brother Thomas was buried at the farthest point in the cemetery and in a very deep grave. Only two brothers were allowed to attend Thomas's requiem.

Two weeks later, Brother Godfrey was found dead in his infirmary bed. Brother Crispin and Lay Brother Evan prepared his body for burial. Godfrey was buried in a deep grave next to Brother Thomas. Brother Crispin told the Abbot that Godfrey and Thomas had given off the same foul odor at the times of their deaths.

SEVERAL PILGRIMS A day visited the image of the Blessed Virgin, the relic given to the abbey by the Archbishop of Canterbury to grace Tintern Abbey's church. The relic was said to have miraculous powers, and it was widely believed that a clubfoot could be cured, a hare-lipped person might be made normal, sex organs might be redeemed, sight might be restored, barren couples might have children, feeble and crippled legs might run, or deaf ears might hear for the first time.

This icon was kept in the lay brothers' part of the sanctuary, near the large west double doors of the abbey church. Brother Benedict, a choir monk, took seriously his responsibility for her care. He covered the image with white linen at sundown and uncovered her at the rising sun. This devoted monk carefully watched over the offering basket and often prayed with timid pilgrims. He kept a careful record of those who purchased Masses and passed this information on to the Abbot. He had no proof of the miraculous powers of the relic, but he nonetheless strongly believed the icon had kept the abbey out of harm's way during these frightening times.

Toward evening of an August day, Brother Benedict was preparing to cover the sacred icon when he heard voices. He looked outside the church and beheld a family coming down the road from Monmouth. When they drew nearer, Benedict could see two sons carrying their mother on a makeshift stretcher. Twin daughters followed behind, carrying their meager possessions. They had finally reached their destination, the place where miracles happened, the site of the cherished image of Mary, the Mother of God.

When they arrived at the church, the older of the two stretcher bearers came forward and spoke to Brother Benedict. "Our mother is sick," he pleaded. "Please, please help us!"

Brother Benedict could scarcely believe his eyes. The mother was small and frail. Her skin was pale and sickly. With her eyes closed she appeared to be sleeping, or something worse. His kind heart went out to this bundle of suffering. "Pray, place the stretcher here on this bench," the monk instructed. Noticing the family's weariness, he passed his water flask to them and invited them to rest and tell him their story.

"Our mother is very sick," the young man said. "We traveled all the way from Dudley. It was a friar traveling through Dudley that told us of the great miracles done by the Blessed Virgin at Tintern Abbey. That friar wrote a note for us to give to the Abbot of Melvern Priory. We did and Prior David of the Priory kept us two days, fed us, and told us how to get to Tintern Abbey.

"We met another friar at Monmouth who begged for food to give to us. He was so thin, he should have eaten the food himself. We have not eaten for two days. We fed all the food we have to our mother. Oh, yes, I have almost forgot, the Monmouth friar wrote a note for us to give to Brother Thomas at Tintern Abbey. It is written in Latin and we cannot read. Are you Brother Thomas?"

"No, I am Brother Benedict. Please let me see the note. I can read Latin."

The note had only six words: *For Christ's sake, help this family!*

The younger son asked to talk with Brother Benedict alone. The two moved a few steps away.

"We are a poor family," the young man said. "But we do not bring our mother to the Virgin without an offering. I have an ancient gold coin that my father found while working a field near Dudley. It is precious. I have shown it only to the friar in Monmouth. He said I should show it only to Brother Thomas."

Brother Benedict shook his head sadly. "Young man, I am sorry to tell you that Brother Thomas died recently. Would you trust me to see the coin?" he asked.

The young stretcher bearer paused for a moment. Then he reached into a pocket sewn onto an undergarment and pulled out a white linen cloth that had been folded around a small object. He handed the package to the monk.

Brother Benedict carefully unfolded the cloth. Inside was a small but heavy gold coin. He examined the coin intently. Roman letters were imprinted all around the outside of the coin, and the likeness of the head of one of the Caesars was stamped in the middle. The back side carried a likeness of the Roman god Apollo.

Brother Benedict knew this family had a small fortune tied up in white linen. His work as keeper of the shrine at Tintern Abbey had made him somewhat of a judge of coins, silver images, and jewelry. Gold had virtually disappeared from commercial transactions; silver was now the main coin used when currency was exchanged, and far more common was simple barter. This coin in his hand was by far the most valuable piece he had seen during his charge as shrine keeper. Benedict also knew many men would murder for much less than this coin was worth.

"What do you intend to do with the coin?" Brother Benedict asked. "Do you know it will buy much food, clothing, and care for you and for your mother?"

"We do not intend to use any of this coin's value on ourselves," the young man answered. "We have come a long way to bring our mother to the Shrine of the Blessed Virgin at Tintern Abbey. We intend to give this coin only to the Blessed Virgin. We know that there is no guarantee of our mother's recovery. We have heard the Virgin heals some and not others. That is all right with us. Our mother must get better or she will die. Whether Mother lives or dies, this coin goes to the Blessed Virgin as our mother's gift."

He carefully refolded the white linen cloth around the coin and gave the package back to the young pilgrim.

A rustle of movement caught the monk's attention. The mother was shifting her body and appeared to be awakening.

"Let me speak to your mother," the monk said.

He and the younger son joined the family. By now the woman's eyes—a deep and stunning emerald green—were open and alert, and she was taking in her new surroundings. Benedict was so taken aback by the gaze that he introduced himself with a flurry of questions.

"I am Brother Benedict, the humble keeper of the Shrine of the Blessed Virgin at Tintern Abbey. Are you hungry? Can I help to make you more comfortable? You do have the most dedicated and loyal children. Are you a free family, and who is your lord? What is your name?"

Raising her hand toward Benedict seemed to be an almost automatic gesture. Brother Benedict took her hand and kissed it.

"My name is Mary. My husband's name was Edward. We are free persons from Dudley. We worked on the demesne of Lord Burton. My husband was accidentally killed in a skirmish between lords. Soon afterwards I became ill, and when I got worse, we met a friar who told us about the image of Mary at Tintern Abbey and her healing powers. My children bundled me up on a stretcher and brought me here. As you may well know, a wife and children, even if we are free, can never be certain of receiving food, shelter, or protection."

"Darkness comes quickly here in the River Wye Valley," Brother Benedict said. "Let us see what we can do before night falls, and then I want to see you after sunup in the morning. Here comes Brother Yoder, one of our lay brothers. He will take you to a place where you can sleep out of the weather. Night rains are frequent here."

"You are most kind," the invalid woman said.

Brother Benedict turned to the lay brother and said, "Brother Yoder, will you take this family to Master Robin's place? He has an empty floored barn that is clean and dry. I am sure this family can spend the night there. Instruct them to be here at the church entrance after sunrise tomorrow. After you have seen to their comforts, go to the lay brothers' refectory and get them enough food for this evening and breakfast tomorrow. Ask Master Robin for a bottle of wine for the family. Tell him the abbey will pay for their lodging and the wine. If I know Master Robin, he will provide them with the best of care. Tell him that the woman's name is Mary. If I am not mistaken, Robin is also from Dudley. They may have mutual acquaintances. Tell him that Mary is sick and ask if he would look in on her and the family."

Brother Yoder picked up the front of the stretcher while the older son lifted the back. The group passed through the abbey enclosure, then disappeared behind some large oak trees.

BROTHER BENEDICT ALMOST missed Vespers. He slipped into his choir stall just as the Sacrist, Brother Araud, and the monks began chanting Psalm Ninety-Eight.

> *Sacrist:*   *O sing to the LORD a new song,*
> *Monks:*   *For He has done wonderful things,*
> *Sacrist:*   *His right hand and His holy arm*
> *Monks:*   *Have gained the victory for Him.*
> *Sacrist:*   *The LORD has made known His salvation;*
> *Monks:*   *He has revealed his righteousness*

> *In the sight of the nations.*
> Sacrist: *He has remembered His lovingkindness*
> *And His faithfulness to the house of Israel;*
> Monks: *All the ends of the earth have seen the salvation*
> *Of our God.*

At the conclusion of the psalm, Brother Araud and the monks chanted the Apostles' Creed together:

I believe in God the Father Almighty, Maker of heaven and earth. And in Jesus Christ His only Son our Lord; who was conceived by the Holy Ghost, born of the Virgin Mary, suffered under Pontius Pilate, was crucified, dead, and buried; He descended into hell; the third day He rose from the dead; He ascended into heaven, and sitteth on the right hand of God the Father Almighty; from thence He shall come to judge the quick and the dead. I believe in the Holy Ghost; The Holy Catholic Church; the Communion of Saints; the forgiveness of sins; the resurrection of the body; and the life everlasting. Amen

Abbot Turhold stepped to the reading stand and asked Brother Araud for the privilege of speaking.

Brother Araud nodded his head in agreement.

"I have shortened our Vespers because I have distressing information to share with you. As you know Brothers Warden and Simon recently returned from their trip to Bristol where they were conducting important wool business. I have asked them not to tell you what happened on their trip, and they have been most mindful of my wishes. Now Prior Frank and I feel we cannot keep you from knowing of this tragedy and our danger. The plague has ferociously attacked Bristol. We know that fifteen members of their town council have died. Bristol's two physicians are dead. This pestilence has left so few alive that they can scarcely bury the dead. The priest of one of their churches took the liberty of opening another half-acre cemetery. It is hoped that the King will pardon this initiative of their priest.

Few have been sick there more than three days before dying. As you know, Bristol is a major shipping port, both receiving and sending great amounts of goods. I believe there were about ten thousand people who lived there. God only knows how many now.

"We have asked Brothers Warden and Simon to move into our visiting Abbot's lodging, where they can be watched and fed. Please do not try to see or talk to them. I can tell you now that we believe that Brothers Thomas and Godfrey died of the plague. They both had many of the signs described to us by our recent visiting monk, Brother Gerome. Because Brother Crispin and Lay Brother Evan prepared our dead brothers for their burial, we have asked them also to take up temporary quarters in the visiting Abbot's lodge. They will continue to do their work, but otherwise will stay at the lodge."

Taking a deep breath the Abbot spoke slowly.

"Now I have one more tragic story. All of you remember the visit from Brother Gerome, who spent a few days here and was liked by everyone. He was on his way to Whitland Abbey to become their new Abbot. I just received word this morning that Brother Gerome's body was discovered dead along one of the roads leading south and west. He had many large buboes, or boils, in his groin, under his armpits, on his face and body. Dried blood was found around his mouth and nose. He must have died a horrible death, all alone. God rest his soul."

Whispers filled the room as the holy men reeled from the news. *Brother Gerome? The gentle man with the small cough? This cannot be... Not here... No, not Brother Gerome!*

Abbot Turhold permitted the disruption and waited patiently. When the monks quieted, he continued. "Every choir monk and many lay brothers had contact with Brother Gerome while he was here with us. We must be in prayer all night. By morning we will have even more measures to take.

"We have our guest rooms that can be prepared and used for any sickness overflow. By shifting around, we will have room for all, and we will care for all our brothers, with God's help."

"Abbot, Brother Gerome drank from your flask!" interrupted Brother Dunston. "I saw that several times while he was speaking!

He was coughing, and you offered him your flask...and he drank from it! What are you going to do?"

"I will carry on with my duties as your Abbot. I have asked Prior Frank to monitor my health. Yes, I did offer my flask, and he did drink from it, and then I continued to use the flask. That might make me a prime candidate for the plague, if indeed the pestilence is spread that way from person to person. On the other hand, we all need to be observant of each other's appearance and behavior."

The Abbot paused.

"We don't really know what causes the plague, or how it spreads from person to person. I have been told that there are those who believe this awful pestilence is a result of sin, even a whole range of sins, from lechery and avarice to the decadence of the church, the secret sins of monks, the greed of kings, drunkenness, pride, disobedience, lust, wrath, envy, treason, deceit, lying, sloth—and only God knows what else.

"Perhaps they are right. If indeed this affliction has been laid down by the Almighty as a retribution for the wickedness of our generation, the punishment fits the crime. God's will must be done. He will wreak vengeance. We cannot question His justice.

"What we can do—and what we must do—is demonstrate to God that we can and do repent. What we must do is show penance. Penance is a means of regaining grace and justice. Penance has two parts, attitude and physical acts. We will be doing both of these. After much thought and prayer, Prior Frank and I have decided on six new measures that might be of benefit under our present situation. I'll let the Prior describe them."

Prior Frank stepped forward. His usually serene face looked battered by grief and worry. He spoke softly at first, and then the urgency of what he had to say brought force to his voice.

"First, the number of psalms will be increased. Each monk will read in silence five additional psalms. In addition each monk will read aloud five psalms.

"Second, each day, each monk will read silently and then aloud the Te Deum Laudamus.

"Third, each monk each day will confess his sins to one of our three ordained monks and seek his absolution. We need to be aware of your hidden sins in properly completing our penance.

"Fourth, pray the Prayer of Saint Chrysostom as you awaken, before you rise from your bed or pad, and also pray to Saint Chrysostom just before falling asleep.

"Fifth, say the Magnificat to honor the Queen of Heaven once on Fridays and once again on Sundays.

Sixth, each Thursday each Brother will find a different partner. Go to one of our four chapels in the transept and present the Decalogue, the Ten Commandments, as a responsive dialogue."

Having given to the monks his instructions for profound penitence, Prior Frank stepped back and nodded to Abbot Turhold, who came forward once again and addressed his community.

"Will these acts be enough?" the Abbot wondered aloud. "Will they please God? That is not for us to judge. We are God's servants. We are God's slaves. God's will be done."

Brother Araud pronounced the benediction on these proceedings:

> Our Father, a time of great peril has come to our abbey and to so many people around us. This grievous sickness has descended among us unannounced. We are frail and uncertain of life. Where can we flee except to You? Father, we have not fled to Tintern to escape Your will or wrath. We have fled here to know You and have our souls shaped by Your will. If we are living, we can praise Your Holy Name. If You call us to eternal rest, may our last acts bring glory to You. We call upon the Blessed Virgin, the holy fathers, the Apostles, and all of Your saints to remember us before Your Holy Throne. Amen.

The meeting over, the monks nonetheless remained standing in silence, as if frozen in place. Were they afraid to move? Were they afraid of what the future would bring, or had perhaps already brought to them? Their only solace was knowing that God's will would be done.

Prior Frank was the first to leave the church. He was followed by Abbot Turhold, who was followed in turn by Brother Araud, the Sacrist. A full minute passed before the remaining monks slowly left their choir stalls and filed out of the church and into God's evening air.

12

Loss, Courage, and Leadership

A MOONLESS NIGHT covered the River Wye Valley. Crickets and melodious Welsh frogs filled the void with eerie noises. High on a silver birch branch an awakening sparrow hawk shifted as it eyed a sleeping sparrow. In the distance a red fox yipped three times, then shrieked.

Most of the brothers had been in prayer throughout the night. Vigils brought them together under the transept. With Vigils completed, a few grabbed a little sleep, while others continued praying in earnest for those who were or might be facing the Black Death, including themselves. This plea worked itself into the prayers and liturgy of the time, just as the peril and fear of the Vikings had been a part of the monastic and church liturgy in the ninth and tenth centuries. "Save us from the Vikings, O Lord!" had been the ancient cry. Now, in the fourteenth century, the cry became, "Save us from the plague, O Lord!"

And indeed, if there was salvation, it would come only from God, for all the armies of the King and all the wealth of the nobility were powerless against this enemy.

It has been thought that the term "Black Death" came from dark and black patches or nodes that nearly always occurred on the skin of plague victims. The nodes or kernels were extremely tender and were surrounded by swollen tissue. Medieval physicians occasionally tried to lance these pus-filled nodes. This was an excruciating procedure for the patient. However, most medieval physicians refused to go anywhere near a person suspected of having the plague.

King Edward III, who ruled at the time Tintern Abbey was besieged by the plague, was believed to have medical talents. He allegedly used his sacred magic to heal thousands of sufferers from scrofula, or tuberculosis, which also attacked the lymph nodes. Although the King may have wanted to help the plague victims with his touch, fear kept him away. In fact, throughout Europe in the fourteenth century, most, if not all, kings and nobles dealt with the plague simply by running way from wherever it was known to be.

Sunrise brought Lauds bell, followed shortly by the Eucharist and breakfast. Brother Benedict spoke briefly to Abbot Turhold before hurrying to the west door of the church, where Mary and her children were waiting to see him. Brother Benedict was not surprised to see that Master Robin had accompanied the new visitors.

Master Robin was more than just a neighbor of Tintern Abbey and an important citizen of Tintern Parva. He also served as the eyes and ears of the lord of Chepstow Castle. As a sensitive liaison he had been helpful to both parties over the years.

As Brother Benedict suspected, Master Robin had taken great care of the family from Dudley. He had fed them and given them each a generous glass of his best wine before bedtime. Straw, blankets, and sheets were provided as padding on the wood floor. A fire was built in the blacksmith's forge, which gave enough light for them to see around in the large barn. Master Robin visited with his ailing guest, Mary, and spoke with her until he was sure she would be comfortable, then he left the family so they could at last enjoy their well-deserved sleep.

Master Robin was almost twice as old as Mary. As a soldier he had learned the art of war, and as a smith, he was known for the strength and quality of his swords, knives, and arrows. He had supplied the superior long arrows that had enabled King Edward's army to defeat the French at the Normandy Battle of 1346. Having been on the victorious side of the Welsh Marcher Wars, he now held several small pieces of land in the fertile Wye Valley. Clean-shaven, with the blue eyes of a Viking descendant, his experience and size had given him a decided edge in any kind of a battle, physical or mental. Like many of the descendants of the Marcher lords and soldiers, Master Robin considered it an honor and privilege to support and strengthen Tintern Abbey.

The pilgrim family and Master Robin accompanied Brother Benedict into the church, where they approached the covered image of the Blessed Virgin in the lay brothers' area. All gathered closely as the monk removed and carefully folded the sheet, revealing the icon, which seemed to glow in the light streaming the length of the church, from the colored glass windows of the clerestory.

Brother Benedict spoke softy. "This icon means a great deal to us," he explained. "Sculpted from an eastern Mediterranean hardwood and stained with a shaded bronze, it reveals superb craftsmanship. The wood grain accents the exquisite natural garment folds. It was probably crafted about two hundred years ago, by some unknown worshipper somewhere near Jerusalem. From there, the icon traversed the burning Syrian sands, crossed the Byzantium peninsula, and journeyed through the mountains of Bulgaria and the Alps. She ended up in France and was smuggled into England, were she was given to the Archbishop of Canterbury. Three Knights Templar, who had carried her from Jerusalem, testified to the Archbishop that she had saved their lives on five occasions and was responsible for many healings on the road, including one girl whose eyesight was restored and a crippled boy who was made to walk straight. King Edward permitted this Blessed Virgin icon to be transported to Tintern Abbey. He and the Archbishop both felt the people of Wales would appreciate having this relic and would welcome it to Tintern Abbey."

The invalid pilgrim, Mary, gazed up from her stretcher with awe at the wooden likeness of the Virgin, Mary, who seemed to smile back down upon her. The icon, wearing a soft lucid radiance, had the face of a young person, almost a child, but with the concentration and compassion of eternity. She wore a simple head scarf that covered her ears and was loose approaching her shoulders. Only one flaw marred the beautiful icon. The Blessed Virgin's right arm ended just below the elbow.

Of the small gathering only Brother Benedict knew of the terrors and tensions that were at this time running through the abbey. He also knew it would do no good, nor help the situation in any way, for these pilgrims to know that two brothers of Tintern Abbey had already died of the Black Death.

Mary stood up from her stretcher and looked intently at the image. Tears welled up in her eyes. She reached out and touched the Virgin's left arm and then moved her hand slowly across to the Virgin's right side, where her arm was missing below the elbow.

She turned to Brother Benedict and said, "Here are two mothers with disabilities. Both of us know what it means to bear children. She does not have her whole arm and I do not have my whole health. But I know this Blessed Mother of Christ has no disability in heaven. Some day, I shall be like her, healthy and full again. If she chooses, this can happen to me now. If not, then I too will be full and healthy in heaven. Either way, I know it will be the will of God."

Brother Benedict did not feel the need to pray or even to speak. He had never experienced such sincerity so eloquently phrased. No, not even in the sacred readings. The fullness and presence of God was evident and felt by all.

The pilgrim Mary turned to her youngest son and asked, "James, will you please give me the golden coin?"

James reached inside his garments and took the white linen from its hiding place, then carefully unfolded it to reveal the ancient gold Roman coin. He cautiously handed his mother the linen with the coin resting on top.

"Brother Benedict, this golden coin my family gives to the Blessed Virgin," said Mary as she extended the gift to the monk.

Brother Benedict accepted the precious offering and folded the white linen cloth around it. He was profoundly moved by the gesture, her faith, and her courage. He at last found words.

"When Lord Bigod gave us this church," the monk began, "we Cistercians stated that no gift we would ever receive would bring us more glory than simply to worship here. Later, when we received the Blessed Virgin from the Archbishop of Canterbury, we all marveled at what she had done for many and what she would contribute to our lives and our worship. Now dear lady, Mary, you have given to the abbey, for the glory of God, this most valuable and expensive gold coin. I say here and now, no gift we shall ever receive can be greater than this golden coin and the utter sincerity that goes with it."

Master Robin took Mary's hands in his and held them for at least a minute. Tears marked their faces. The children smiled at the gesture and then at each other. They were fond of Master Robin and supported the special friendship that appeared to be growing between him and their mother. *Maybe,* one of the daughters thought, *God will bless us in more ways than one.*

Master Robin took Brother Benedict aside and said, "Do not worry about this family. I will take care of them. And you do not need to send any payment for the use of my barn or the wine."

They turned back to the pilgrim family from Dudley, and they were surprised and pleased to see that Mary had not returned to her stretcher, but had remained standing. Color had returned to her cheeks, and her eyes shone with the presence of grace.

"I am feeling much better," said Mary. "Master Robin, if you will lend me your arm for a little support, I believe I will be able to walk!"

The family and Master Robin left the church and headed toward the large oak tree. Mary and Master Robin walked together, talking about friends they both knew in Dudley. Walking behind were the four children—Michael, Sara, Susana, with James carrying the unneeded stretcher under his right arm.

Brother Benedict rushed off to deliver the golden Roman coin to the Cellarer and then joined the brothers at Eucharist.

TWO WEEKS PASSED by without further incident. However, one morning Abbot Turhold stumbled into the church for Lauds, looking drawn and shaking with a fever. After consulting with Prior Franks, the Abbot went to his private quarters, lay down upon his small bed, and spent the next few hours in restless tossing.

The following day, the Abbot appeared for Compline, but left after the prayers and shuffled away without speaking to the choir monks. Prior Frank followed behind and watched the Abbot carefully, but out of sight, to make sure Abbot Turhold was able to get to his private quarters.

When the Abbot failed to appear at the ringing of the Vigils bell, the Prior went quickly to his quarters and rapped softly on the door. Hearing no answer, Prior Frank tiptoed carefully into the darkened room. The Prior lit several candles before he was able to get a clear look at the Abbot. He touched the Abbot's forehead. Although burning with a high fever, the man was still and sleeping. The Prior made some cool compresses to wipe Abbot Turhold's forehead.

As the Lauds bell was sounded, the Prior joined the rest of the monks. Each was in his proper stall in front of the high altar. Before Brother Araud could begin Lauds, the Prior announced that their Abbot was ill and would not be joining them in any of their regular activities that day.

Immediately after Lauds, the Prior rushed to the visiting Abbot's quarters to speak with Simon. Simon had not experienced any symptoms and was as strong as ever. Staying with Simon was Lay Brother Evan who was also without symptoms.

"When Abbot Turhold did not appear at Vigils, I went to see him in his quarters," said the Prior. "At daybreak he had a very high fever, but was otherwise sleeping. I am going to ask both of you one more time to enter the lions' den. This could be dangerous to both of you. Will you go with me to examine our Abbot?"

"We have already buried two bodies that surely had the plague," said Lay Brother Evan.

"We are now experienced and skilled in facing and identifying this pestilence. Perhaps this illness is only a cold," Simon said hopefully.

"But if it is more serious," continued Evan, "then we are the most prepared here in our abbey. We may be even more prepared than most in all of Wales!"

"Bless you both!" exclaimed Prior Frank as he turned to leave. "Please come with me to the Abbot's quarters."

There was no answer when they tapped lightly on the Abbot's door. Two windows allowed in some light, but to get a better look, Simon lit three candles.

Abbot Turhold was laboriously trying to breathe. Then suddenly his mouth was full of blood when he tried to open it. He opened his eyes, but only to stare blankly at nothing. He did not respond when

Simon tried to get him to talk or communicate by moving his arms or legs.

All at once the foul, sickening stench of this wicked disease filled the room, as if trying to make this kind, generous, almost saintly man into a grotesque, revolting creature that no one could stand to endure. Silence throbbed as the Prior and two brothers looked down at their beloved and once powerful Abbot.

"Prior, you go about your business. I do not envy you," Simon said. "Evan and I will take care of him. If there is a drastic change one of us shall quickly notify you."

"I take my leave of you, then," Prior Frank said. He moved toward the door, hesitated, then looked back to Lay Brother Evan and said, "Evan, I am pleased that you are learning to read. If we survive this plague, I intend to reward you. Brother Simon is an able teacher."

Evan blushed and said, "I did not think anyone knew of this secret. Particularly you, Prior Frank. I did not want you to know Simon was teaching me how to read. It is not allowed for lay brothers."

"That is true. And yet I have a feeling I was meant to know your secret, and to respond with my honest feelings. What I know at this moment is that you are doing your Abbot a great favor, and Tintern Abbey owes you something in return."

Prior Frank nodded to both brothers, then left the Abbot's quarters.

Before he could reach the chapter room, he was approached by Brother Benedict, who told him, "Master Robin is at the church entrance and urgently wishes to have an audience with you."

Prior nodded, his face grim. Brother Benedict could sense that something frightful must be troubling the Prior. The monk offered a brief silent prayer on behalf of his Prior and his Abbot as he walked with the Prior toward the church, where they found Master Robin waiting at the western door.

"Brother Prior," was Master Robin's greeting. "I am here to offer you my support. If you have any needs, declare them and I will see to it they are met. Troubled rumors abound that this dreadful illness has reached into the abbey. A physician by the name of Samuel from

Monmouth is a houseguest of mine. While with me he has been treating my other houseguests, Mary and her four charming and bright children. In the week that Samuel has been with us, Mary appears to have completely recovered." Master Robin paused, then added. "I praise the Virgin Mary. I feel she was instrumental in getting Samuel to visit me at this time of our greatest need. Samuel has offered his services to all who are in need."

"God bless you, Master Robin," Prior Frank responded. "All the brothers at the monastery have been elated at the rare, valuable, and special gift of the golden Roman coin. We have named your guest, 'The Gold Coin Lady.'" The Prior's face brightened for the first time in several hours. "Brother Benedict just this morning told me that in a dream this little phrase came to him: 'The gift of the golden coin was from Mary to Mary to God.' The gift came at an auspicious and needful time. Please convey to The Gold Coin Lady that I intend to show my gratitude in person. And notify Physician Samuel we will be calling upon him shortly. I have heard of Physician Samuel before. I understand he is one of those physicians who takes his Hippocratic Oath seriously."

ANOTHER DAY PASSED without further incident. The Abbot's condition did not improve, but neither did it seem to worsen. But the following morning, Lay Brother Evan rushed into the refectory and interrupted Prior Frank.

"Prior! Will you come with me? There have been changes, and you are direly needed!"

They hastened down the cloister to the Abbot's quarters, where they pushed open the door and entered quietly. Noting Abbot Turhold's shallow breathing and no other movement, the Prior pulled his priest's cross from under his garment. Knowing that this man of God lying before him had lived daily with a contrite heart, the priestly Prior absolved the Abbot of all his sins. At that moment, Abbot Turhold received the holy sacrament of Extreme Unction. Then the Prior left his beloved Abbot in the loving care of Lay Brother Evan, and he went back along the cloister to the chapter room in order to let it be known among the community that their Abbot was not long for the world.

Abbot Turhold of Tintern Abbey died that night, at a little past midnight. The following afternoon he was laid to rest with appropriate ceremonies in an unmarked grave next to the latest plague victims. By order of Prior Frank only he, Brother Simon, and Lay Brother Evan were present at the burial.

STRONG FEARS GREW and spread through the abbey. The customary formality of life in the abbey was changing. Monks were keeping their distance from one another and even a light cough would startle a brother and cause him to move away. Nevertheless, in spite of the turmoil in their hearts and minds, there was no disorder. And curiously, despite their fears and their caution, there was no loss of love among the brothers.

As they met here and there about the abbey, they greeted each other warmly, using first names. Occasionally, a monk would ask an approaching brother how he was feeling, or he would ask if all was well, using a traditional Welsh greeting, "What goes with you?"

Brother Dunston, the Cellarer, stopped Prior Frank near the refectory one morning to complain, "I don't know what has been happening or why, but we have been experiencing a heavy infestation of black rats. We are taking extra precautions to protect our food, but at times we are fighting a losing battle. I have instructed our workers to place all food of any kind in large clay jars, but we have run out of jars. In the past I have sent to Bristol and Monmouth for large jars, but now, of course, because of their plague, we cannot accept any containers from Bristol. Furthermore, I'm told Monmouth is running short of jars also. My supplier there said he is selling them out as fast they are made, but he will save us ten large and several smaller ones and have them sent to us by next Saturday. If this shortage keeps up we may be forced to make our own clay jars. We have the knowledge among our lay brothers, but the task will take much time from their work."

"Do what you think is best, Brother Dunston. How is the health of your refectory workers? Have any complained about fever, sore throats, or unusual sores?" asked the Prior.

"No, praise God. You will be the first to know if any of them become sick in any way," the Cellarer responded.

Prior Frank now found himself the chief administrator of his abbey, a position he had never wanted, but knew he must fill. With his close friend the Abbot gone, he did not have anyone with whom to share his thoughts. Priors and Abbots did not usually form strong bonds with the monks under them. A formal distance had always been considered proper for the abbey hierarchy.

However, Prior Frank realized this was not the time to be dealing with formalities. He needed help. He knew it might take months for a new Abbot to be chosen.

The Prior decided to reach out to Brother Dunston, requesting that the Cellarer meet with him in the Prior's quarters.

"Thank you for coming, Brother Dunston," the Prior said. "Our entire brotherhood will be meeting momentarily with Master Robin and his houseguest, Physician Samuel. But before that meeting, I want to take you into my confidence and give you a brief summary of our dire situation. The crisis at Tintern Abbey seems to have been slow in developing, but compared to the decades it took to build our church, this pestilence has roared in like a storm. Somehow the plague was well established before any one of us realized it. No one here thought of responding when the visiting Brother Gerome told us of the dire pestilence that had struck Sicily and Italy. There appeared to be no urgent crisis as far as we were concerned when Brothers Warden and Simon brought news of Bristol's devastation. Not even the death of two of our monks produced any practical responses. But now our Abbot is dead, and we can no longer pretend we're safe. Practical, useful measures must be undertaken at this very moment, if it is not already too late."

Brother Dunston nodded silently. Before he could answer, the bell of the hours rang and kept ringing, calling everyone—choir monks, lay brothers, and visitors from Tintern Parva—to the cloister. Among the citizens of Tintern Parva was its leading citizen Master Robin, and his house guest, Physician Samuel. The lengthy ringing of the bell was only used in a crisis.

It took very little time for the entire monastic community to assemble in the cloister. However, a head count revealed that two monks and seven lay brothers were not present. The Prior quickly designated Dunston and Evan to check on the lay brothers, while Crispin and Warwick went to search for the absent choir monks. These four moved swiftly with their tasks.

Prior Frank called the group to order with a brief prayer that few would forget.

> Lord, we are your servants that have been given a task of life and death. We know a great pestilence has come among us. Many have died in Bristol and far-off Italy and France. Among us at this abbey you have called three into Your bosom, including our beloved Abbot. Our bishops and leaders have told us this pestilence has been caused by lechery, avarice, irreverence by and toward our knightly class, the greed of our kings, the drunkenness of our peasants, flagrant adultery, and sins we cannot even recall. If this Black Death has been decreed by You, O Holy One, then, we Thy servants admit and confess our guilt. We are overwhelmed by a sense of inevitable doom. As You have shown mercy to Your people in times of old by slaying their enemies, so lift Your mighty hand from our necks and deliver us from this doom. Amen.

The monks and lay brothers responded with a murmured chorus of "Amen." They raised their bowed heads slowly, and no one claimed his innocence.

When he had all of their attention, the Prior addressed his community. "The question in all of our hearts is 'What else can we do?' I can address this question. A plan has been created, based upon what others are doing in their time of peril," the Prior began.

"It appears that more contrition on our part is essential. How much more contrition on our part is required? We do not know. We are not even sure that all of our penitence and contrition will be enough. How then will we know? We shall know when the Black Death, the plague, is gone from our abbey, from Tintern Parva, and from the River Wye Valley. We shall know when we cease to be sick. Health and wellness will be our sign from God. We cannot fail to notice our deliverance."

The Prior paused and looked at the assembled faces. Then he continued. "What acts of contrition will we now do? I will ask our brothers, both choir and lay, to walk around our abbey barefooted twelve times, one time for each Apostle. As we walk, we shall read chosen psalms and other sacred passages. This will be done each day for twelve days. We shall ask our choir monks to fast every other day. We shall ask the lay monks to give up one meal every other day. These will be the abbey's acts of contrition.

"Now, I ask Master Robin to come forward. He is well known to all of you as a leader in Tintern Parva. He will tell us of the conditions at the village and what actions the people outside our abbey have taken."

Master Robin acknowledged the Prior and then addressed the abbey gathering. "At this point I do not know how many of our village people have been stricken with this sickness," he said. "Our village priest is on a pilgrimage to Rome and will not return until late in the fall. We have sent a messenger, on horseback, to request his hasty return. I feel most humbled to have been asked by Parva people to lead them in this trial. Prior Frank has pledged one of his priest-brothers to hold Mass in our Tintern Parva church on each Lord's Day. In order to keep the congregations small, the priest-brother will hold two services, one in the afternoon and another at eventide. We are holding two services because we have been advised against gathering too many people at one time in the church building.

"I have consulted Parva's leaders and here is our plan of contrition. We shall march in bare feet around our village church seven times each day for seven days. We shall pray in our homes three times each day to be delivered from this death. Our merchants have agreed to give half of all their earnings for the next six months to the Tintern Parva Village Church. Extra alms will also be given to our needy each Monday and Thursday, with Friday being fasting day.

"Finally, I have had as a houseguest a physician friend of mine, named Samuel from Monmouth. He has consented to stay in our Tintern area until this crisis is over. You need not worry about his fees or payment. I will absorb all of this. I have known this man for over twenty years. He is one physician that will not fleece his fold or run from danger. He is here today to give us his appraisal concerning this terrible sickness."

With that, Master Robin stepped back and Samuel the physician stepped forward.

"I knew your Abbot Turhold from his many visits to Monmouth," Samuel began. "A finer man one could never meet.

"Now, listen carefully, for in addition to your acts of contrition, I have a few suggestions of other things you can do. To start with, I have been told that there is an infestation of black rats at the abbey. I have also seen many in Parva. These are nasty vermin that always find their way into dark, damp rubbish heaps, but are also known to attack our food, our grain, our clothes, and even our water. I believe they carry sickness. Many of my physician colleagues do not agree with me about this, but nevertheless, I urge you to clean up your property, remove rubbish of any sort from your buildings, and burn that rubbish. If there is an empty house or shed that is not useful, burn it! Do not try to salvage the wood for your own use. Black rats do not dwell long in coal cinders or in clean places, so I repeat: keep all your buildings clean.

"This next recommendation may be the most difficult. Do not admit anyone to your town limits or to the abbey! The Prior has appointed one of his monks to stand guard and prohibit any boats or rafts from putting in at the Tintern dock. This monk, who is also a knight and who has traveled to Jerusalem and the Holy Land, will have a seven-foot staff, and he knows how to use it to defend his abbey and Tintern Parva. His instructions are to allow no one to dock or come ashore in our area. If one knight is not enough to keep the dock safe, Master Robin will send one of his workers to the dock with a bow and a supply of Master Robin's legendary longbow arrows.

Nearly everyone in Parva has seen these arrows. Many of you have helped craft them.

"The roads coming into Parva and Tintern Abbey from the north and south and the trail from the west must also be guarded. Admit no one! If the people insist, call Master Robin, who will dispatch his armed bowmen.

"If you become ill or uncomfortable, please contact me immediately at Master Robin's manor home. God bless you and may the presence and power of Tintern Abbey's Blessed Virgin be with you. I will answer your questions as I am able."

Brother Dunston raised his hand and was recognized.

"I have a shipment of clay jars arriving next Saturday from Monmouth. What shall I do about them?" the Cellarer asked.

"This could be a problem," the physician replied. "If the jars are absolutely essential, have them unloaded on a nearby sand bank. Before the jars are unloaded, however, they must be removed from any cartons. The people transporting these materials must take the cartons back to Monmouth and leave only the jars. When this is done and the boat has left, have your men pick up the jars and take them to the refectory, where they must be scrubbed, then placed in sunshine to dry. The same men who picked up the jars on the sand bank are to do the washing. When this work is finished, these men are immediately to remove their clothes and take a bath. Their clothes must be washed in water soaked with leaves and lavender flowers, then dried in the sun. Most important! Our men must remain at least three hundred feet from any persons coming from Monmouth. If these procedures are followed, I feel it will be safe to use the jars."

"These procedures are terribly stringent," responded the Cellarer. "Nevertheless, if ordered by the Prior, they will be done."

"We must do as the physician instructs," said Prior Frank.

"It will be done as you request," Brother Dunston replied.

Brother Crispin returned alone from his search. "We have two choir brothers who appear to sick be in their beds," he reported. "These are Brother Eudo and Novice Warden. Both appear to be afflicted with something."

Murmurs went through the assembly.

"Are they dying?" called out a lay brother from the back.

"What can we do?" another cried. "May Christ preserve us!"

"We must leave this place! It is polluted!" declared Brother Garron.

"No, No, *No!*" appealed Samuel. "If indeed we do have cases of the plague, we must not leave. Where would you go? To your friends? To your relatives? To your neighbors? If we do have the Black Death here, you would take it with you, and you would spread the plague to every home, every barn, every tavern, to every abbey, and to anyone with whom you came in contact. They say the plague places a miasma about all who are infected, and even the touch or eye contact can spread the disease."

"Brothers!" Prior Frank spoke forcefully over the commotion, calling for the assembly's complete attention. He so rarely spoke with such intensity that a hush fell quickly over the open-air cloister. "I agree with and support all of Physician Samuel's recommendations. We must stay here. Tintern Abbey is our home. It is here that we do God's work and follow God's plan." His words, which echoed off the cloister walls, had the desired effect. The audience was focused again. "Samuel, pray continue."

"Thank you, Brother Prior. Let me point out that you are relatively isolated here at Tintern Abbey and Tintern Parva. That is good. We know the plague is south and west as well as probably east. If you ran, where would you go? You would be running right into face of doom. It will not be easy for anyone to get in or out of this valley without our knowing about it. We have adequate food and good water here. We have priests on hand for whenever they are needed. I am a physician. I will be staying with you throughout this crisis.

"Now, with the Prior's permission, you need to isolate all persons known to be afflicted. This procedure will not make it worse for anyone who may already have the plague, but it may save those who have not yet been taken down with this pestilence. If others become ill, they can be moved into your isolation rooms or houses."

"Those who are well will remain in their present dormitories," the Prior said. "They will be fed from the choir refectory. For the time being sacred hours will be observed. Indeed, our sacred hours will be an important part of our contrition.

"This is the considered plan for our abbey. We will move all afflicted brothers, both lay and choir, into the infirmary hall, which has an adjoining refectory where food will be kept and prepared. The infirmary has several rooms, so that we may isolate the very sick from the others. There is also water running under this infirmary that can be used to dispose of all waste. Our waste will be carried out and away from our abbey, into the River Wye, which will carry it on to Bristol Bay and finally out to the ocean.

"Brother Crispin and Lay Brother Evan have volunteered to care for all those who are sick enough to be moved into the infirmary. They have experience. They have already been tending to the sick, for which our community is most grateful."

The Prior next turned to the leading citizen of Tintern Parva. "Master Robin, what other measures will be in place in the village?" he asked.

"We will set up a clearing house for Parva at my manor," answered Master Robin. "The sick will be moved to my manor barn. I have already moved the pilgrim family from Dudley into the manor house, so the barn is available, and it is large enough to handle all of our Parva infirmary needs. It is floored, and it has a forge which can be used to prepare food and to provide warmth. Parva also has four fine widow women who have volunteered to offer care for the ill under the direction of Physician Samuel. These ladies will be staying full-time at the infirmary.

"When we leave here, Parva women will inventory every home to see if anyone needs to be moved to our infirmary. We will mark every house in which persons have come down with the sickness. Everyone should stay away from those houses. At the same time the women will take an inventory of all food that is available and check on all the wine our people have. I want you to know that I have plenty of grain and a large stock of wine that will help us through this crisis. There will be no charge for the wine. And what I have left now is my best wine!" Master Robin smiled and held his hands out, to show he wanted to be the best host he could be in troubled times.

"As for water," he continued, "there are several wells to provide us with all the water we need. We also have several able women in the village who produce excellent beer. That will be their task. Beer will be more healthy for us than our water from wells or the river.

"I believe we have enough fodder and grain to care for our horses. We must keep them safe. We will certainly need them for moving supplies and for seeking help.

"If needed, our church grave digger, Coleman, has said he will be available on call at all times. Coleman is a dedicated man, an asset to our village. I have known few men who work harder than he does. I have already mentioned that priestly brothers from the abbey will hold Mass every Sunday and requiem Masses in our Parva Church, when needed. Physician Samuel has suggested wisely that we bury anyone who dies of this pestilence on the edge of the cemetery. Tintern Abbey is already doing this. Physician Samuel has also advised against large numbers of people attending any requiem Masses. For that matter, any large gathering is discouraged."

The Prior raised his hand, and when he had the attention of all those gathered, he thanked Master Robin for his leadership commitment, then faced the gathering of men. His face became grave, and everyone in the group could sense he was on the verge of an important announcement.

"I must also inform you of some news I received from a courier a couple of days ago," he said. "The King is vitally interested in all of us. He asked the Archbishop of Canterbury to organize penitential prayers for the port cities which have experienced the most devastation. Two weeks after his request, the Archbishop died of the pestilence. Sadly, the King's daughter Joan, on her way to marry Infante Pedro of Castile, died of the plague in Bordeaux. Even though we are far from London, we are saddened by the news. The King and the Archbishop will be included in our prayers, as will the King's daughter."

Prior Frank concluded the meeting with a prayer of hope. Were his decisions sound? Were his words the right words? He yearned for one more conversation with his friend, Abbot Turhold. The Prior had tasted the flavor of monastic leadership and revered his late Abbot even more.

When the meeting was over, Brother Dunston and Lay Brother Evan approached the Prior and asked for a moment of his attention.

"We have checked on the lay brothers," Evan began. "Although seven did not show for our meeting, two of the seven were caring for three who were too ill to attend. Two others, Jesse and John the Minor, could not be located. They have disappeared before. They could be fishing or maybe even hunting, although they know that is not permitted."

"The three sick lay brothers are Remis, Gothrom, and Nigis. We should prevail upon Physician Samuel to look at them," Brother Dunston recommended.

Physician Samuel and Master Robin went to the lay brothers' dormitory. Remis, Gothrom, and Nigis were grouped together on the second story in the northwest corner of the building. All three had fevers. Remis appeared to be bleeding from his nose. All three nodded affirmatively when asked if they had sores or pain in their groins and under their arms. At this point all could walk. The physician recommended that they all be moved quickly to the infirmary and that they be kept together in one room if possible. He instructed them not to talk to anyone until they reached the infirmary.

Shortly afterwards, the ailing lay brothers were bedded down in one of the smaller infirmary rooms. Samuel, who had accompanied them to the infirmary, met Brothers Simon and Evan. With their recent experience, these two had more firsthand familiarity with the Black Death than Samuel.

The three caregivers discussed with one another what they had learned. They agreed that foul, noxious odors should be avoided. Upon death, bodies should be buried as quickly as possible, in deep graves far from habitation. Those who showed blood running from their noses or mouths should be given last rites. Those who were moved to the infirmary should be urged to confess their sins to a priest, and if no priest was available, then to a lay brother or a secular man, or even, if conditions worsened and no man was available, to a woman.

Physician Samuel said he would ask the women of the Parva Church to create little packets of sweet-smelling herbs made from marigold, dittany, lavender, or thyme. These were to be worn around necks or attached to the clothing of all, monk or lay person. The physician also said that he had heard of a potion that had been used after a person has contracted the plague. The victim was to be given a potion made from rue, columbine, marigold, and a fresh egg, which was roasted, but not burned. The potion was to be combined with good ale or wine and given to the sick to drink three nights and mornings in a row. If they could keep it down, they might survive.

"This concoction seems like a tall order, even for the healthy to hold down," Brother Simon remarked. "But we must try it. Our lay brothers will gather the plants and bring them to you. If you will have your women prepare the potion, we will administer it to our suffering brothers and see if it helps or not."

Physician Samuel nodded. He thanked the brothers for all they were doing for the sake of the Tintern community and perhaps for all humanity. "And now Master Robin and I must return to Tintern Parva," he said. "There is much to be done."

TWO DAYS LATER Remis, Gothrom, and Nigis were lovingly buried.

After that, nearly two weeks elapsed without incident. Then, on the thirteenth day, two lay brothers, gathering driftwood along the riverbank for a fire, found the bodies of the missing lay brothers, Jesse and John the Minor, about three miles north of the abbey. Caked blood covered their lips and cheeks. Swollen lymph nodes marked the agony which must have filled the last hours of John the Minor with unrelenting pain. His arms were covered with blotches of gray and then black caused by bleeding under the skin. One large knob with a top resembling a seed wart distorted his left cheek. Trying in vain to ease the torture, his feet had dug deep into the sand bank.

Lay Brother Jesse had evidently expired some time before John. His body was laid out on his back with his arms folded in a praying position. In all probability, John had prayed over Jesse before crawling a few yards away for the final hours of his life.

When the news of these two mortalities reached the abbey, Prior Frank concluded these brave lay brothers had endured their death struggle alone because they did not want to carry the pestilence back to Tintern Abbey.

Tintern Parva's life was also filled with pain and death. Coleman had placed twenty-one bodies in the northwest section of the graveyard. At the request of Master Robin, Coleman kept a careful record of the location and name of each grave. Master Robin told the villagers of Parva that he would have appropriate markers placed on each grave after the pestilence had passed. Three of the women who had attended the sick in Master Robin's infirmary were among the twenty-one bodies.

Mary was a source of strength to the fearful and the living of Parva. On several occasions Master Robin had tried to get Mary to shut herself off in his manor house, but to no avail.

"My children brought me to this place when there was little or no hope for me," Mary insisted. "The Blessed Virgin rescued and redeemed me, perhaps for this purpose. God has a way of moving us to wherever we can do His will and fit into His overall plan. If God wishes me to be with the Blessed Virgin in heaven, where she has a complete right arm, He knows where to find me, at Master Robin's infirmary."

With that answer, Mary gave Robin a smile that shone with love, then turned and walked confidently into the place of sickness.

Samuel had witnessed the whole conversation. Laughing gently, he turned to Master Robin and said, "You must be living right, Robin, to have a gracious woman like that step into your old life."

"I am hardly an old man, Physician," Master Robin retorted with a smile.

One mid-afternoon in October, Prior Frank asked Brother Araud to sit with him following the liturgy hour of None. After a minute or two he spoke what was on his mind.

"Brother Araud," he said, "I know that you are the most accomplished writer of all of us, with the greatest command of Latin. I am also aware you have been keeping some notes concerning our beloved Tintern Abbey, relating tales of brothers who have gone before us, telling of how the abbey was founded by Abbot Henry, how the church was built, and so forth. We have allowed you parchment for this purpose, knowing you will make good use of this valuable material."

"I am grateful for that, Brother Prior. I hope my writings may serve the abbey and the greater glory of God, but I also confess that writing about Tintern has given me some pleasure and, though I hate to admit it, some pride."

"I encourage you, Brother Araud. In fact, I instruct you to continue this good work. And now you must keep a careful record of the trials we are going through. This is most important, and I urge you to be thorough and truthful."

Brother Araud rubbed his face with both hands. "God knows what is happening here," he said. "God only knows."

"Yes, I know God is aware how we are facing these trials. But I do not want the struggle made here to vanish from the memory of those who will come after us. What you write will be read by people in the unknown future. They will look at this abbey, marvel at its beauty, and walk in the shaded cloister, but unless you write what truly happened here, what agony was faced here, what triumphs were made here, the stones of Tintern Abbey may one day resemble Hadrian's Wall, an empty monument in the wind. The spirit of all the monks who have lived here, beginning with Abbot Henry and his pioneers, inhabit these walls and grounds. Make them live, Araud!" the Prior urged. "Make them live again! The spirit of the fair ladies and brave knights who are buried here must speak out. Your chronicles must tell all who come to the Wye Valley that we lived here, confessed our sins here, praised God here, gloried in the Blessed Virgin's greatness here—and that we went through the Valley of the Shadow of Death here. I have confidence in you, Araud. Make our Tintern Abbey live long after you and I, and all of our brothers and successors, have gone."

"What a task you have given me!" Brother Araud answered. "I am humbled, but I'm also frightened. I am so near death every day.

Suppose I become stricken, so that I am unable to write. What will happen then?"

Prior Frank smiled wistfully. "Write while there is time. What more can you do? Always leave a few parchments from your allowance, should others need to continue your chronicle." The Prior laid his hand on the monk's shoulder. "Brother Araud," he whispered, "we are prepared to lose some of us, but we shall never be prepared to lose all of us. You will make certain of that."

13

The Plague's Legacy

BROTHER ARAUD RUBBED his temples, scratched his head, and stared at the blank parchment before him. "We are prepared to lose some of us," Prior Frank had told him, "but we shall never be prepared to lose all of us!" What a fearsome responsibility the chronicler had. "Make the spirits of the fair ladies buried under our abbey floor live again! Make the spirit of the noble knight Lord Bigod live again! Make the spirit of our founder, Abbot Henry, live again! Make the spirit of our six-fingered knight live again! Make their chants, Vigils, Lauds, Vespers, and Complines live again!"

Will what I write here and now be read by unknown monks, knights, Abbots, nobles, and kings? What will our abbey be like in 100 years? What will our abbey be like in 500 years?

"Make them live Araud! Make them all live again!"

What a tall order! Can I truly accomplish this? I am just a monk, he thought. *Yes, I do know Latin. I can read and write Latin better than most. But, I am not the Venerable Bede! I am just a monk. I cannot be expected to write like the Apostle Paul or Saint Bernard.*

Make them live Araud! Make them all live again!

BROTHER ARAUD SPENT most of that night turning, tossing, and dreaming. *Make them live Araud! Make them all live again!*

The Vigils bell called Araud to the transept where, as Sacrist, he led the choir monks' night prayers. Prior Frank closed Vigils requesting each monk to offer a personal prayer. "I am asking each of you to audibly call upon God on our behalf. Let us begin with Brother Dunston."

"O Lord, deliver us from this pestilence as You protected and delivered Moses," prayed Brother Dunston.

"Father, it is not suffering that I want to avoid, for many saints have suffered. True suffering is a mark of fidelity," petitioned Brother Benedict. "If this plague comes for me, I pray that I will face it bravely and without complaint. No matter what happens to me or us, we know it is Your will and it is in keeping with Your overall plans."

"Lord, if I should be brought down by this vicious plague, do not look upon my appearance such as I will be at the time of my death," asked Brother Garron. "I pray You look upon me instead as a forgiven and resurrected monk who is called to the heavenly cloister, if it be Your pleasure."

Each monk appealed to God in his own way. Prior Frank finished with his own prayer: "First, remove from us all fears. Reach down and touch us with Your hand. Help us to sense that touch. Second, make us bold in the face of tribulation. Help us to see that we are surrounded by a great cloud of witnesses—martyrs, holy saints, angels, and apostles. Finally, we know that You, O God, are stronger than all the devils over all the earth. We know You are greater than all the plagues and greater than death itself. For this reason, we entrust our lives and our souls to You forever. Amen."

FOR TWO MORE days Brother Araud continued his emotional battle against the Prior's assignment. Finally, he surrendered his personal feelings of unworthiness to his Creator and accepted the charge. He gathered up several rolls of parchment and placed one on his angled desk. Though parchment was expensive, the abbey's prosperity afforded an ample supply of the animal-skinned vellum. Araud gazed at the blank page. The brother's quill, sharp knife, and small glass of iron gall ink waited patiently for his inspiration.

Araud's thoughts drifted back to Bede, the prolific monastic writer and scholar who had lived over 600 years earlier. What had inspired him? Araud had read a number of Bede's accounts and appreciated the simplicity of his expressions. He drew a deep breath, recalling one of Bede's prayers. The monk whispered. His body relaxed.

Christ is the morning star
Who when the night
Of this world is past
Brings to his saints
The promise of
The light of life
And opens everlasting day.

The monk reached for his quill and sharpened the nib. He dipped it in ink, then paused with the quill poised above the parchment. Feeling a wave of emotion, he lowered the nib to the parchment and began to write, first slowly and then more rapidly, but always in a clear and careful hand and logical, forceful Latin sentences.

I Brother Araud, of the Cistercian Order at Tintern Abbey in Wales, write in this chronicle of those events that happened in this time in which I am a witness or have heard from people not known to lie or exaggerate. I write these words in order to prevent these happenings from vanishing from the memory of any who may come after me. I have seen and heard of so many evils that if I wrote them all down, they would fill all of England. At the writing of these notes, I am in good health, being strong in body and spirit. Our beloved Prior, Brother Frank, has asked me always to place some empty parchments under my most recent pages in order that another monk may take up my words if I am called home to be with the Lord. Unless all the world perishes in this conflagration, then for those who are left, this is our record of how Tintern Abbey faced its darkest hour. And if, in the midst of fear and trembling in the Valley of the Shadow of Death we can carry on our work to the glory of God and the salvation of our souls and the souls of those for whom we pray, this will surely be our finest hour as well.

By the fifteenth of November, no new cases of the Black Death had occurred in the abbey or at Parva in more than a month, but the devastation was by no means over, and the losses already suffered had been substantial. Of the two, Tintern Parva had been the more devastated. Three of the four women who had volunteered to work at Master Robin's Infirmary had been buried. Twenty-one others, including four merchants, had died. Coleman buried them all, working alone, and the villagers wondered, could any village find a finer example of a saint than Coleman?

On the Thomas demesne only one son and one daughter survived. Of the four tenant families, two men and three women perished. All of the Thomas livestock succumbed except for their best horse and two pigs. The surviving son blamed a Cistercian monk who stopped for water and stayed until the middle of afternoon. Young Thomas said he was told that a white-robed monk, ravaged by the plague, had been found after that on the west trail, about halfway to the coast. Young Thomas sent word that as soon the imminent danger passed, he wished to have one of the priest-monks come and consecrate the family cemetery.

Another tragedy struck at Tintern Parva when their village priest lost his life to the Black Death five days after returning from Rome.

BROTHER ARAUD REPORTED no new occurrences of the pestilence at Tintern Abbey until the middle of December, 1348. On the fifteenth of the month, however, Prior Frank complained of stiff muscles and a headache. The Prior attended Compline and returned to his bed in the dormitory. At Dunston's urging the Prior did not attend Vigils. Before the Lauds bell rang, Dunston helped Prior Frank to the infirmary, where he was placed in one of the private rooms. The next day his sickness had worsened to the extent of coughing up blood. Dunston knew he would soon be the only priest left at Tintern Abbey. Following instructions given by the late Abbot Turhold, Brother Dunston received the confession of Prior Frank. A few moments later Prior Frank received the sacrament of Extreme Unction.

Tintern Abbey's Prior died while the Brothers attended Lauds the next morning and was buried a short time later in an unmarked grave next to Abbot Turhold.

THE LOSS OF Prior Frank caused a great sorrow among the remaining monks. The Black Death had taken a terrible toll on the abbey. By January, 1349, one-half of Tintern Abbey's monks had died of the plague. Brother Dunston assumed the responsibility of acting Abbot. Brother Benedict was selected as acting Prior. Brothers Crispin, Simon, and Evan continued to tend to the afflicted in the infirmary. Brother Warden lost his only novice. The fifteen remaining lay brothers now reported to Brother Simon.

Brother Araud remained Sacristan leader and continued his chronicles. Many monks suspected Araud suffered the most with the death of Prior Frank. Ironically, the two men had not always seen eye to eye on issues for many years, but from the moment Araud accepted his assignment of recording the history of Tintern, a strong bond of friendship had developed. Araud regretted their friendship was so short-lived.

BY SEPTEMBER, 1349, the pestilence was on the wane. Here and there a case would occur. Evidently the efforts of Master Robin, Physician Samuel, and Abbot Turhold, along with Prior Frank and the monks and lay brothers of the abbey, as well as Tintern Parva, had all contributed to turning a corner to better times. But ultimately, it was God who had mercy upon the Tintern environs.

Early in 1350, Brother Darnhall arrived from Citeaux to be the new Abbot of Tintern Abbey. Darnhall was in his fifties, some say even older. He had been an Abbot at Cistercian Quar Abbey on the Isle of Wight, which had been created just a year after Tintern by Lord Baldwin de Redvers. In recent years, Quar had established two daughter houses under the leadership of Abbot Darnhall. Later, his health failing, he was sent to Citeaux to end his years there. However, the climate and healthy conditions at Citeaux brought about a miraculous recovery. Then, when the plague brought personnel shortages in monasteries everywhere, he asked for assignment to Tintern Abbey. Citeaux was reluctant to send their younger brothers to such a dangerous place, and so, at his persistent request, Darnhall was chosen.

Darnhall was born in Normandy, the third son of Robert Curthose,

Duke of Normandy. Dedicated to becoming a priest or monk, he was educated at home with private tutors and later in Paris and Oxford. He became a novice at Le Relecq Abbey in Normandy, where he was ordained as a priest.

Darnhall's blue eyes and light complexion, as well as his stature of slightly larger-than-average height, gave away his Saxon and Viking lineage. His long face and gray hair did not give him a dominant appearance, however; it was his voice that made him stand out. The deep resonance was ear-catching and commanded attention. Like many Abbots, Darnhall was at his best in crisis situations. A more stressful situation than Tintern Abbey in the mid-fourteenth century could hardly be found. If he had any extraordinary plans for the abbey, he kept them to himself. If he wanted to lead Tintern to be perfect, or big or powerful, he told no one.

Abbot Darnhall moved into the Abbot's quarters. He requested no additional furniture, writing stand, or bed covers. If it were not for his incessant questions, no one would hardly have noticed him. Realizing this group of monks had lived through deadly circumstances, he went about asking every monk and every lay brother his name, how old he was, where he was from, whether he had been to any other abbeys, what his specialty skills were, and what his assignment was. The new Abbot acknowledged that silence was golden in a monastery, but he also knew it was sometimes not very therapeutic.

No special meetings were held the first ten days. Abbot Darnhall just went about smiling, encouraging, and speaking. He did not break in or try to dominate Vigils, Lauds, Vespers or Compline. In fact, in groups he hardly spoke except to ask questions at Chapter.

Finally the Abbot called a general meeting in the cloister for choir and lay brothers. He opened the assembly with prayer, then turned to their Cellarer, Brother Dunston, who had led the abbey since the death of Prior Frank. Dunston stepped forward to give an overview of Tintern Abbey and its holdings.

"Since the plague commenced," Brother Dunston began, "one half of our choir brothers lie in the cemetery. At present we have only fifteen lay brothers, yet God has left us with brothers who are extremely skilled and dedicated.

"Our Trellech Grange suffered, but is functioning. Sadly, our Lay Brother Johybert, who represented our abbey for seven years at Trellech Grange, has succumbed to the devastating illness.

"We have seven churches under our care. We do not know their status. Nor do we know the condition of Llandaff Village southwest of us. We are able to report on Tintern Parva, the village that has grown around the western lands of our abbey. We know that thirty-three of their people have died of this pestilence, with their priest being among the victims."

Brother Dunston reached for a sip of water, then resumed his report.

"We isolated ourselves, and this choice may have helped us have fewer deaths than other communities in Wales. We fared far better than Bath, which was devastated by the pestilence. We were warned on good authority that even a slight encounter with the dying would prove to be fatal. Yet those of us still here today have all survived despite our close contact with the diseased. Our beloved Prior Frank once told us how we would know if our prayers and efforts of penitence were successful. 'We shall know when we cease to be sick,' he declared to us. We can now bear witness that our prayers have been answered."

Brother Dunston lingered before the group after completing his report. He had been their leader for over a year. It felt strange stepping down from those duties. He nodded to his new Abbot and stated, "We pledge our support and obedience to you, Abbot Darnhall."

Abbot Darnhall stepped to the side of the podium and began speaking. The freshness of his deep voice commanded attention to every word.

"Thank you for your gracious reception of me as your Abbot," he began. "I have been a Cistercian monk since I was a young man and I can say that not all Abbots are received in the way you have accepted me. A while back I thought my life as a Cistercian monk was all but over. I went to Citeaux to die. The way I was received there and God's favorable treatment of me gave me new life. I am as strong now as I was when I was forty. Please do not ask me how long ago that was."

Light laughter rippled through the gathering.

"The Cistercians, the Benedictines, and others have been ravaged by this pestilence," the new Abbot continued. "Under ordinary circumstances I would probably have been buried at Citeaux. But once I heard of your fate I fasted for a week. In my prayers for you, I asked God how I might be allowed to help. I was prepared to request Abbot Amaury to send me to you as a fellow monk. But before I could ask him, he said to me, 'Darnhall, I am sending you to Tintern Abbey to be their new Abbot! Can you leave in the morning?' He could tell by my grin that I was ready to go, even that night if need be."

Stretching out his arms to point to the surrounding valley, Abbot Darnhall said, "Your beautiful buildings and grounds, vast holdings and majestic location make Tintern Abbey the envy of many other Cistercian monks." The Abbot paused. "Please forgive me. I shouldn't have used that word. Cistercians do not envy. Let me just state what Abbot Amaury of Citeaux said to me before I left his abbey. He told me that no Tintern brother had ever requested a transfer from here, nor had it ever been reported that a Tintern brother had spoken ill of his fellow monks.

"Cistercian history has a place of honor for your first Abbot, Abbot Henry. He must have been a unique man of God. If the Cistercians permitted monuments or markers, Henry's would be counted among our finest.

"I just yesterday renewed an old friendship. I have known Master Robin for many years. He embarked at the Isle of Wight during the wars against France. His arrows, furnished to the longbows, brought victory to England. He stayed at Quar Abbey several days waiting for the boats to leave for Normandy, and he stopped by our little abbey on his return. All of our monks lifted him up in their prayers, pleading for his safety.

"Brother Dunston has relayed to me the courageous actions taken by Master Robin as well as those of Mary, the Gold Coin Lady, from Dudley, and the physician Samuel. Mary must indeed be blessed person; I know of no greater tribute than to be called the 'Gold Coin

Lady,' with the generosity that name implies. She would be a rare person in any gathering, village, or town. God has surely blessed Tintern Abbey and Tintern Parva with such people of strength during the crisis.

"Please allow me one more personal comment before going on. In the ten days I have been among you no one has complained or said ill of any Tintern Abbey monks. Abbot Amaury was right; this is indeed a remarkable abbey.

"I want you all to know that I have come among you as a brother and a fellow monk. True, I am your Abbot. But that does not make me your lord. I do have a lifetime of experience. If I can help any of you, choir or lay brother, please talk with me about yourself, your concerns, or what you see to be the abbey's needs. Do I mean the two of us just talking to one another? Yes, that is exactly what I mean."

Taking a deep breath, the Abbot resumed his speech.

"Brothers, I am new among you. My conversations with you have aided me considerably in grasping the tone of our situation. Brother Dunston has also been of great service. We have met regularly over the past two weeks and have created a list of six actions our abbey must accomplish.

"First, we need to evaluate the condition of our churches. We have resources that may be of help to them. Second, we need to evaluate the condition of our Trellech Grange. Can we help them? Third, we must evaluate the needs of the Thomas Demesne. Again, how can we help? I understand they have not always been treated correctly. Fourth, we should recruit young Welshmen and other young men to become a part of our lay brotherhood. Young men everywhere are in short supply. This may be hard to do, but we can make a serious effort. To that end, Brother Dunston and I have decided Tintern Abbey shall establish an abbey school for teaching young boys to read and write, in order to prepare them to be novices. And finally, we need to select a Prior."

A murmur moved about the gathering, then settled down to allow Abbot Darnhall to continue.

"Brother Dunston has requested that he be allowed to return to and concentrate on the responsibilities of Cellarer, and I have approved that request. He is to be commended for the skill with which he led this abbey after Abbot Turhold was called home to his eternal reward and rest.

"The Archbishop of Canterbury notified my office that we will soon be receiving a new priest who wishes to become a monk. His name is Brother Gilmore. This canon should arrive next week. Until then, Brother Dunston and I will conduct Masses both here and at Tintern Parva. Master Robin has informed me that a priest may be on duty there by the end of the month. Although Bath is shorthanded, the bishop plans to send a priest from his own staff. See, it is not unheard of that bishops work with one another!"

Abbot Darnhall smiled. "I'm nearly finished. I thank you for your patience. But before I leave the podium, there's one more brother in our midst whom I wish to acknowledge and thank. It is largely thanks to the labors of our Sacrist, Brother Araud, that I have been able to learn so much, so quickly about Tintern Abbey. I wish to pay tribute to his gifts as a scribe and master of Latin, and thank him for converting the events of this abbey into a chronicle that acknowledges the courage of brothers who have gone before us, men of extraordinary faith." The Abbot smiled at the chronicler and respectfully nodded in his direction.

Brother Araud humbly bowed his head. He was both touched and embarrassed by these tributes from their new leader. Araud's thoughts summoned up the words of his friend Prior Frank. "The spirit of all the monks who have lived here, beginning with Abbot Henry and his pioneers, inhabit these walls and grounds. Make them live!" Araud had accomplished his assignment. He made the lives of these devoted men of God live again. Uniting the power of Christ and the inspiration of Bede with a collection of simple words, he had produced a manuscript of distinction.

"I request of Brother Araud that he continue the chronicle detailing the life of Tintern Abbey," Abbot Darnhall continued, his voice slightly subdued, as if there were only two men in the chapter room and he was asking a personal favor from a fellow monk.

Brother Araud looked up in surprise. He had assumed his task was completed. He felt a hint of a smile crossing his face. Dare he admit that the assignment he had protested and resisted so adamantly had become a source of gratification? Araud nodded to the Abbot.

Abbot Darnhall's tone returned to its customary resonance as he concluded, "We do not know what the future will be for us. We pray this pestilence is past. You have already demonstrated that whatever comes, with the help of the Blessed Virgin, God's work will prevail. Now I invite your questions or comments."

The first to speak was a lay brother, Robert, from the village of Llandaff. "Brother Abbot, I have heard rumors that some of the lay brothers elsewhere are leaving their abbeys for paying work at nearby demesnes or manors. Others are fleeing to cities, with the hope of bettering themselves. And some peasants, both free and not, are fleeing their manors with the hope of a more prosperous life. Some of us lay brothers here, myself included, wonder what these changes mean as far as we are concerned. Can you tell us the present status of lay brothers among the Cistercians? Are we free or not free?" Lay Brother Robert's bold question caused an expectant hush to fill the room.

Abbot Darnhall nodded. "You are right. Profound changes are happening, both in England and throughout Europe. Before leaving Citeaux, I had several long discussions with Abbot Maury about the collapse of the social and economic structure outside our abbeys, and how these changes might affect us within our walls.

"Before the pestilence came, it was well known that there was a surplus of labor. At that time every lord was obligated to take care of his peasants, free or servile. Most lords took this obligation seriously, devotedly trying to meet the needs of those on his manor or estate. As a rule, the lord of the manor paid cash out to free peasants during the harvest time, when he did not have enough servile labor to gather his crops. The lords of the manors, including our Tintern Abbey, had to grow enough food and produce for all of its inhabitants, including the lord, plus an excess to sell, which paid for those items the lord's serfs and free peasants could not produce. It was a society that benefited all.

"But as we all know, times have changed since the plague ravaged our society. In some areas up to seventy percent of the population has died from this dreaded malady. Some villages have been wiped out, although a few others escaped less damaged. In general, most of the victims were serfs, leaving the lords with a shortage of servile labor."

Looking directly at the lay brother who had raised the question, the Abbot said, "What you have pointed out, Brother Robert, is happening all over England. Nearly every estate owner or lord has found that he does not have sufficient labor to plant his crops, and in the harvest season he does not have enough labor to gather in his yield. Many serfs, or free men for that matter, appear to be unwilling to work under the old system. They want their rents reduced and their pay increased for work that they do.

"Many land owners resent and resist such changes. I have heard some of the nobility call these peasants 'miserable creatures, unfit for mankind.' But the fact is this: any landlord unwilling to make concessions to his tenants now might find that they have vanished from his land and are seeking greener fields elsewhere. They must realize that many people who labor now expect to be paid.

"And, as you have pointed out, Brother Robert, these changing times have created opportunities for many laborers, opportunities that never existed before the pestilence changed the face of Europe."

"I understand all of that, Abbot," said Robert of Llandaff. "But I still do not know how these changes might affect the lives of lay brothers in the Cistercian Order. My question, again, is: what is our status? Are lay brothers free or not free?"

An uncomfortable murmur moved over the assembly. Some of the choir monks appeared annoyed or embarrassed that their new Abbot should be asked to respond to a question that appeared more challenge than question. As for the lay brothers, clearly some of them had the same questions and concerns as Brother Robert, and were waiting for Abbot Darnhall's answer.

When the group settled back into silence, the Abbot spoke. "I understand your question, and I can answer it this way. Lay brothers are not slaves. Lay brothers are not serfs. Brown-robed lay monks have the same social status as white-robed monks. And like choir monks, you have certain requirements and obligations. One requirement is obedience to the Abbot. Another is that you combine physical, agricultural, and building labor with spiritual exercises. You are required to take certain vows, but not all the vows of the choir monks. For example, you do not need to meet for nighttime prayers. Nor do you have to read and meditate on the holy writings or copy Scriptures; in fact, you are not permitted to be able to read or write. Finally, you must act as a connection between the abbey's choir monks and those outside our grounds. Lay brothers duties in this regard give the choir monks more time to continue their daily prayers and other necessary religious activities.

"In exchange for your devotion and work, you are granted a roof over your head, two meals per day, and a dry bed. You are not asked to work any harder than you would on a feudal lord's land. You are asked to attend services more frequently than most peasants, which is probably not a burden and may bring rest to both body and soul between periods of work. However, there is a more taxing requirement for some, and that is to forgo the company of women. Much work and prayer enables all brothers to overcome their passions.

"All of us at the monasteries have taken a personal vow to serve God in the monastic way. The choir monks do this by transcribing holy documents and by repeating the litany of the canonical hours, seven times each day, saying prayers, intercessions, and praises to God, to the Blessed Virgin, and to the saints. It is fitting, therefore, that choir monks wear white robes. Lay brothers, on the other hand, wear brown habits which are a little shorter, making work easier. Lay brothers work from sunrise to sunset, as agricultural workers, in order to feed the choir monks and themselves. As you can see, you make possible all of the prayer and praise services to God and the Blessed Virgin.

"This division has been called the natural order of things and has been accepted by all for hundreds of years."

"May I repeat my question, Abbot Darnhall?"

"There is no need to, Brother Robert. You have asked the status of the lay brothers. To repeat, when you entered the abbey as a lay brother, you took a vow to obey your Abbot in all things. I do not have the power to release you from that vow. However, the Archbishop of

Canterbury or the Pope does have this power and the way is open to them. If you leave without their permission, to seek employment elsewhere or to forsake your vows and travel, will you be hunted down and brought back here in chains? I think not. This was not done before the plague, and I think it is far less likely to be done now in these times. You may not leave, that is true, but you can probably leave without punishment; that is also true. What I am doing is placing the question and responsibility squarely back on your shoulders and in your heart."

Abbot Darnhall smiled at Lay Brother Robert to show that he was done with his lengthy explanation. Robert of Llandaff stared back without smiling, and there was a long moment of tense silence. When the monks and lay brothers posed no additional questions, Abbot Darnhall closed the meeting with prayer. As the assembly filed out of the chapter room, he distinctly heard disgruntled mumbling resounding off the walls.

IF LAY BROTHER Robert and any of his brown-cloaked companions had doubts about the compassion of their new Abbot, those doubts were put aside at least temporarily the following week, on Maundy Thursday. Following the example set by Christ, who showed His humility and devotion to service by washing the feet of His Apostles, the Abbot of Tintern Abbey did the same for his brotherhood. It was a yearly ritual, as it had been since the founding of the abbey by Abbot Henry. Indeed the Maundy Thursday washing of feet was a tradition throughout the Cistercian Order, as well as throughout most of Christendom.

During supper, Brother Araud read from the thirteenth chapter of John's gospel:

> Now before the Feast of the Passover, Jesus knowing that His hour had come that He would depart out of this world to the Father, having loved His own who were in the world, He loved them to the end. During supper, the devil having already put into the heart of Judas Iscariot, the son of Simon, to betray Him, Jesus . . . got up from supper, and laid aside

his garments; and taking a towel, He girded Himself. Then He poured water into the basin, and began to wash the disciples' feet and to wipe them with the towel with which he was girded.

So He came to Simon Peter. He said to Him, "Lord, do You wash my feet?" Jesus answered and said to him, "What I do you do not realize now, but you will understand hereafter." Peter said to Him, "Never shall You wash my feet!" Jesus answered him, "If I do not wash you, you have no part of Me."

... So when He had washed their feet, and had taken His garments and reclined at the table again, He said to them, "Do you know what I have done to you? You call me Teacher and Lord: and you are right, for so I am. If I then, the Lord and the Teacher, washed your feet, you also ought to wash one another's feet. . . . If you know these things, you are blessed if you do them."

Brother Araud, the Sacristan, sat down and finished his meal.

"Let us now go before the high altar under the transept," invited Abbot Darnhall.

They all assembled in front of the high altar, and the Abbot invited everyone to sit. When they were all seated on the floor in front of the altar, Abbot Darnhall began to wash their feet, one by one. He was careful to kiss each foot after he had washed it.

This reenactment of Holy Scripture took the place of Compline. Afterwards, the monks quietly retired to their beds. Many of the monks deliberated over the power and holiness of the event, and some wondered if any of them could ever be as humble as their Abbot.

Even the most discontent of the lay brothers had seen that their new Abbot was a humble man, a man whose only ambition was to serve his God, and by extension, to serve all men, including themselves.

BASED ON CELLARER Dunston's analysis of recent events and their effect on nearby society, Abbot Darnhall launched three expeditions to determine the extent and devastation of the plague. The first team included Brothers Benedict and Araud, who headed across the Wye to visit the Manor of Woolaston, which contained the village of Ashwell. Abbot Darnhall and Master Robin led the second group toward Llandaff Village. Two lay brothers accompanied them. Brother Dunston was uncertain of the distance of these two journeys, but he estimated about seven to ten days would be needed. He anticipated that Benedict and Araud would complete their mission first, and so he and the Abbot assigned them to the third expedition, a trip to Trellech Manor.

THE WOOLASTON EXPEDITION crossed the River Wye and came upon Offa's Dike. "This twenty-five-foot-high earthen dike, built in the late eighth century by King Offa of Mercia, is longer than Hadrian's Wall," Brother Araud said, "and it has never been garrisoned."

"You know your history," Brother Benedict said. "That's all very well, but right now the thing to do is to get to the other side of this thing."

Soon after crossing the dike, Brothers Benedict and Araud came to the old Roman road, which stretched south from the town of Monmouth. About ten feet wide, made of large cobblestones, the road led past the ruins of a Roman temple. Brother Araud wished they had time to explore the temple, but they stopped only for a cool drink at the fresh water spring that flowed there.

The monks reached the Woolaston Manor fields, and about an hour later they spotted the village of Ashwell. Brother Benedict was disturbed by what they saw: the hamlet appeared nearly deserted, as if the population had disintegrated. The monks counted twenty-two houses, only two of which seemed to be occupied.

They approached Saint Mary Magdalene Church, the stone building in the center of town. Brother Araud, with his passion for history, found the church building fascinating; like most architecture, it told a story.

"What do you see, Brother?" his fellow monk asked.

"Well," said Araud, "it appears that this church was built in Anglo-Saxon times, because of its tall narrow windows installed in pairs. When the church was built, it probably had a thatch roof, but that has been replaced by a new slate roof since the coming of the Normans." The monks also found a round Norman tower to the west that was just a few feet above the gable, forming a bargeboard style.

The door of the church stood open. "Let's go inside," Brother Araud urged. A north wind followed them through the door, whipping up sand and tossing it into the church. Someone had chopped up the stalls, probably, for firewood. Dung on the wood floors showed that animals had used the building for protection against the elements. No trace of the parson could be seen.

The brothers left the church and moved toward a cottage at the edge of the village. They found two elderly women conversing near the front door of the small house.

"Greetings, good women," Brother Benedict called.

The women jolted and turned to face the monks. "Holy men of faith, you frightened us!" one of the women said. "Our visitors here are so few. But welcome. I can see by your cloaks that you are Cistercian. My name is Marian and here is my friend, Marthyn."

"We are Brothers Benedict and Araud from Tintern Abbey," said Benedict. "Our purpose is to gather information concerning the condition of these lands and to see how we might be able to help you. May we offer you bread and wine this late in the afternoon as gifts of friendship?"

Marian and Marthyn welcomed the two monks into the cottage and gestured toward a large wooden table. The women brought out plates and cups and served their guests.

"It appears Ashwell has suffered the plague disaster in an agonizing way," Brother Araud said. "Where is your priest? Will you tell us how this village became almost empty?"

Marian, her mouth full of bread, nodded to her companion to start their story.

"Did you see that large mound of freshly dug dirt at edge of the cemetery?" Marthyn asked. "Our Parson John is buried there, along with twelve of Ashwell's finest. Marian and I buried them by ourselves. About a dozen or more of our villagers fled to the woods to escape the plague. We do not know if they are dead or alive. Neither

Marian nor I had the courage to see if they survived or are out there putrefying. We have been living off of what food was left in their houses. A few hens have provided some eggs, and we discovered some grain in a large crock. Nearly everything else has been eaten by those large black rats. I observed too many rats to count. A few cows also survived. We have been milking them and making butter and whey. Now, thanks to you, we have some bread to put our butter on! God has seen fit to spare us, but we do not know why."

"It is clear God saved you for a purpose," said Brother Benedict. "For one thing, He needed someone to bury your people and the parson. I expect God has many tasks for you to do before He calls you home," the monk continued, smiling kindly. "You must be the salt of the earth."

"And a light set on a hill," added Araud. "We have some food left. Would you join two tired monks for dinner this evening? Your presence would honor us."

The two widow women grinned at each other, and Marthyn asked, "Shall we eat at your cottage or mine?"

"Mine," said Marian, indicating with a gesture that where they were sitting was where they'd be enjoying their evening meal. "I swept my house just this morning!"

"Fine," said Araud. "I will gather some wood and build a fire in your hearth."

"We are in for a real treat tonight," Marthyn told them. "Marian set a trap this morning, and it caught a rabbit. It has already been skinned and quartered. We found some leeks hanging in the reeve's home, as well as some apples. We knew the reeve had salted pork and fish, but unfortunately the black rats discovered them in the attic before we got there. One house had a crock full of apples, which was soaked by rain. An unfortunate loss, we thought, and then we discovered it had turned to wine and was quite drinkable—and did we have fun! Another house had a barrel of nuts of assorted kinds. We will also enjoy them this evening."

Brothers Benedict and Araud left the cottage to collect wood, and when they returned they built a blazing fire in the hearth. Soon the aroma of fresh cooking filled the air.

"Please tell us about yourselves," Brother Araud asked the widows, once they had prayed and begun to eat the fine meal set before them.

The monks learned that both women were longtime widows. Both had settled in Ashwell as young brides many years ago. Marian's husband had been a merchant, Marthyn was the daughter of a carpenter from Monmouth.

"I don't want to pry," Brother Benedict said, "but I cannot contain my curiosity. In spite of your age, you both appear to be good health. Why are the two of you still alive when every one else in the village is dead? Was there some potion that you took? Did you bleed one another? Did the two of you march around your church reading holy words? Did you touch or handle the dead? Your healthy condition indicates that you did not overly fast."

"Brothers, you have not asked any questions that we have not pondered and discussed," Marthyn answered. "Maybe it was as you said, Brother Benedict. God had something for us to do, and when that is done, He will take us."

Marian added, "As to how close we were to the dead, the two of us dug graves. We found the dead in the streets, in homes, and in barns. The two of us dragged the dead to that big hole by the church where we prayerfully placed them side by side, with their heads to the west, so that when the resurrection comes, they will sit up and greet the Lord. We buried them in the clothes they were wearing when they died.

"Were you afraid?" Brother Araud asked.

Marthyn said, "There is such a thing as being too busy to be afraid. We had our Compline just after sundown every day. We did not venture into the night. We often discussed between ourselves what had caused all our people to die such horrible deaths. We fell asleep before we had answers."

Brother Benedict nodded. "We have eaten and talked right through Vespers, and now it is time for Compline. Marthyn, Marian, would you join us in Compline?"

The women accepted his offer and the four of them walked to the church. Following Compline the women went to their homes, and on advice from Marian, the brothers spent the night in the reeve's home.

THE MONKS SLEPT through Vigils, but were up before sunrise and held their own Lauds. They spent the entire morning cleaning Saint Mary Magdalene Church and repairing the door so it could be latched. Marian and Marthyn brought a light noonday meal and some wine they had found in the reeve's house. The women spent the afternoon assisting their newfound monk friends.

Late in the afternoon the four gathered around the freshly dug graves of the unfortunates at Ashwell. The women repeated each victim's name, concluding with Father Griggston. Brother Araud, the Sacrist of Tintern Abbey, knew the funeral service well, and he spoke each word with grace and emphasis. Brother Benedict understood each word, but the women understood only a few of the Latin phrases. When Brother Benedict said, "The Lord be with you," Brother Araud and the two women distinctly repeated, "And with you also, sir and madam, Amen."

THE NEXT DAY, while investigating the conditions of the village houses, Brother Benedict and Brother Araud decided fifteen were still habitable. The monks gathered from the other dilapidated houses a huge pile of wood for the women, then set fire to the useless buildings.

Threatening weather encouraged the monks to cut short their tasks and return to the abbey. The monks hastened their goodbyes to their good-natured hosts and started their journey home to Tintern.

THE PURPOSE OF the second expedition—led by Abbot Darnhall and Master Robin and including two lay brothers from the abbey—was to determine the condition of Llandaff Village. From Araud's chronicles, the Abbot had learned of a previous Sheriff of Llandaff and the Welshmen's efforts to rid the village of Cathars, an infestation brought to light by Brother Hugh and William the Templar, two of the first Cistercians to live and worship at Tintern Abbey. Now there was another infestation to investigate, the plague.

Going by boat down the River Wye, Abbot Darnhall, Master Robin, and the two lay brothers reached Chepstow Castle by mid-morning. By evening of the second day they reached Llandaff Village. They walked by the cemetery and the church. Just a glance at the cemetery revealed many new graves. Except for the unusual tombstones on the north side of the cemetery, no traces of the Cathars remained. Abbot Darnhall had no firsthand knowledge of the heretic group, but he had heard of some of their unusual beliefs.

A converted long house was now occupied by the current sheriff, Bredon, who was pleased to welcome the Tintern Abbey caravan. "We have been anxious to hear from our lord Tintern Abbey," he told them. "Visitors to our village have said that your abbey suffered great losses. Both Abbot Turhold and Prior Frank are known to me. I hope they have been spared from the sickness."

"Regretfully, both have gone on to their heavenly rest. I am Abbot Darnhall, and this is Master Robin from Tintern Parva," replied the Abbot.

"May the good brothers rest in peace," responded the sheriff with a solemn tone. Then he turned to Master Robin and said, "I have heard of you, Master Robin. In fact, I own a dozen of your famous longbow arrows. I hope I must never use one in anger."

"With all that has befallen us, we have not been able to learn how the plague has affected your village," said the Abbot. "We are here to see if the abbey can be of any service to you. Can you tell us how you have fared under this dreadful pestilence, which has mortally struck so many areas?"

"Yes," the sheriff answered. "I have in fact been preparing a written report of how we fared. But first, let us go over to my home, where you can be refreshed while my wife and servant girls prepare an evening meal for us. Do you think your Pope will forgive you if you shared some roast lamb?" asked the sheriff.

"I think the Pope would be pleased by your generosity, sheriff," the Abbot answered with smile.

"And I know that I will be pleased!" added Master Robin.

As they approached the large manor house, they saw in the

distance several children playing tag happily, apparently unscathed by the plague.

The men entered the manor house. The inside room included a large rectangular raised hearth, several chairs, and a long table at which the sheriff often entertained visitors. Leeks were hanging from the rafters. Large earthen jars contained assorted nuts and other foodstuffs. A smoked lamb quarter hung high on the wall to protect it from varmints. At one end a buttery and wine press revealed that the sheriff's family and servants ate well.

A small altar marked the center of the manor house as a place of meditation and spiritual exercises. A large tapestry told the story of Mary and Jesus walking through the woods with guardian angels nearby to keep them safe. The altar was adorned with four icons representing Matthew, Mark, Luke, and John. An ornately decorated wooden cup stood in the center.

One corner of the large room contained the sheriff's armor, shield, and longbows, along with twelve of Master Robin's crafted arrows — neatly arranged, but quickly available in case of danger.

Since the old Celtic barn was still useable, no animals occupied the Manor House. Sweet-smelling herbs made the home refreshing and inviting. Red and brown cloth draped in vertical strips set the sleeping area apart from the rest of the lodge.

The Sheriff of Llandaff smiled at his visitors and said, "Brothers, I welcome you to my home. Now please sit at the table and let us enjoy refreshment while we discuss matters that concern us all."

As Abbot Darnhall, Master Robin, and the two brown-cloaked lay brothers sat down at the huge table, a kindly, comely woman approached the table, and the sheriff introduced her as his wife, Rotha.

"Brothers, what can I get for you?" the good woman asked. "We have wine and beer, and both are well aged."

"Kindly bring wine for all of us," Master Robin replied. "One round will be plenty."

Rotha curtsied with a smile and turned to fulfill the men's wishes. Sheriff Bredon grinned with pleasure and pride in his gracious, beautiful wife. Then his expression became serious, and he began his story.

"One week before anyone fell ill, a peddler came through, telling us of many hamlets and villages that had become deserted. He said a great pestilence was taking many lives in Italy and France. We were not alarmed by this news. Our parson had told us of a great death coming from the East, but we took no heed. Priests are always predicting doom.

"This time, sadly, the prediction came true. Our village suffered greatly, and quickly, and before long we had fifteen empty houses. This scourge was so sweeping and unsparing, without any visible cause, that we believed it must be a divine punishment. But for what?"

Before they could speculate on the Divine cause for such a disaster, Rotha returned to the table, bearing cups of wine. The gift was a momentary respite from the sad tale unfolding.

"We quickly decided that we must have no contact with the infected," Sheriff Bredon said. "Many kinfolk became aloof from one another. Some fathers and mothers even abandoned their own children. All love appeared to vanish among us. Led by the finest priest we have ever known, all of our church people paraded around the church repeating holy phrases. Father Deon visited all of the sick persons, received their confession, prayed for them, and gave last rites to the perishing. A week later, Father Deon himself died horribly."

The visitors from Tintern Abbey and Tintern Parva nodded in sympathy. They were well acquainted with the sorrow that the sheriff was describing.

"As you entered our village you may have noticed a small house set apart from the others. Aging Maggie and her black cat named Demon lived there. Maggie was always considered different. She was often pestered by the children, who one day tied a stick to Demon's tail. She ran the children off with her broom. While tying the stick to Demon's tail one of children's arms was scratched. The boy ran home claiming that Demon had attacked him. Some of the villagers, drunk on too much wine, panic-stricken by the plague, and looking for a scapegoat, rushed to Maggie's house and battered the old woman to death. They even smashed the poor cat's head against her wall."

"God rest Maggie's soul," Abbot Darnhall said.

The sheriff nodded in gratitude for the Abbot's kindness. "Mansus, our bailiff, had been remarkably successful in raising our sheep and leading us through the best times our village has ever seen. I remember the day he and I were discussing the price of wool. He stretched out his arm and complained of stiffness. I told him he had been working too hard, that he should go home and get some rest. The next day Sarah, his wife, came running down the street crying, 'My husband! My husband!' I rushed to her home where I found Mansus stretched out on his bed, bleeding from his mouth. His eyes were focused on the ceiling. His legs twitched and stiffened. He had a high fever and was talking incoherently. I asked Sarah if he had any sores. She said he had several on his body and his groin was swollen. I felt so impotent. I was neither a priest nor a physician. I repeated some comforting verses of Scripture, but to no avail. Three days later our bailiff died.

"Our sexton and cemetery keeper has buried thirty-one persons. He was overworked. No one in the village would help him. I felt obliged as sheriff to pitch in. What I remember most was the suffocating stench."

The sheriff took a sip of wine, as if to erase the memory of the scent. He shook his head; clearly the scent was with him still, and might be there for the rest of his days.

"For a while our cows, pigs, and sheep wandered around aimlessly. Many of them died. Every dog and cat in town died. Pessimism and renunciation took over our village. I really do not know how any of us survived this. We lived one day at a time, feeling each day was precious and was God's gift to us. Knowing, too, that we might not know another.

"One day, a traveling friar came through our town. He just showed up. He said he was on his way north. We felt overwhelmingly that at last God was bringing a message to our village. God had not deserted us. He had not left us to rot. Friar Matthew visited every house in town, sick or well. He heard our confessions. He listened to our woes. We had so many present for the Friar's Mass that we had to hold the service outside. Fearful of our children's souls, we asked him to baptize the little ones. He said he was not authorized to perform baptisms. He said our bishop should do this. We told him we had not heard from our bishop. We pleaded. He eventually consented. After being with us a week, one morning, he said he had to go on. Again we pleaded. This time he said he must leave. We gathered some gold and silver and offered them to him. However, he refused all gifts. He said he would take with him his memory of us and some cool water."

"I expect God was calling the friar to another village. He had done what he could do here in Llandaff," Master Robin suggested.

"We will never forget his kindness," Sheriff Bredon said. "Nor will we ever forget the Mass he offered on our behalf. And remembering that occasion, which brought hope and joy to our devastated community, I have this request of you, Abbot Darnhall. Would you lead our village in a Mass before you return to Tintern Abbey?"

The next morning the brightly colored interior of the Llandaff Church was packed as Abbot Darnhall lifted the Chalice and Host heavenward, celebrating the mystical reality of the celestial banquet, the blood and body of Christ. Never before had the Mass meant so much in this church where for centuries many kinds of Christians—Celts, Anglo-Saxons, Cathars, and followers of Rome—had gathered for the worship and glory of God!

After the Mass, Abbot Darnhall promised to have Cellarer Dunston visit the Llandaff Village soon. The following day, the men began their journey home.

BROTHERS ARAUD AND Benedict returned from their trip to Woolaston while Abbot Darnhall was still at Llandaff. They permitted themselves a two-day respite to catch up with their spiritual and monastic activities. Then the monks freshened their supplies for their second expedition, up the River Wye to the Trellech Grange.

The two monks, accompanied by four lay brothers, headed north, reaching the dock at Llandogo by late that afternoon. The wooden dock had been built by merchants who traded wool for other goods. These traders regularly traveled the river, selling their wares on their way to the Black Mountains. During the high-water season they would dock at the Trellech Grange and proceed on foot, because not far up the river, the swift current posed danger for larger boats. The dock was large, with ample room for four barges or boats.

When the company from Tintern Abbey arrived, however, they found the dock unoccupied and unattended. Brother Benedict said, "We seem to have this place to ourselves. It's too late in the day to impose ourselves on the grange unannounced. I propose we settle down here for the night. We can camp beside the river and rest until morning."

The four lay brothers, who had done the rowing, were quick to agree that a rest was in order. But it was too early to retire, and so after the boat was secured and the camp was set up, Brother Araud entertained his friends with another historical story.

"Have you ever heard the story of the Golden Tara Brooch?" he asked.

Brother Benedict shook his head and smiled. The lay brothers had not heard of this story either.

"Well," Brother Araud began, "back in the time of Abbot Henry, some children were playing nearby—they were in fact in the sand around those stone circles over there. They probably should have left those old stones alone, but children will be children, and they began turning them over. Under one of the larger stones they found a gold brooch, the kind that was once used by the Celts to pin their clothing or as an adornment. The children were rewarded and the golden brooch was given to St. Dogmaels Abbey. Abbot Henry learned this story when he was camping in this very spot. You see, we have a connection to those who went before us."

Brother Benedict said, "Let's go turn a few of those stones over. Who knows, maybe there is another gold or even a silver something under one."

"You must not be superstitious," Brother Araud chuckled. "Although Abbot Henry said to Brother Galandas, right here on this spot as they camped that night, that he believed everyone is a bit superstitious."

Perhaps to prove they were not superstitious, the four lay brothers spent the next two hours turning stones. Under one they found a dog's skull. Brother Araud reasoned that the dog's skeleton head had been placed there by the Celts or an earlier people as a part of some ritual.

"A ritual?" said the brown-cloaked brother who was holding the skull. "Perhaps we should bury this skull, put it back where it came from."

"Yes," agreed another lay brother. "And quickly!"

"Very well," Brother Benedict said with a laugh. "And then we'll have supper."

"Followed by Compline," Brother Araud added. "And a good night's sleep."

THE NEXT MORNING two of the lay brothers stayed with the boat as guards while Brothers Araud and Benedict and the other two lay brothers took the old Roman trail northeast.

By noon the monks reached a rise from which they could see Trellech Grange. The grange was the center of a two-thousand-acre sheep enterprise. The landscape included four large stone barns, as well as two manor houses and quarters for about twenty-five workers. Empty foundations indicated that some worker houses had been torn down. The last communication from Trellech Grange had brought news of the sad loss of Lay Brother Johybert. He was buried at the Grange, although Cistercian custom maintained that his body be moved to his own abbey. Brother Araud was relieved that the exhumation and transportation of Johybert's body was not included in their current expedition.

The descendants of Gruffudd ap Rys ap Tewder had managed this grange since the invasion of the Normans. His son Owain ap Gruffudd established the original working arrangements with Abbot Henry in 1132, and those arrangements still existed. Owain and his brother had been instrumental in cleaning out the Cathar infestation in Llandaff Village. They were handsomely rewarded with both land and sheep.

Despite several rebellions in Northern Wales, the close contact the Gruffudd family maintained with Tintern Abbey and Normandy had kept their property from being ravaged by either Welsh princes or English kings. Control of the grange passed through generation after generation of Gruffudd leaders, a series of strong Welshmen named Owain. These recently included Owain Lawgoch—known as Owain of the Red Hand—who held power throughout that area of Wales called Powys. When the Red Hand's responsibilities to Trellech Grange limited his funds to further his ambitions, he relinquished his interest in the Grange to his nephew, the son of Glyn Dwr. By the time of the plague, Glyn Dwr's nephew, Owain ap Owain was managing the grange.

It was this Owain ap Owain who warmly welcomed Brothers Benedict and Araud and their two lay brother companions to the main hall of Trellech Grange. He was a burley Welshman from a long line of powerful military and political leaders, but this Owain was clearly also a farmer, a trader, and a manager of a business.

He also looked weary. As they sat at the long table and shared a simple meal, he told the monks, "It is good to receive a visit from Tintern Abbey, and I thank you for coming. We have all been through so much during the last couple of years, but now it is important that we reestablish our ties. We were pleased to have your Lay Brother Johybert among us, and we mourn his loss, as I'm sure you do."

"We do indeed," Brother Araud said.

"Johybert's compassion and care offered comfort to many during this wretched ordeal," Owain said. "He gave much help and comfort to the dying, offering cup after cup of cool water from our well. He had no fear of touching the sick, or lifting them and helping them find more comfortable positions. That holy man spent much time praying for and with our ravaged young men. When his time came and he had horrible symptoms, he continued his work until he could not stand. He drew his last breath kissing his small cross."

The room was silent for a sorrowful moment, until Brother Benedict returned to the business at hand. "How severely was the grange affected by the plague?" he asked. "Brother Araud and I were sent to assess the loss and devastation among all our neighbors, whom we include in our prayers."

"For which I'm grateful," said the Welshman. "We lost more than half of our workers, forty-three souls, to be exact. We also lost over two thousand sheep and nearly a hundred pigs. We are still staggering from the pestilence, although, thanks to God, we have not been afflicted in recent months. Let us pray the affliction has passed."

The monks and lay brothers nodded, and Brother Araud softly said, "Amen."

When the refreshment was consumed, Owain ap Owain said, "I expect you'll want to visit the gravesite of your departed lay brother, Johybert. I shall lead you there. We have been told by travelers and traders of wool that we no longer need be afraid of the cemetery."

STANDING BESIDE THE grave of their departed lay brother, Brothers Araud and Benedict said prayers on the behalf of his soul. Their two brown-cloaked companions were not so reserved, having worked alongside Johybert for many years; they remembered him as a man of virtue and good humor, whose love for his friends almost rivaled his love for his God.

Leaving the gravesite, Owain asked Brother Benedict, "May I hope you brothers will be our guests here at the grange for a few days?"

"You are most kind to offer us this hospitality," Brother Benedict replied, "but we must leave you now and return to Tintern. Our Abbot will have returned from his own travels, and he is anxious to hear what we have learned."

"Very well," the Welshman said. "But before you go, can you assure me that the new Abbot of Tintern Abbey will honor the agreements we have had between grange and abbey through the years?"

"I expect so," Brother Benedict replied. "I assume he knows the terms of those agreements. They must be written down. Is that correct, Brother Araud?" He turned to Owain and explained, "Brother Araud is our chronicler, and if documents exist—"

"I confess I haven't seen any documents relating to the agreements made between Trellech Grange and Tintern Abbey," Brother Araud interrupted. "Like Brother Benedict, I am certain Abbot Darnhall will honor them, but it would be wise for us to make it clear to him exactly what those terms are. Can you tell us, Owain?"

Owain nodded. "Please return with me to the great hall. We can

enjoy another cup of wine, and I shall tell you the terms of our relationship with the abbey. I too trust Abbot Darnhall to be honorable,
but people in my family still tell stories about one Abbot John, who
had a different philosophy concerning agreements. It would be wise
to avoid any such misunderstandings with your new Abbot."

Araud nodded. "I have heard similar stories about Abbot John,"
he said. "Let me assure you, Abbot Darnhall is cut from a finer
cloth."

SEATED AT THE long table in the great hall, Owain ap Owain
explained the contractual agreement between Owain ap Gruffudd
and the Abbot Henry of Tintern Abbey. He explained many details
concerning sheep, crops, and so forth, but they all supported a basic
division of monies. They called for one half of the net profit to go to
the grange and one half to be given to Tintern Abbey. "I am happy
with this arrangement, and I would be grateful for your assurance
that it will continue."

Brother Benedict answered, "We don't have the authority to speak
for the Abbot. But I can assure you he is a reasonable man, and we
will present your request to him as soon as we get back to Tintern."

"Thank you, brothers, for your help," Owain said.

AS THE BOAT floated downriver from the dock at Llandogo to the
dock at Tintern Abbey, Brothers Benedict and Araud discussed what
they had learned from Owain ap Owain.

"Frankly, I think the arrangement is more than fair to Tintern
Abbey," Brother Araud said. "After all, Trellech Grange is a most
profitable enterprise, worth many hundreds of pounds. The abbey
would not have manpower or lay brothers to take over an operation
of this size, nor would we have the soldiers to take this large grange
from the Welsh if there were a dispute."

Brother Benedict agreed. "Furthermore, in spite of the losses
inflicted by the plague, it is clear that the grange will be a flourish-
ing business again. And I feel that the abbey deserves its share of
the profits. We are the ones who established markets in Europe, and
our wool is under contract to French and Italian buyers. Between the

abbey and the grange, the marketing of wool is a thriving concern. The grange can take advantage of our contacts abroad. So this alliance seems to benefit both sides."

"It amazes me that our abbey has such power in the temporal world," said Brother Araud. "It appears that Abbots have been elevated to the status of lords, counts and barons. If this is so, then only the King outranks them!"

"In that case," added Brother Benedict, "and if Trellech Grange belongs to the King and by extension to our Lord at Chepstow, and again by extension to Tintern Abbey, then why would we allow Trellech Grange to keep one half of its earnings? Reasoning tells me, as I expect it told Abbot John, that Tintern Abbey should get all the earnings, less any expenses. The more I think of it, the more it seems a complicated arrangement. Well, these matters are not for you and me to decide."

"Look ahead," Brother Araud said, pointing and smiling. "Just around the bend, we can see the spire of our church. We're home in time for Vespers."

VESPERS WAS FOLLOWED by supper, which in turn was followed by Compline. After Compline, Brothers Araud and Benedict approached Abbot Darnhall and asked if they might have a word with him before retiring.

"Of course," the Abbot replied. "Let us go into the warming room. The room is empty, so we may speak privately. I've asked that the fire be lit, so we will have light and warmth. The spring day was warm today, but the evening is chilly, and I'm anxious to meet with you and hear what you have learned from your expeditions."

The men entered the warming room and stood around the fire pit, stretching out their hands to gather heat from the blaze. It was a comfortable and attractive room, with a fine vaulted ceiling and benches along walls for seating. The great central fireplace burned continuously from the first of November until Good Friday. Choir monks gathered in the room and around the fire often during the long, bitter cold winter months. At Abbot Darnhall's request, the fire had been lit that evening expressly for this meeting with the two returning brothers.

"First of all, before I hear your report, I have some important, joyful news to announce to you, Brother Benedict. Your devotion and hard work beyond what is asked of you has not gone unnoticed. In your absence, the Tintern monks selected you as our new Prior. I trust you will be at ease with your new official position."

The warm glow that Brother Benedict felt was more than just what emanated from the fire pit. He looked at the smiling faces of the Abbot and his friend, Brother Araud, then bowed his head humbly.

"I am honored that my brothers continue to deem me worthy of such responsibilities," Brother Benedict responded.

The Abbot answered, "Of course they have great confidence in you. After all, you have been serving as acting Prior since the death of Prior Frank, and you've been capable and wise. But lest you be tempted to engage in feelings of pride, which of course would not be proper for a Cistercian monk, let alone a Prior, let us get on with our business." His smile revealed that his stern remark was at least partially in jest. "Araud, tell me how the Woolaston investigation fared."

"Ashwell has disintegrated," Brother Araud began. "When the plague invaded the village more than a dozen villagers fled into the woods. We have no word of them. The only people remaining in the whole village were two resourceful old women. These two brave women went through a living hell. In the first five days their priest and reeve suffered horribly before dying. Then, one by one, others perished until they alone were left. These women actually buried all of the dead from Ashwell! Their great faith and grace from the Holy Mother enabled them to touch and handle bodies of persons who were filled with death and horrible sores. I do not see how they were not overcome by the stench. They survived by setting traps for rabbits and scavenging what was left behind by the dead and those who fled."

"God bless those courageous women," the Abbot murmured. He closed his eyes as if better to absorb the enormity of Ashwell's loss. When he opened his eyes, he nodded for Brother Araud to continue.

"Saint Mary Magdalene Church had become a haven for animals. We cleaned up the church and held graveside services over the victims.

Concerning the remaining properties, by our count fifteen houses are still habitable. Two of these are manor houses. Several cows and pigs are running loose. After piling wood up for the old women we burned the dilapidated houses. The ground around Ashwell appears to be fertile. This village could thrive if about three or four families took over what was occupied earlier by fifteen or so families. But if Ashwell is reoccupied it will need a sheriff and a bailiff, as well as a steward responsible to our abbey.

"After visiting Ashwell, we returned to Tintern Abbey early because of threatening storms. We will need to go back to complete our mission, to investigate the rest of the Woolaston Grange lands and properties."

"Thank you, Brother Araud," the Abbot said, "for providing those important details. If it is God's will, Ashwell will thrive again one day. Now, Brother Benedict, tell me about the Trellech Grange."

"This extensive grange holds about two thousand acres and is used for both crops and sheep grazing," Brother Benedict began. "More than forty of the grange laborers suffered dreadful deaths. The plague also devastated their animals. Two thousand sheep and nearly one hundred pigs perished."

The monk suddenly lost concentration and tears came to his eyes. "We witnessed Brother Johybert's grave," he said, when he could find a voice. "He was buried with his cross, and his gravesite has a small stone marker with the words 'Johybert, An Angel Who Visited Us When We Were Sick.' His body will be moved to our cemetery this summer, when the ground is soft again."

The three men offered their fallen brother a moment of quiet tribute and extended their prayers for the many lives lost during the tragedy.

"Who runs the grange now?" the Abbot asked, breaking the silence.

"Owain ap Owain," replied Brother Benedict. "His ancestors go all the way back to the founding of our abbey. According to Owain, the Grange receives one half of the net profit from wool and other products sold by Trellech. The other half comes to Tintern Abbey. It appears the abbey makes all of the arrangements for the sale of the wool. Neither Brother Araud nor I had been aware of this long-standing agreement, so the two of us were not prepared to speak on the subject, nor did we feel we had the authority to continue or discontinue such a significant arrangement. We did not voice an opinion about this agreement before we left, but we did say we would bring you Owain ap Owain's request that the arrangement be continued."

The Abbot nodded. "Well done. I am proud of both of you. You have served Tintern in the correct manner by your quiet tact. After I accepted the position as your Abbot, I read all of the records at Citeaux concerning Tintern Abbey. The fifty-percent division has been a part of our generous agreement with Trellech from the very beginning. Abbot Henry made this agreement in order to control some of the ambitions of Welsh princes and lords. The secret agreement was approved by Lord Walter Fitz Richard of Clare. The idea was to keep Tintern Abbey out of the struggle for domination between Welsh princes and the English Crown. So far it has worked. As you may know, Owain of the Red Hand has wanted to become the Welsh prince or even king. He has been playing both sides against the middle with the hope he can prevail. Red Hand borrowed huge sums of money from King Charles of France. It has been rumored that the English government is tired of Red Hand's intrigues and may send a spy to assassinate him. What will come of this we do not know. But whatever happens, Tintern will appear to be on the side of right. Our contrived neutrality has served us well, and we have never been attacked like many other Welsh abbeys.

"And now," the Abbot concluded, "the time has come for me to bid you goodnight. It will soon be time for Vigils. I thank you both for your excellent reports. It is reassuring for me to know this abbey has such a fine Prior, as well as such a fine Sacrist and chronicler. Most of all, I value you both as brothers."

After Abbot Darnhall left the warming room, the two monks lingered at the fire absorbing a bit of radiant warmth before exiting into the chilly passageway.

PRIOR BENEDICT, THE monk thought. He liked the sound of his new title. Having served as acting Prior for many months, Brother

Benedict did not expect to feel any different now that the abbey had bestowed the full title upon him. But that act of selection by the Tintern monks meant more to him than he wanted to admit to himself. Whatever the nature of his true feelings, one thing he knew: his sense of responsibility was stronger now than it had ever been. And he was eager to work, for he was dedicated to the service of his new official role.

Now that the heavy clouds of the plague were lifting, he was free to pursue other monastic endeavors. High on his list of goals was creating a new shrine to house the carved figure of the Virgin Mary. He wanted to move the icon from its current location, just inside of the entrance to the lay brothers' chapel, and create a separate, smaller chapel dedicated to the Blessed Virgin.

That morning Prior Benedict conferred with Brother Dunston about the project. Both saw the advantage of having the icon in a more visible position, with a secure place for offerings to be deposited. As the Cellarer, Brother Dunston saw a practical advantage in the move as well, since it would relieve some of the need to have a monk on duty all the times, although a monk would need to be available to assist in the prayers and to give guidance and comfort to any pilgrims who might visit the shrine.

"How do you suggest we proceed?" the Prior asked. "And can you give me any idea of the cost of building this small chapel? Can the abbey afford a suitable shrine for our precious relic?"

"I think we should discuss this matter with Master Robin," Cellarer Dunston answered. "He is a practical man, and he could give us wise counsel."

"That is an excellent idea. And let us also include Mary in those discussions. She is a wise woman, and she has personal and spiritual reasons to know how valuable the icon is to our abbey."

Two days later Cellarer Dunston and Prior Benedict walked to the Robin manor house. As they approached the manor, they spotted Robin and Mary, walking in the herb garden.

"Good morning Master Robin and Lady Mary," Cellarer Dunston called out. He immediately put his hand to his mouth. "Forgive me,

Mary," the monk said quickly. "I meant no offense. You are known by all of us as the Gold Coin Lady. I intended to say—"

"Fear not, my brother. Bestowing upon me a title of nobility could be construed as a hint of flattery," Mary teased. The monk's face turned a pale shade of crimson. Mary smiled to rescue the self-conscious brother from embarrassment. "Now, now, there is nothing to forgive. God knows you graced me with words of honor and respect."

Brother Dunston sighed with relief.

Master Robin said, "This noble woman, whom you call the Gold Coin Lady, does indeed merit your compliment, Brother Dunston. She is perhaps too modest to mention this, but was born the daughter of a minor knight and her late husband, Edward, was the son of a lord from Dudley."

"Let us be honest, Robin," Mary said. "Edward was an illegitimate son, and his father was a minor lord. So there's no need for any title, nor do I want one. I do feel honored, though, to be called the Gold Coin Lady, knowing that the coin serves Tintern Abbey and the worship of our Blessed Virgin."

Master Robin beamed at her, and Prior Benedict noticed for the first time that there was something more than friendship between the two of them.

"Master Robin, we seek your advice concerning a needful and honorable project," the Prior said. "I've spoken to our new Abbot and he supports this cause, that a new chapel be constructed for our Blessed Virgin image. We feel the best site would be just outside of the west door of our abbey church. This chapel could be closed in inclement weather, but otherwise we feel it should be kept open. We can build a depository for offerings and gifts into the structure. More and more pilgrims are now seeking the Virgin's power to enhance their lives. We need an attractive, but not elaborate structure. We seek your advice and your opinion. And yours as well, Mary."

Mary's eyes widened as she listened to Prior Benedict's ideas. Emotionally touched and unable to articulate, she nodded to Master Robin to speak for her.

"I have been deeply thankful that Mary, her children, and I

survived this dreadful plague that has struck down so many. Mary knows firsthand the miracle-working power of the Blessed Virgin. If you will be kind enough to draw the plans and sketches, it will be my honor to build and pay for the new chapel. I suggest that the chapel might be called the Mary Mary Chapel, to honor both the Virgin and the Gold Coin Lady."

But Mary would have none of that. "Please do not do that," she protested. "I do not want an honor of that sort, nor do I deserve to have my name placed alongside that of the Blessed Virgin. I would be pleased, however, if somewhere, where it cannot be seen, the name 'Mary' could be cut into one little block of the stone that will be placed in an inconspicuous location."

"I bow to your wisdom," Robin told the woman. "But the two of us, and the brothers at Tintern Abbey, and especially the Blessed Virgin will know what that single name means."

"The Virgin will be pleased," asserted Cellarer Dunston. "Your generosity far exceeds our expectations. Blessings to you both."

Mary nudged Master Robin and whispered a few words to him. Master Robin nodded, then smiled at the monks. "Ah yes, Prior Benedict, congratulations on your new duties," he said. "Mary and I have been praying for this to happen ever since Prior Frank died. I hope you do not consider our prayers meddling in Tintern Abbey's affairs."

"No, to the contrary," the Prior responded. "Your prayers are important to us. You have given us so many gifts. I cannot imagine Tintern Abbey without your support."

"Good men of faith, my heart is filled with gratitude for your kind words," Mary said. "I am alive today because of Tintern Abbey's kindness as well as the Virgin's compassion."

Virgin Mary's Chapel was completed in less than a year, thanks to the generosity of Master Robin and to Cellarer Dunston's many connections with English and Welsh builders.

Thirty days after the Blessed Mary's chapel dedication, the choir monks of Tintern Abbey received a written invitation to attend the wedding of Master Robin of Tintern Parva to Mary of Dudley, daughter of Sir William Oswalk of Dudley, on the day following Saint John the Baptist Day.

Brother Araud wrote of the ceremony in the chronicle of Tintern Abbey: "God provided us with beautiful friends. God provided these friends with a beautiful love for each other. And God provided us all a beautiful day for their marriage. Praise be to God!"

PART IV
The Last Monks of Tintern Abbey

14

End of an Era

By the end of the fourteenth century, the Black Death had ceased to be a menace in the Wye Valley, and the monks of Tintern Abbey no longer lived in constant fear of pestilence. Other problems beset the abbey, however. When Owain of the Red Hand was assassinated by an Englishman, Welsh uprisings brought turmoil to southern Wales, and as a result the abbey lost its lucrative interest in Trellech Grange.

The fifteenth century saw great political upheaval in the British monarchy and a series of civil wars that lasted for decades, until the Plantagenet kings were replaced by the Tudors, starting in 1485 with Henry VII. During those turbulent years, the English throne left Tintern Abbey and other monasteries alone for the most part, so the monks could go about their business of prayer and devotion without interference from the world outside.

There was no denying, however, that the world was changing, and the changes were affecting life at Tintern Abbey. Some of the older monks could still remember Abbot Darnhall's explanation to Lay Brother Robert of the increasing economic opportunities for laborers outside the monastic life. As a result of these continuing changes to society, monasteries all over Britain, including Tintern Abbey, were losing their lay brothers to the outside world, and fewer and fewer free men were joining the orders as monks. By the end of the century, the abbey had lost over half of its lay brothers, and the number of choir monks was reduced to thirteen. Thus, during the fifteenth century Tintern Abbey became a less influential, poorer enterprise, both in land holdings and in labor force.

Nevertheless, life continued throughout the century at Tintern

Abbey. Sir William Herbert of Raglan, the ambitious and contro-
versial Earl of Pembroke, became the abbey's steward, and he set
about making physical improvements to the abbey. With far less
room needed for lay brothers, parts of their dormitory were made
into private rooms for senior brothers. Sir William also built a lavish,
imposing new hall on the northeast side, to be used as the Abbot's
private quarters, with two windows, a wooden bed, a working table,
and a fireplace. The Abbot even had his own latrine, with under-
ground flowing water that carried waste back to the River Wye.
Two additional rooms gave added space for important visitors. This
open-timbered great hall was connected to the Abbot's refectory by
a covered walkway with six painted glass windows running nearly
to the dock.

Sir William of Raglan left a provision in his will for the building
of his tomb at Tintern Abbey. Any money not used was to go for
cloisters. Involved in a rebellion, the Earl was captured at the Battle of
Edgecote and was quickly executed. He was buried at Tintern Abbey,
as was his wish. However, his elaborate tomb was never built, as the
money he had left was needed elsewhere to keep the abbey going.

By the end of the fifteenth century, Tintern Abbey was still surviving, although its influence did not reach far outside the River
Wye Valley. The monastic community had survived the ills that had
ravaged Britain all through living memory, the plague of the fourteenth century and the civil wars of the fifteenth. Henry VIII, a Tudor,
was now on the throne, and the monks at Tintern had reason to hope
for stability at last, and a period of continued peace in which they
could carry on their spiritual lives.

What would the sixteenth century bring? As long as the King of
England maintained a cordial relationship with the Church of Rome,
the Cistercians had every reason to believe all would be well.

ON A COLD, rainy afternoon in February, 1531, a boat traveling north
on the River Wye docked at Tintern Abbey. Prior Nicholas was there
on the dock, waiting to greet and welcome Richard Wyche, the new
Abbot. The Abbot stepped onto the dock and bowed to the Prior, who
said, "I am Nicholas from Kingswood, your Prior, and I am pleased

to welcome you to Tintern Abbey." The Prior offered the Abbot his hand, which the newcomer accepted, and a smile, which the new Abbot did not return.

"Thank you, Prior Nicholas. I am pleased to be here."

He doesn't look all that pleased, the Prior thought. *Perhaps he doesn't like traveling by boat.*

"Allow me to take you to your quarters, Abbot Richard," he said.

"I am eager to become acquainted with the monks," the new Abbot said, as they walked through the covered passage to the Abbot's quarters. "When shall we have a meeting?"

"I assumed you would want to rest after your travels. Perhaps tomorrow morning?"

"Why not this afternoon? I don't need any rest, and I prefer to do what must be done. Can you arrange it?"

Prior Nicholas nodded. "Of course. The choir monks are eager to meet you as well. I shall tell them to gather in the chapter room in one hour, and I'll return here to your quarters to show you the way."

PRIOR NICHOLAS ASKED Brother Waldo to help spread the news of the new Abbot's arrival and of the meeting in the chapter room.

"What is he like?" Brother Waldo asked, wringing his hands. "We've heard rumors."

"There's no need for rumors, Brother Waldo, and there's no need to fret. I'm sure we'll be quite happy with our new Abbot."

"But what is he like?" Brother Waldo repeated, insistently.

Prior Nicholas smiled. "He is middle-aged, perhaps forty-five years old. He's tall, he has a long nose, and a ruddy complexion. He seems energetic, intent on getting things done. As you know, he was the Cellarer at Furness Abbey before he was assigned to us."

"I knew it," Brother Waldo said with a wince. "A long nose. He's going to put us to the task, I just know it. Cellarers care about every penny, you know."

"As they should. And I for one am glad of it. It's no secret that we are in trouble financially, and I'm sure Brother Odo will welcome the advice of an Abbot who knows how to mind finances. Perhaps between the two of them they can turn our fortunes around. I am told Brother Richard was noted for keeping track of every penny at Furness, but also that he was lavish in providing for the comforts of his fellow monks. If we do as we ought, I'm sure we'll have no problems with our new Abbot. He knows about the politics of monastery life, just as he knows about politics outside the walls of the abbey."

"He knows about that as well?" Waldo asked. "Does he know government forces are just waiting to grab the wealth of the Church and her monasteries?"

"I expect so, Brother Waldo."

"But what's going to happen to us?" the troubled monk pleaded.

"God's will be done."

"Yes, but—"

"Brother Waldo, we have a meeting coming up. Please inform your brothers."

WHEN THE CISTERCIAN brothers were assembled, Prior Nicholas began the meeting by introducing the choir monks to their new Abbot.

"Performing the task of Sacrist is Brother Evarder. Your able Cellarer is Odo of Normandy. Overseeing the infirmary is our youngest monk, Brother Gordon, who is also a gifted herbalist. Brother Payen looks after the Blessed Virgin Mary Chapel. Waldo of Bath is in charge of the novices, when we have novices, although we have not had any novices for some years now. Brother Waldo also directs the abbey school. Brother Alvin assists Brother Evarder in copying and preserving documents. Brother Homer assists Brother Gordon in the infirmary. Except for Brother Gordon, all of the brothers are over fifty years of age. Three of our brothers, Elias, Cecil, and Knute, are confined to the infirmary. Elias is our oldest monk, at eighty-one, but he is still able to come to Lauds and Vespers. Cecil and Knute are bedridden." Prior Nicholas paused, smiled broadly, and announced, "Brothers, your new Abbot."

Abbot Richard stepped before the monks and spoke clearly,

without smiling. "My name is Abbot Richard from Furness Abbey. As a young man I looked after my father's estates. When I became a monk at Furness I was immediately assigned the duty of Cellarer and have performed that task all of my monastic life.

"I expect you want to know what sort of person I am, and what sort of Abbot I shall be. I speak plainly and have been known to show anger. I do not claim to be a saint. I have been told that I am too stern at times, that I care more for numbers than I do for people. That may be true, but I know I must learn to be more amiable as your Abbot than I ever was as a Cellarer. I ask for your help. If I am too blunt or if I offend, please let me know. If you raise your hand with the palm facing me, I will understand your meaning."

Prior Nicholas saw many of the monks looking at him with questioning eyes, as if to ask, *Is the Abbot speaking the truth? Would I dare show such a response?* In truth, the Prior did not know the answer himself.

Abbot Richard continued, "As monks, with years of service, you know what a monk is expected to do. I am instructing you to do your work as best you can. I believe strongly in the monk's day, from about halfway between midnight and sunrise to the time we retire, an hour after sunset, just following Compline. Our big bells will ring out the hours of our gathering. Every meeting will start shortly after the bells. I know you know them by heart, but they will be posted in the chapter room. Brother Evarder will lead all of liturgy of the hours. In case he is absent because of sickness, Prior Nicholas will preside. I will preside at all Chapter meetings."

Abbot Richard paused. He realized his first statements could have been more amiable. "I want you to know I am genuinely pleased to be here," he stated, trying on a smile. "Tintern Abbey offers a most agreeable setting. I understand you have a thorough chronicle of the history of this fine abbey, and I do intend to read it. I've been told that the chronicle was begun during the years of the plague. Is that correct?"

"That is correct," answered Brother Evarder, the Sacrist. "Brother Araud began the chronicle to record the devastation of the Black Death, but he also wrote down as much as was known about the founding of the abbey and the building of our church. After Araud's death, the task was taken on by each succeeding Sacrist, and it now falls to me, although I rely heavily upon the labors of my friend, Brother Alvin, who has a most agreeable hand. We have treasured this document and have endeavored to keep it up to date, including the eagerly awaited arrival of Abbot Richard."

"Thank you," Abbot Richard said. "I also want to say it appears that the abbey is performing well, even though you have lost all but a few of your lay brothers. I understand their work is now done by servants. I approve of that, because if a man does not do his tasks, he can be replaced. It is true, of course, that the lay brothers of old had a love for their tasks and on the whole were more sincere than hired laborers are."

Realizing that the warm tone he had tried to exhibit had grown cool, he turned once again to business. "You'll find I am an exacting director," he said. "Fair, but exacting. When I call on any of you for a report, I expect you to report on that matter. When I am not present, the Prior will preside, and should he not be present, the Cellarer will take charge. As you would expect, I believe the Cellarer knows nearly everything that goes on in a monastic setting. So I am asking Brother Odo to give us a report, now, on the state of our enterprise. This is largely for my benefit, but it is also important for all of us to be aware of how we are faring."

The Cellarer was surprised. He had not expected to be called upon for a report, nor was he comfortable making extemporaneous statements. Yet his angel seemed to guide him on this one occasion. He had prepared a report for an earlier meeting, and was blessed with an excellent memory.

Brother Odo stepped forward. "Tintern Abbey was founded four hundred years ago. For all this time the monks of Tintern Abbey have worshiped and proclaimed the glory of God here in the River Wye Valley. At present we have twelve monks including our new Abbot. We have six lay brothers.

"Our largest grange holding of Trellech was swept away by Welsh uprisings. The nearest battle in that war was as close as Monmouth. The Trellech Grange included around two thousand acres with over two thousand sheep. Still in our domain is our Woolaston Grange, which has five churches and three villages scattered in it. Seven miles west of the abbey is our one-thousand-acre Rogerstone Grange, with a chapel and mill. Rogerstone is leased to some Welsh families in Chepstow Village. We have one piece of town property in Chepstow Village. We have fishing rights from about two miles up the River Wye to the bend of the river near Chepstow. We have some disputed and scattered properties ten miles west including Merthygeryn and Moore. On the River Usk we hold Monkswood. This is a good piece of farming land with a small chapel. The land is leased out.

"We hold our Abbey Court over at Tintern Parva two times year, which yields under twenty pounds a year. We also have two other sources of income. One is the leasing of abbey holdings to merchants on the main street of Tintern Parva. Another is the Blessed Virgin of Tintern Abbey within her own chapel. These bring in between ten and twenty pounds a year.

"For many years the profits of the abbey were large. Most of our income has gone back into buildings. We have no new buildings planned or in construction, but many of our existing structures need repair. Also, as Abbot Richard has pointed out, we must pay for much of the labor that was once done by a larger community of lay brothers. If I have not missed anything, these are the holdings of Tintern Abbey," the Cellarer concluded.

All of the brothers present remained silent. Brother Waldo knew he was not the only choir monk who felt uneasy. What would be the response of their new Abbot? He seemed to be all business and not in the least spiritual. Was this to be the future of monasticism here and everywhere? With Tintern's finances on the wane, would their earthly lords continue to protect them? Would their King protect them? *Surely God will protect us,* Brother Waldo thought. *"Won't He?"*

"Thank you for that valuable information, Brother Odo," said the Abbot. "Though I am concerned about our finances, I am relieved to be told we are not yet without money or resources. We also have other resources we can draw on. I suspect there are more than a hundred abbeys still available to help us, if need be."

Brother Waldo offered a silent prayer of thanks. God did not often answer prayers so quickly.

The Abbot, however, did not allow the feeling of relief to last. "Unfortunately, the financial state of Tintern Abbey is not what alarms me at this time. You may be surprised to hear me, who was trained as a Cellarer and whose emotions are largely influenced by numbers, tell you there are forces to worry about that are dreadfully more important than money," stated the Abbot. "What I am about to tell you about is more powerful than sheep, more powerful than our land, more powerful than our earthly lord, more powerful than our King.

"To put it simply, people beyond the walls of our monastery are changing their ways of thinking." The Abbot did not speak with a commanding, resonate voice, but his audience was captivated by his topic, his apparent sincerity, and his knowledge of the secular world.

"There is an alarming change in people's attitudes toward God, toward the church, toward monasteries, toward the holy order of things, toward the very foundation our world has been based upon. Listen to me! Ponder this! To many people God is not even real anymore. Many of those who do believe in God have lost the fear of His power. We seem to be a people looking at the future through a dark glass, as the Apostle Paul said. At the same time we are fearfully looking over our shoulders toward the past. The older people can remember the devastation of the plague. The younger ones have no fear that the dreaded Black Death will return. No fear of a catastrophe. No fear of God or the devil. As you look at our present world, fix your thoughts on what I am saying: it was our fears that pushed so many of us into the monasteries and convents. Our monasteries offered a safe haven. They offered food, shelter, and a sure dock to which we could tie our souls. Our souls have been anchored on this rock." The Abbot waved his arms in a sweeping manner that brought in all people. "But now, in the world around us, all manner of people—mothers, fathers, nobility, and even the poor—see the monastery as an unreal place, a place not of this world. Some even see us as places that shelter slothful or perverted, even evildoing demons.

There is no longer the same rejoicing in the family when a boy wishes to become a priest or monk. Often now when a boy joins the church, his parents feel they have failed."

What is he telling us? Brother Waldo wondered. *Does he mean that a monk's work is no longer valued? Surely our Tintern Abbey — our secure and safe home — cannot be in danger. What does all this mean for our futures?*

"You must understand this," exclaimed the Abbot. "We are facing times when money will not save our way of life. I look about here and at other abbeys and see old men waiting to die with no one ready to pick up our banner. I sense dark storms threatening to sweep away all we have and all we have stood for. One by one I can see our little abbeys dying, closed, vacant, and lost."

For a moment the Abbot paused, gazing fiercely over the monks' heads, lost in his own thoughts. *As an Abbot I am bound to relay this state of affairs to my brothers. Tintern, isolated as it is, has been spared much political turmoil. But will Tintern continue to be spared? I fear it will not.* A soft cough from Prior Nicholas jolted the Abbot back to the present. He sighed and forced himself to smile. "But enough of my sermon," he concluded abruptly, and he left the chapter room.

The choir monks rose from their seats full of talk. Many saw their new Abbot as a practical and knowledgeable man. He was a monk who knew the ways of the world and the harsh wind that was gathering over religious life in the British Isles. Prior Nicholas had told the curious monks before the Abbot's arrival that Abbot Richard was one who knew the politics of the land and was attentive to the dangerous power struggles brewing in the Royal Court. This Abbot might be more rigid and forceful than leaders some of the older monks had known in the past, but it was important that this Abbot Richard seemed aware of the large-scale events that could change Tintern forever.

Of all the monks, Brother Waldo was the most fretful. He sat alone in the chapter room and tried to find solace in prayer, but solace eluded him. Finally he left the hall and found his way to the room of his friend, the herbalist, Brother Gordon.

"Brother Gordon, what does he mean?" Brother Waldo cried out in anguish. "Is Abbot Richard preparing us for doomsday? I have always thought that if our abbey were to close, I could find another. But if all of the abbeys close, where can I go? I gave up my relatives to come to the Cistercians. Over the years I have lost contact with all of them. I have no place to go. Tell me what I can do. Surely God will not let our way of life end. There have been monasteries since the third century. What is going to happen to all of those who have purchased everlasting prayers and Masses?"

Brother Gordon put a steady hand on the worried monk's shoulder. "You are taking on too much worry, my friend. In the first place, closures may not come. In the second place, you have a good classical education. If necessary, you will be able to find a place in a school or college or maybe even start your own school. Who knows? God may be leading you to another place or time."

"Yes, but we are Catholic and the winds are blowing against us. Who's to say England will not break from the Church of Rome one day, and if that happens, who will hire a Catholic educator?" questioned Waldo.

"God will not desert us, Waldo. He may require that we change, but He will not desert us."

SEVERAL WEEKS WENT by. Neither time nor prayers calmed Brother Waldo's worries. One day he came upon Brother Odo in the warming room, the one place where brothers might speak, share opinions, and ask questions freely.

"You seemed distressed, Brother Waldo," the Cellarer observed. "Your face is lined with worry."

"I continue to be troubled by Abbot Richard's remarks to us," Brother Waldo admitted. "Did you get the idea that our abbey and all other monastic holdings are doomed? Our days here may be numbered. Is our new Abbot preparing us for doomsday, when all abbeys will close? How does he know this? Did his information come from God, the Pope, Clairvaux, or where? I gave up my relatives and a promising future as the second son of a knight to become a Cistercian. I've abandoned direct contact with my relatives and virtually all who knew me. I have no place to go! I became a Cistercian to serve the

Blessed Virgin and her church, I thought for a lifetime. Can you tell me what is going to happen to us monks of Tintern Abbey?"

"I know nothing beyond what the Abbot said," Brother Odo answered. "God's will be done, and I can't imagine God would permit our abbey to be stolen from us, or from Him. I do believe it would be downright robbery if the holy monastic properties were seized. We and our fellow brothers before us have carried on here for four hundred years, and think of all the lives that were lived here in devotion to the Blessed Virgin Mary." Odo pointed toward the cemetery south of the chapel. "Besides, no one but the Pope can close an abbey. I suppose King Henry might, but we're told he cares only about making a male heir. I doubt if he even knows that we exist."

Waldo gazed at the fire, placed his hands inside his cowl, and walked slowly from the warming room. He spent another night tossing and turning, with no sleep until Lauds.

During the morning work hours Evarder approached Brother Waldo and asked him to read the Scriptures at Vespers. "You seem tired, Waldo. Are you getting enough sleep?"

Brother Waldo asked if they could talk. Evarder nodded. It was always permissible talk if the conversation had to do with abbey work.

"I have done all of my work and more. But sleep? At night with the only the frogs sounding, I can think of nothing else but the possible closing of the abbey." Waldo wrung his hands and scowled. "What would I do? I have lived most of my life within these walls. I came here as a novitiate, and I gave my youth and my strong middle years to Tintern. I have no hands-on trade, and there is little place for chanting in the outside world. I have no living parents. Both my sister and brother are dead. But I'm not worried only for myself," Brother Waldo added. "I worry about all those blessed souls who gave their own money, not to mention the money given by their loved ones, for Masses and prayers to get them out of purgatory. What will happen to those souls, and what will happen to us, if—"

The Sacrist smiled sadly. "God's will be done."

"Yes, but we have taken money to be the caretakers of bodies and souls. Some rest in our cemetery, some in our village, and some in the hills around our valley. We must not leave them without the comfort and care of our Blessed Mary. How will the families of those for whom we pray judge us? How will God judge us if we can no longer do His work?"

"Waldo, since the founding of Tintern Abbey, we monks have done what we could for these souls. We have heard their confessions, sung with all the emotions we are capable of, we have shared the blood and body of Christ in their honor, and we built a great church which is the castle for housing that moment when the finger of Christ and His creation meet. We have done all that is humanly possible. The rest is in God's hands. God will take care of them and us. Have faith in God. Reach for His trust, His truth, and His trenchant. God's will be done."

WEEKS WENT BY, and the storms of early spring gave way to the warm sunshine of May; but Brother Waldo's spirit stayed in a dark winter that was observed by all. Prior Nicholas decided this was a pressing problem for the Abbot to solve. Hailing Abbot Richard as he was leaving the chapter house, the Prior told the Abbot of his concern.

"Brother Waldo appears moody and listless, and he does not have the ability to focus on his tasks. He complains that when he lies down to rest or sleep, he can do neither. He has been feeling and acting this way ever since your opening remarks when you first arrived."

"I knew monks with similar concerns at Furness," Abbot Richard replied. "It is dangerous to the soul to worry about what we cannot control. I suppose I must speak with Brother Waldo. As you know, I am not as personable as some of your past Abbots have been, but I shall try my best. Promising nothing, I shall see what I can do, short of discipline."

The following day, the Abbot found Brother Waldo sitting on the south bench of the cloister. Since Waldo's head was covered by his hood, the Abbot could not determine, even at short distance, if the choir monk was reading, silently praying, or staring. Slipping down beside him, the Abbot spoke softly.

"Brother Waldo, first I want to thank your for your hard work over the years you've been at Tintern Abbey, even though we have no novices or schoolchildren for you to teach at this time. Over the past couple of years, I have talked with other Abbots, both in England and in France, about novices. The numbers are dwindling in monasteries everywhere. I have my own ideas about the causes, but I would like to hear yours."

Waldo looked up from his hands, which were folded in his lap. He sighed. "I'm afraid I don't know the answer. I have not been thinking about new novices lately. I would not ask them to be a part of monastic life. As you so rightly told us all when you first arrived, our world has changed and is still changing. People no longer fear God or Satan. You said the people do not even believe in God anymore. You also said the outside people see the orders as unreal places, not of this world, a shelter for people who would steal their land and animals. I once believed that monasticism offered a safe haven from the storms of life. You quoted from the Holy Bible when you said in olden times the life of a monk was built on solid rock, but now our foundations are nothing more than shifting sand. No wonder fewer young people are deciding to become priests, monks, and nuns. No wonder I have no novitiates to train."

"It is discouraging," Abbot Richard admitted. "But I have found, as a Cellarer, that the best cure for problems is action. If you are doing something, and doing your best work, you can stay busy and not feel guilty for the changes that threaten us. That's the best we can do. I want you to stay active Brother Waldo, even though there are no novitiates to train or children to teach."

"Busy?" Brother Waldo asked. "I wish I were busy, but what am I to do?"

"I have given this matter some thought, and here are a few things I instruct you to do for me. First, when you are approaching others, look at them and smile. Perhaps you will even go so far as to raise your arm in passing.

"Second, find out from Brother Odo which families in and around Tintern Parva have children. Visit the house of every one of them, and try to persuade those families to send their children to the school we have set up on our premises. Have Brother Odo go with you. He knows most of them.

"Third, yesterday I instructed Brother Odo to arrange a pleasure outing for the people of Tintern Parva, here on the abbey grounds, and I want you to help him make this a splendid occasion, with roasted lamb, beer and wine, and games for the children. All our monks will participate."

Brother Waldo still looked worried. "Can we afford this?" he asked the Abbot.

"We have received a generous gift from a physician named Lewis, a descendant of Samuel, that Monmouth physician who braved the plague and helped to save so many of our choir monks and lay brothers, as well as so many people of Tintern Parva. Physician Lewis is eager to meet the families of people whom his great-grandfather cared for, and so has offered to pay for the outing. The event will happen sometime next month."

Brother Waldo breathed another heavy sigh. "But Brother Abbot, what if we make plans for an outdoor feast, and it rains heavily that day?"

Abbot Richard smiled and laid a hand on Brother Waldo's arm. To his own surprise, he found that the smile came easily to him, and so did the gesture of friendship. "We have no control over the weather," he admitted. "God's will be done. But that must not stop us from making plans and doing what needs to be done. I am instructing you, as your Abbot, to go find Brother Odo right now and get busy visiting the families of Tintern Parva. Tell them about the outing, and encourage them to have their children come to the abbey for schooling. I also want you to keep close contact with Physician Lewis, whom I shall introduce to you. I shall also send you to Monmouth with Master Robin's great-grandson. You and Odo are to report on your progress with the Prior and me. Brother Waldo, I am going to see to it that you are too busy to worry!"

Abbot Richard wondered if he had been too stern in his instructions, but his fears were put to rest when he saw on Brother Waldo's face the first smile he'd ever seen there. This was the kind of a smile that showed a monk's teeth!

THE OUTDOOR FEAST was a huge success. Physician Lewis established a strong connection with the inhabitants of Tintern Parva—and also with Brother Waldo. Whenever the physician would visit the area, the news of his presence would spread through the village, and many sick folk came to the church to see him. On rare occasions, very sick folk from the village would be taken to Monmouth by one of the many boats passing the abbey's dock. On his visits Lewis would always check on the monks of Tintern, especially his new friend Brother Waldo. As a guest of honor, the physician would be served a meal along with the best wine available.

IN EARLY 1534, the Act of Supremacy was passed by Parliament. This act placed the King, below God, as Supreme Head of the churches in England and Ireland. In fact, by this act, King Henry owned all monasteries, convents, and priories in England and Wales. But taking possession of them and their riches would be another matter.

Abbot Richard was summoned to Rome to advise the Vatican on the matter of King Henry's intentions. His clear, but blunt predictions did not go well with the cardinals. He told the purple-robed fathers what they did not want to hear, but had to accept as truth: that there were strong winds of rebellion against the Church blowing in England. The King's henchmen, first Cardinal Woolsey and now Thomas Cromwell, had been busy closing scores of monasteries and confiscating their wealth for the Crown. King Henry had already disobeyed the Pope in the matter of divorce and remarriage. Now the Act of Supremacy would close many more monasteries and would make wearing a Catholic priest's garment a crime. Anyone who disagreed with the King on these matters would be judged guilty of high treason.

Still, the monks of Tintern Abbey carried on as if the winds of change would never sweep them from their home and their place of worship.

IN SEPTEMBER OF that year Abbot Richard received a letter from Secretary Cromwell, King Henry's Vicar-General of Spiritual Affairs, summoning him to court in London. The Vicar-General made it quite clear that Tintern Abbey would be on the list of possible closures.

The following week Physician Lewis made a hurried trip down the River Wye, hoping the Abbot would have time for a long chat to discuss information just made known to the physician. Brother Gordon, the young herbalist who admired Lewis for his talent as a healer, greeted the physician at the dock and pointed to the refectory, where he knew Abbot Richard would be at this time of day. Lewis crossed the cloister and in moment he found the Abbot drinking hot tea at the table next to the monks' kitchen. Rising quickly, Abbot Richard issued a warm greeting to Lewis.

"Lewis, it is a great pleasure to welcome you again to Tintern Abbey. Let me help you with your cloak. While you're here, if you have time would you have a look at Brother Cecil? He has slipped some in the last week."

"Of course."

"Now, what can I get you? We have fine wines, tea hot or cold. Oh yes, we also have a new and different drink, made from a rare and exotic bean raised in Turkey. It is called 'coffee.'"

"I have heard of this drink," the physician said. "I have never tasted it."

"I would like you to try it and let me know what you think. Since our cooks are taking a rest, I will brew it for us. It needs to be served in small cups. A little bit goes a long way."

In a few moments the two were seated across from one another, sipping the bitter black beverage. "Very pleasant," Lewis remarked.

"Unfortunately, it is also most expensive," the Abbot said. "A disappointment, because I'm beginning to depend upon it. Now, what was it you wanted to discuss with me?"

"I just returned from Oxford two days ago. I was there visiting my father, who is a physician as well as a teacher. His high-level contacts in London have passed along information I felt you should know. My father is most distressed about what the King is planning for the English Church. As for me, I'm especially concerned about what these developments mean with respect to the abbeys, and particularly Tintern Abbey. How do you see the future, my friend?"

Abbot Richard shook his head sadly. "God's will be done," he said, "but I dread the future. The struggle between the Church and the Crown is ongoing, and getting worse. I sense that it's not only a matter of power and control, not even primarily a matter of finances. At the root of the problem is a changing attitude throughout society. There has been a change in attitudes toward God, toward the Church, toward holy orders and monasteries."

"I agree," the physician said. "And so says my father. He tells me his students do not fear God; indeed they believe God does not exist. They believe there is no heaven and no hell."

"Most distressing. But what can be done about it?"

"It is even worse," Lewis said. "My father told me that Cromwell has already set in motion the machinery for the partial dissolution of six hundred monasteries, priories, and convents." The physician expected his friend to cringe at such numbers, but the Abbot only confirmed the news.

"Yes. Cromwell told me the same, only last week," Abbot Richard said sadly. "I do not know how he expects to complete his mission."

"We have learned of his tactics," Lewis responded. "Cromwell has a direct access to the King and he is carrying out His Majesty's orders. They are most ingenious, and most devious. They begin by blackening the reputations of monasteries and convents. They've already begun sending out 'preachers' all over the land to educate the people against monks and nuns. These orators speak at public gatherings, to the common people as well as the nobility."

"What on earth are they saying against us?" Abbot Richard asked. He no longer felt like a leader in charge of a business, but like a shepherd whose flock was being attacked by wolves.

"There are different kinds of slander. Some of the orators, called 'railers,' harangue against religious groups, labeling them hypocrites, sorcerers, and idle drones who live off everyone else's wages. Others pose as 'preachers,' going about the land to every meeting, saying that monks make the business and lands unprofitable. Monasteries and convents pay no taxes, they point out, while other land owners do. A third group includes 'gentlemen and merchants,' who spread the idea that if monasteries, convents, and priories were taken over by the King, he would cease taxing the people. All lies, of course." Physician Lewis rattled his coffee cup in one hand, and drummed the fingers of his other hand on the table. "All lies."

"Please continue," Abbot Richard urged. Have you come across any of Cromwell's groups in Monmouth?"

Lewis nodded. "Yes we do have a few. They are making lots of noise. I fear people will listen, especially if they are foolish enough to believe their taxes will be reduced or abolished."

"People tend to believe what they want to believe. Our opponents know that."

"Wait. There's more," the physician said. "They've also been disseminating scandalous literature. For all I know, some of the stories may be true, or partially true, but certainly most of them are false. At Lamley Convent, Sister Mariana reportedly gave birth three times and Sister Joana six times. It appears that two nuns at Litchfield Convent may be with child. At Ford Abbey, the Prior was accused of fathering six children. At Pershing Abbey, monks were accused of often being drunk at Mass. At Lincoln Abbey, the Prior was frequently intoxicated, while the monks played dice and other games for money. The lord of Peterborough Abbey has often appointed lazy monks to lead the monastery, while brothers sold wood and kept the money. Peterborough Abbey was said to have no beds, even for receiving guests. When the King visited the abbey, he had to be put up in a nearby inn, and was furious about it.

"And Tintern Abbey was not left out, either, my friend," Lewis continued. "According to one of the articles, you have been accused of wrongfully cutting and selling timber, then dividing the proceeds with your Prior. I am afraid you must prepare, for the worst is yet to come."

Abbot Richard groaned. "These are bad tidings indeed, but I must thank you for keeping me aware and prepared for what lies ahead."

Physician Lewis stood. "I shall soon be on my way after my visit to Brother Cecil—and a few quick words with Brother Waldo. Thank you for introducing me to this drink you call coffee. It has restored my energy. It could become a new favorite."

"God bless and protect you." Abbot Richard bade farewell to his friend and confidant. The Abbot reflected upon their conversation. He felt compelled to pray, calling upon his Lord for strength to face this uncertain future.

THE PHYSICIAN'S DIRE predictions came to pass. The following year, 1535, Secretary Cromwell, the Vicar-General of Spiritual Affairs, appointed commissioners to call upon all the dioceses in Wales. These special investigators reached Tintern Abbey in February of 1536. After examining Brother Odo's figures, they assessed Tintern's income at one hundred ninety pounds, and Commissioner John Vaughn sent his letter to Cromwell, recommending that the abbey be closed.

Abbot Richard was furious. His records showed that his abbey earned well over the two hundred pounds necessary to escape closing. But some of the abbey's income was disallowed, for reasons the commissioners chose not to reveal. Abbot Richard made every effort possible to change the report, but to no avail.

"I am sorry, Abbot Richard," the unctuous commissioner said, flatly. "According to the Act of Dissolution passed by Parliament, all monasteries, priories, and convents with an income of less than two hundred pounds or fewer than twelve monks are the property of King Henry, to do with as he chooses."

"My records indicate that our abbey has twelve monks with an income of two hundred thirty pounds," stated Abbot Richard.

Commissioner Vaughn shook his head, gave the Abbot a condescending half-smile, and was on his way.

ABBOT RICHARD GATHERED the choir monks and lay brothers in the chapter room late that afternoon to tell them the dismal news. A rumble of protest rose from the assembly, but the Abbot raised his hand for silence.

"There is nothing we can do," he said. "The numbers they used were falsified, but we have no higher authority who will hear our case, at least in this life. We are not the first to be robbed, as you all know. Many monasteries have already succumbed to the King's greed and the spiritual disease of our society. But there is nothing we can do. Nothing."

The first to respond to the Abbot's announcement was Brother Waldo. His voice—no longer heavy with anxiety and worry—offered traces of determination and concern. He asked the questions his fellow monks were most mindful of. "Abbot, all of us, including myself, are resigned to God's will, whatever that may be. But I cannot understand how King Henry, to whom we have always been faithful and for whom we have offered our prayers, could treat us this way. We were given this land by the first King Henry. Tell me what power the eighth King Henry has to take this abbey away from us and from the Cistercian Order? Does he not care that some of us have no place to go? And more, what is going to happen to Brothers Cecil and Knute? When will this happen? Will we be given a chance to find other homes where we may carry on our lives?"

Concerned murmurs again filled the room, and once again Abbot Richard called for silence.

"I have not been told when we will have to leave or what arrangements there will be to give us any money when we leave, but I am hopeful we will be given some money. As to Brothers Cecil and Knute, we might be able to place them in one of the larger monasteries. I shall send messages to Bath, Bury Saint Edmunds, Ramsey, Saint Albans, Gloucester, and Westminster. I do not know which of these are among the ones to be closed, but they are all large and wealthy abbeys.

"Until we learn the date of our closing, we shall keep to our regular duties. If any of you have family that might be willing to offer you a home, by all means write them. If you receive a firm offer, I shall grant you leave to visit your family so that you may make arrangements for your future. I shall also allow you to visit other abbeys, if you think they will offer you a place. By the time you are ready to return, in all probability this abbey will be closed."

AFTER THE CHAPTER meeting, Brother Waldo took the opportunity to speak to Brother Gordon. Waldo started the conversation:

"Brother Gordon," he said, "my initial fears were finally confirmed today. Yet with all my worrying, nothing changed this outcome."

"But *you* have changed," Brother Gordon responded. "In time, you released your anguish. I noticed a distinct change in your manner once you and Brother Odo began planning the festival with Physician Lewis. We all noticed."

"Yes, my acquaintance with the good physician has blessed me in more ways than one," Waldo agreed.

"Have you received his letter yet?"

"No. He has been attending his mother's illness," Brother Waldo answered. "We will see what plans God has in store for me." He then looked at his friend in a curious way. "And where will you go?"

"I plan to go to Oxford," the herbalist answered, his eyes shining. "There is so much more to learn about the art of healing. I am fascinated by the powers of herbs, but I'm also intrigued by the causes of disease. I would like very much to talk to other scholars of medicine about the Black Death that so afflicted our forebears. One day we will discover the real cause of the plague, and I believe it will not be sin, evil, or vapor. When we find a connection between two persons with the plague, we may be close to finding out the real cause, even if that cause be as small as a flea. With knowledge like that, just think of the suffering we may be able to eliminate."

"You have another calling, it appears," Brother Waldo said.

"I have enjoyed being a monk," Brother Gordon said. "I think I could also enjoy being a physician. I would still be doing God's work."

Brother Waldo nodded. He remembered Physician Lewis's dedication to healing others and witnessed the same commitment from Brother Gordon. Perhaps Waldo and the herbalist monk would cross paths again. "God be with you," he said to his friend as he left the chapter room.

"God be with us all," Brother Gordon replied.

WHAT WILL THEY all do? Abbot Richard wondered. *Where will they go?*

In the few short years he had lived in Tintern Abbey, in the splendid, quiet valley of the River Wye, the stern Abbot who had always thought of himself as a Cellarer had become deeply fond of each and every one of his monks, and he now found himself agonizing over their fates, as if he had failed them in some way.

I needn't worry about the monastic servants, he thought. *Because of the shortage of labor, they'll have abundant opportunities for work.*

Prior Nicholas, he reasoned, was a strong and resourceful man; he could find his way in any kind of situation.

Brothers Evarder and Alvin had a trade, as scribes. They would survive. Perhaps they could learn to operate one of those new machines, a printing press. *Yes,* the Abbot thought. *They will survive.*

Odo was capable with numbers and finances. He would find work, even if he had to leave England to find it.

The Abbot had arranged for Brothers Cecil and Knute to be taken in by a kind family in Tintern Parva, descendants of the Gold Coin Lady who still lived in Master Robin's manor home. Elias had gone to his rest, the last choir monk to die at Tintern Abbey. He was buried in our cemetery, and Cecil and Knute would be as well.

The others?

Brother Payen could leave the order and become a village vicar. He would be serving the King that way, but he would be serving God as well. The Abbot would give him his blessing.

Homer had decided to leave the Cistercian Order and would join Brother Gordon at Oxford, where they could study the healing arts together.

The newest choir monks, Brothers Gavin and Simon, had joined the abbey from nearby villages. Their families would take them in again until they made other plans for their futures.

As for me, I shall go, at last, to Citeaux. I am no longer needed in England.

And as for Waldo…?

Abbot Richard took a deep breath. His mind focused on the last of the monks. On his desk was a letter from Physician Lewis bringing good news. The physician's brother was searching for a private tutor for his son. The Abbot smiled and nodded. Waldo had learned to accept the will of God, and now God had repaid that trust.

One more important matter remained to be done. The Abbot reached for the pile of parchments—the document that told the history of Tintern Abbey. He now knew who would be the keeper of the chronicles. He wrapped the packet in a monk's robe to disguise its contents and asked his servant to store the item in the small chest on the boat. Brother Gordon would guard the precious chronicles well until he could entrust them to the medical library at Oxford, where they would remain forever, a record of four hundred years of service to God and the Blessed Virgin. Four hundred years of praise and prayer in the beautiful Valley of the River Wye.

ON THE AFTERNOON of 3 September 1536, Abbot Richard Wyche surrendered Tintern Abbey to the King's commissioners. The Abbot received twenty-three pounds. The remaining twelve monks each received eight pounds, eight shillings. "It's not much," Commissioner Vaughn admitted without apology, "but I expect your order will provide for you and your brothers. All right then?"

As they came out of the Abbot's quarters after the papers were exchanged, Abbot Richard's eyes were drawn to a golden eagle circling above Tintern Abbey. Storm clouds were gathering over the mountains in the north.

BROTHER WALDO WALKED one last time around the grounds of the abbey he had called home for over two-thirds of his life. Yet he knew that his life was of no great importance; it was only a moment in the greater life of Tintern Abbey, which had lasted more than four hundred years.

Tintern Abbey had started as a few wooden structures in a soggy green valley, and now it stood handsomely in stone still echoing with the prayers and chants of centuries. The hills around the valley of the River Wye still reverberated with bells calling monks eight times every day to their prayers. In their prayers the monks had confessed sins, asked God to protect the King, praised the glory of the Virgin Mary, and lifted up God and Christ above all that existed in the world. They had hoped for nothing more than the salvation of their souls and the souls of those whom they honored in their Masses.

Wandering once more around the magnificent church, the monk

contemplated his future. In his hand was the letter Abbot Richard had passed along to him from Physician Lewis. *God's will be done.*

Brother Waldo smiled, quickened his pace, and walked down to the dock to join the Abbot and his fellow brothers to board the boat that would carry them all downstream.

Epilogue

SAM LEWIS WALKED into Father Ignatius's office Tuesday afternoon, carrying the manuscript of the priest's translations of the Chronicles of Tintern Abbey in one hand, a paper sack in the other. Father Ignatius rose from behind his desk and gave Sam a warm smile. "You're back," he observed. "And you look refreshed!"

Sam handed the priest the manuscript and grinned. "Indeed I am. I thank you so much for letting me read that book in English. And for suggesting that I go to Tintern. I walked the grounds of the abbey, in the footsteps of those Cistercian monks! And reading the Chronicles helped me glimpse into their lives. I could almost hear their prayers and devotions, their stories of servitude, courage, and grace. You and Brother Araud have made them live again. I wish others could experience what I've been through this past weekend. Father Ignatius, we need to get this story out to the world!"

A look of satisfaction radiated from the old priest's face. "One step at a time, my friend. But tell me, what else fills you with so much joy today? I can see there's more."

"Well, that place, you know, and the book too…they're both eye-openers."

"And…? There's more, Samuel. What is it?"

"I spoke with my wife this morning," Sam said. "And—I spoke with my mother!"

"How is she?"

"She's…she's…she's fed up with hospital food, and she will be going home tomorrow! The tumor was benign. No more tumor, no more pain, no more worry! Father, I don't want to get too sentimental on you, but I owe you a lot for those prayers. Thank you."

Father Ignatius chuckled. "You think they did any good?"

"I'm sure of it," Sam declared.

"Well, don't thank me. You can thank God. In fact, you *should* thank God."

"I already have. Believe me."

"I do believe you. Shall I put the kettle on?"

"Why not? I brought scones." Sam set the paper sack on the desk.

When Father Ignatius served the tea, they sat back in their chairs and grinned at each other across the desk. "So," the old priest asked. "Tell me. Do you think those Cistercian monks did any good with all that chanting and praying during their darkest hour? All that marching around in the rain?"

"I don't really know," Samuel said. "But they certainly did no harm, and for all I know they may have prevented the plague from wiping out Britain entirely." He thought a moment and continued, "Yes, that was a dark hour, but I believe the monks did what they had to do. I believe it was their *finest* hour."

Further Notes and Resources

Author's Notes

THE SECRETS OF *Tintern Abbey* is a fictional novel set in medieval times, prominently featuring the lives of the Cistercian monks at that monastery. In the course of my research, I found a number of discrepancies among dates, the spellings of names, and other historical details. For the sake of a consistent story line, I have modified some of the dates and made decisions among other conflicting records. For example, I have introduced the first abbot, Abbot Henry, earlier than he appears in some accounts, and the last abbot, Abbot Richard Wyche, later.

For the Holy Bible verses quoted in this novel, I have used the *New American Standard Bible*, published by The Lockman Foundation.

Maps in this book were created by Catherine Snow, who has a gift for taking rough, hand-drawn scribbles and turning them into clear and attractive drawings. The maps were designed to show the reader the approximate locations of important places mentioned in the novel and are not drawn to scale. Partial river flows were drawn. Borders of some countries changed over the book's timeline of 400 years. For the sake of simplicity, the lines representing the borders of France show the modern boundaries.

The diagram of the building and ground plans of Tintern Abbey was provided courtesy of Cadw, the official guardian of Tintern Abbey as well as the governmental service that conserves and protects the historical monuments throughout Wales.

My professional photograph printed on the back cover of this book was furnished by Prestigious Images of Kennett, Missouri, and is copyrighted 2008. The studio granted permission to reprint the image for publication.

A Monk's Day

THE MEDIEVAL CISTERCIAN monks spent the majority of their time praising, praying, chanting, and contemplating. At Tintern Abbey, the schedule was influenced by the seasons. In the summertime, the monks rose about an hour earlier and retired to bed about two hours later than in the wintertime. The table below provides a schedule approximating the monk's day in the winter. The italicized words collectively are referred to as canonical hours, horarium, the liturgy of the hours, or the Divine Office.

2:30 a.m.	Rise
3:30 a.m.	*Vigils* (or *Nocturns*) — early morning prayer
6:00 a.m.	*Lauds* (or *Matins*) — praising the dawn
	Prime — first hour of the daylight praise
	Reading
8:00 a.m.	*Terce* — reading of the psalms
	Mass, Chapter Meeting, Work
12:00 noon	*Sext* — midday prayer/psalms
	Mass
1:30 p.m.	*None* — reading of the psalms
	Dinner, Work
4:15 p.m.	*Vespers* — evening prayer at the lighting of the lamps
	Collation — reading in the chapter house
6:15 p.m.	*Compline* — prayers at the end of the day
6:30 p.m.	Retire to bed

Tintern Abbey Groundplan

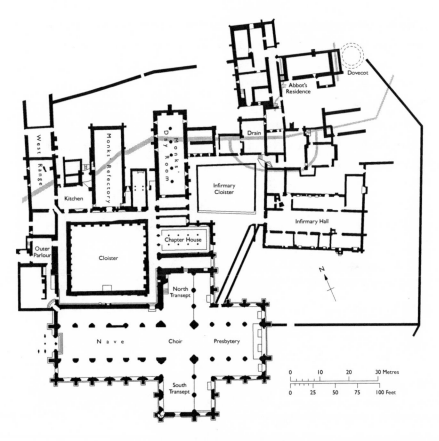

Groundplan courtesy Cadw
Cadw.Crown Copyright

Resources

The following resources include books and website information that were available and accurate at the time of publication.

Cadw

Tintern Abbey and Chepstow Castle are historic sites in Wales connected with the Welsh Assembly Government service called Cadw. Cadw, pronounced "cad-oo," is a Welsh word that means "to keep." Its website provides information about its mission, its many historic sites, and its publications.

Cadw website: http://www.cadw.wales.gov.uk/
Cadw e-mail: cadw@wales.gsi.gov.uk

Visiting Tintern Abbey

Details about visiting Tintern Abbey, including days and hours of operation and entry fees, are available at the Cadw website, listed above or visit the Tintern Abbey site information by the direct links listed below.

Visitor's information:

http://www.cadw.wales.gov.uk/default.asp?id=6&PlaceID=132

Historical information and resources for teachers:

http://www.cadw.wales.gov.uk/default.asp?id=240

Further information and advice about visiting Tintern Abbey is also available from the custodian at the monument.

Custodian, Tintern Abbey

Tintern, Monmouthshire NP16 6SE United Kingdom
E-mail: tintern.abbey@cadw.co.uk

Drawings of the Abbey and Monastery Grounds
The Cadw organization created a four-page handout that presents an overview of Tintern Abbey, an excellent diagram of the monastery grounds with key locations, a list of educational activities, and basic visiting and contact information.
http://www.cadw.wales.gov.uk/upload/resourcepool/Tintern710.pdf

Another great online resource that provides 3-D renderings of Tintern Abbey buildings at full completion is through the timeref. com website. Browse the site for additional time lines, glossary, and maps.
http://www.timeref.com/tint3d.htm

Guidebooks for Tintern Abbey and Chepstow Castle
The guidebooks published by Cadw are all well researched, beautifully illustrated with full-color drawing and photographs, and designed to give the reader a glimpse of the historic sites during their construction, use, and history. The Tintern Abbey guidebook also includes details about the Cistercian monastic order.

E-mail address for ordering guidebooks:
cadw.sales@wales.gsi.gov.uk

Tintern Abbey Guidebook
Revised Edition, Copyright 2002
David M. Robinson
ISBN 1 85760 163 7
Published by Cadw, Welsh Assembly Government
(Crown Copyright)

Chepstow Castle Guidebook
Revised Edition, Copyright 2006

Rick Turner
ISBN 1 85760 229 3
Published by Cadw, Welsh Assembly Government
(Crown Copyright)

Cistercian Monastic Order

A web-based learning program funded by EnrichUK has been created to illustrate and describe the life and history of the Cistercian monks. Although the website features abbeys in the Yorkshire area, the information on the monastic order in general gives a comprehensive look into the lives of the medieval monks.

For an overview of Cistercian life:
http://www.cistercians.shef.ac.uk/cistercian_life/

For slideshows illustrating a day in the life of monks and lay-brothers:
http://cistercians.shef.ac.uk/multimedia/games/intro.html

http://cistercians.shef.ac.uk/multimedia/games/layintro.html

Order of Saint Benedict

A wealth of information about the Order of Saint Benedict, including translations of the Rule, is available at their website.

Website for the Order of Saint Benedict (OSB):
http://www.osb.org

About the Author

AFTER HIS RETIREMENT from serving as a Christian Church (Disciples of Christ) minister for twenty years, Gordon Masters completed his Masters degree at Central Missouri State College and joined the faculty there as an Assistant Professor of Sociology. He later went on to earn his Doctor of Ministry degree at St. Paul School of Theology in Kansas City, Missouri.

During a trip to Wales in the spring of 1997, Dr. Masters visited Tintern Abbey and was inspired to learn more about the medieval abbey's 400-year history and the dedicated Cistercian monks who lived there. With the encouragement of his late wife, Martha, Dr. Masters started his personal investigation, which led him to put pen to paper and write his first novel, *The Secrets of Tintern Abbey*.

Gordon Masters lives in Melbourne, Florida, with his feisty dog, Yip Yip. For more information about Dr. Masters and Tintern Abbey, visit the author's website at www.gordon-masters.com.

Printed in the United States
208415BV00001B/89/P

9 781604 940749